THE KNIFE TRICK

I spread the paper over the heap of cards. I picked up the dagger, clutching the handle so tightly that my fingers ached. I looked toward the bedroom and hoped that Roth would stay in there a bit longer. I didn't want him to witness the mockery I was making of his star trick.

I poised the knife over the newspaper. And heard a dripping sound. The paper was wet ... dotted with tiny circles of gleaming red. The dagger clattered out of my hand. Fresh blood ...

I ran down the hall and shoved the bedroom door open. I could see a man sitting on the floor, his legs splayed and his back against the bed. A bib of red covered his chest and trickled down, soaking his trousers and part of the rug. His throat had been slit ...

Other Avon Books by
Patrick A. Kelley

SLEIGHTLY INVISIBLE
SLEIGHTLY LETHAL
SLEIGHTLY MURDER

SLEIGHTLY DECEIVED

PATRICK A. KELLEY

AVON
PUBLISHERS OF BARD, CAMELOT, DISCUS AND FLARE BOOKS

AVON BOOKS
A division of
The Hearst Corporation
105 Madison Avenue
New York, New York 10016

For Walter V. Eichenlaub, my great-uncle,
whom I have gotten to know through his wonderful letters

CHAPTER ONE

Fifteen years of deceiving people for a living have left me a hopeless skeptic. That's why I doubted all the tales about Arlen Roth and his ivory-handled, double-edged dagger.

But the stories persisted. I heard them in hotel bars at weekend magic conventions. In the dressing rooms of nightclubs. And in the dusty back rooms of conjuring shops. Gradually my skepticism gave way to curiosity. And curiosity eventually gave way to obsession.

Everyone's story about Roth seemed to end with the same line: "Just wait till you see him." My wait was longer than expected: over ten years. In the beginning, it was hard to find time to track him down. I made little progress. However, in the past couple of years I had involuntarily had a lot more spare time than I ever dreamed of. In a few hours, my search for Roth and his magical dagger would end.

I had spent the last two hours nursing beers and smoking cigarettes in a tavern called the Willis Café. The Willis consisted of twelve tables and a bar that specialized in boilermakers. In the corner beside the bar were a shuffleboard bowling machine, a flipperless pinball machine that paid off in cash, and a cigarette machine that displayed brands they don't make anymore.

Sipping my beer, I gazed across the street at the Pritchard Hotel and wondered which room was Roth's. The Pritchard's crumbling gray facade reminded me of an archaeological relic awaiting exploration.

The whiskey clock above the café window now showed almost

twelve noon. Soon it would be time to drift to one of the back tables.

"Something wrong, sir?" Hovering over my table was the café owner, a pleasantly round man in a fresh white shirt with sleeves neatly folded halfway up his forearms.

"Everything's fine, Mr. Willis."

"Actually, Willis isn't my real name. Folks started to call me that way back in high school. Funny how a nickname can stick with you."

"Must be nice having two names. Sometimes I wish I'd change mine. It might come in handy sometime."

He smiled politely but didn't tell me his real name. I didn't tell him mine, either. "Thanks for your concern," I said, "but everything's fine here."

I leaned toward the window as the door of the Pritchard Hotel swung open. A man wearing jeans with holes in the knees left the hotel and crawled into a taxi. Too young to be Roth. Besides, I knew that Roth usually traveled by bus. In fact, the desk clerk at the Pritchard had told me that Roth arrived here in Maylene, Indiana, three months ago by Greyhound. This was the longest that I ever knew Roth to stay in any one town . . . which was probably why I had finally caught up with him.

The owner said, "I was afraid that something was wrong with your lunch."

My hamburger and french fries lay untouched in front of me. "I guess I'm not as hungry as I thought."

I looked down at my belt, now cinched two notches tighter than a month ago. I felt fitter now than I had in years, even though I was still a few pounds heavier than the last time I was on TV. I wanted to look my best for next week's appearance at the Magic Oasis nightclub in L.A. It was my first real break since being blackballed by the TV networks over five years ago. Once I had rid myself of this obsession to learn Roth's dagger trick, I could get back to polishing my show. Maybe I could shed another pound or so in the few remaining days.

Just as I was reaching in my pocket for my cigarettes, I turned to watch the hotel door open. Two women carrying shopping bags walked out and went in opposite directions. Somehow the cigarettes didn't feel right in my hand, and I looked down to see that I had mistakenly taken out my deck of cards. There was no name on the card box, just a drawing of a swan. They were privately manufactured and cost twenty dollars a pack.

The café owner said, "Do you play cards?"

I sighed. Ordinarily I delighted in performing impromptu magic. But not today. I wanted to keep my eyes on the hotel entrance. I didn't want to spend another five years catching up to Roth again. I lit a cigarette and puffed on it hard and fast, with the faint hope that my clouds of smoke would chase off the owner. But when you run a joint like the Willis, where it smelled like the exhaust fan above the grill was running in reverse, you probably thrive on stale air. He smiled through my haze and said, "I know someone else who uses cards like that."

"Oh yeah? Then he must be a bridge player. That's what I use them for. Bridge."

He looked at me doubtfully. "This guy told me that the surface of his cards were treated to give a better grip. He does tricks with his cards. Do you do tricks?"

I tapped the box on the table, debating whether a quick trick would get rid of him or just whet his appetite. Instead of actual tricks, I decided on a few flourishes—flashy demonstrations of skill. Taking care to avoid the wet bottle marks on the table, I ribbon-spread the cards, stretching them out in a perfectly straight line, making sure that every index of every card was visible. I slipped a finger under the first card and turned it over, causing the rest to flip over—one by one—in a chain reaction, like cardboard dominoes. I scooped up the cards and did a slop shuffle, mixing the cards faceup and facedown. Squaring the deck, I waggled my finger in quick little circles above the cards. I again ribbon-spread the cards, showing that they were now all faceup again. I reassembled the deck, put it back in the box, and started to hand it to him. As his fingers closed around the box he flinched. "What . . . ?" The deck had suddenly vaporized. His hand was squeezing thin air.

I glanced back at the window in time to see the door of the hotel glide closed as someone entered.

"Not bad," Willis said, ". . . for an amateur. If you practiced, I bet you could get real good. That guy I told you about—his name's Roth—performs here regularly. The customers love him. We could never afford to pay him what he's really worth. Would you believe that he works here for free? He usually comes

in a little past noon. Then he sits here all day, reading newspapers
and drinking beer. He's a real private guy. Doesn't talk to
anyone. But every night at about nine, Roth takes out his deck of
cards and starts doing magic. Better stuff than you'll ever see on
TV."

Nine o'clock? The prospect of eight more hours at the Willis
Café depressed me.

The manager said, "Roth's been a real boon for business.
People stop in just to see him work. I offered him a small salary,
on the condition that he perform more than once a night, but he
turned me down flat. He said that ten minutes a night is plenty.
Even so, I keep him in good supply of free food and drink. Plus,
he gets to keep all his tips. With the kind of crowds that he draws,
it's worth it. Say, I got an idea. Why don't you stick around?
Maybe he could give you some pointers. He does a dagger trick
that's dynamite."

I held my breath, hoping that Willis wouldn't say: "Just wait
till you see him!" But he did anyway.

Using many gestures, Willis described to me Roth's star trick—a
feat with a razor-sharp dagger. According to Willis, Roth was
still at the top of his form.

I said, "Say, I think I've heard of that fellow. Is he about sixty
years old? Kind of sickly-looking?"

"Yeah. That's him. Every time he starts coughing, I hold my
breath. But when he picks up that deck of cards, you forget all
about how sick he is."

The waiter approached my table and apologized for interrupting. He said, "By any chance, is your name Harry?"

I nodded and smiled graciously, thinking that he had recognized me from TV. But of course I was wrong. An absence of
nearly six years from television is an eternity.

He said, "There's a telephone call at the bar for you. It's not a
woman, but if you still want me to say you're not here, I will."

I looked around at the buzzing lunchtime crowd. Almost all
the table were filled and the bar customers had to take care not to
knock elbows. "How did you know my name? Did the caller
give a description of me?"

"No. All the guy said was he wanted to talk to the man sitting
by the window with the café's name painted on it. He said your
name was Harry."

I looked down and saw the name of the café written in a misshapen shadow that stretched the whole way across the table.

"I'll take that call."

On my way to the bar, I glanced back. The owner was on his hands and knees, looking for the vanished deck of cards. Some people just hate to admit it when they enjoy a magic trick. The waiter, misunderstanding, told Willis that I had already given him his tip.

The television above the bar was tuned to a talk show. The guest was a beauty expert who was doing makeovers on the studio audience. As each subject came onstage the men at the bar whistled and clacked their glasses.

I took the phone from the bartender and pressed it hard to my ear. With my finger in my other ear, I said hello, trying not to shout. Although the connection was free of static, the caller's voice was faint. He said, "Mr. Colderwood? Ah, I thought that was you sitting there. How come you didn't eat your lunch? Willis's cholesterol-enriched burgers don't meet your fancy?"

"Who is this?"

"First, Mr. Colderwood, I want you to look out the front door."

I didn't know what to expect. Was it some kook on the street with a wireless telephone playing a prank? Maybe he had just stripped my van and now wanted to enjoy the expression on my face. The voice added, "And please look up at the fifth floor of the Pritchard Hotel."

I did as requested and saw a white-haired man standing at one of the windows, holding a phone in his hand. He wore small, round spectacles and a butter-yellow shirt. He waved at me. And I, not wanting to be ill mannered, waved back.

The TV talk show was now featuring swimwear fashions. The whistling and glass tapping intensified.

"My name is Arlen Roth," the man on the phone said. "I take it you want to see me. Or more precisely, you want to see me and my dagger."

I swallowed hard and hoped that I wouldn't sound overanxious. "I've been looking forward to this for a long time, Mr. Roth. There's a seat waiting for you at my table."

"I'm afraid I'm not going to visit the café today."

"Why? Aren't you feeling well?"

"Of course I'm not feeling well. How would you feel if someone was trying to kill you?"

The bar customers boisterously competed to come up with the most absurd sexual remark about the models parading across the screen. I again looked up at the fifth-floor window. Roth was gone.

I said, "I'll be right over."

But all I heard was the dial tone. And a bar full of loud, lonely men.

CHAPTER TWO

Seven years ago in St. Louis I had missed Arlen Roth by a scant four days. The owner of the poolroom where Roth performed nightly said that Roth had fled town without any explanation. A few months later, I received a reliable tip that Roth was attending a regional magic convention in New Orleans. Missing the start of a nationwide theater tour, I chartered a plane to New Orleans—eight hundred miles out of my way—only to find that there was no Arlen Roth registered at the New Orleans Hilton. Coincidentally, a conventioneer named A. Ross had checked out of his room an hour after my plane had touched down at New Orleans International Airport.

What brought me to Maylene, Indiana, today was a phone call from a ghostwriter named Warner Huston. Only two days ago I had been holed up in a motel room near Pittsburgh, entering into the fifteenth hour of a marathon rehearsal session. Slowly and painfully I was resurrecting my pantomime act for my engagement at the Magic Oasis. I had gotten out of practice because silent magic simply didn't work in the dives that I'd been playing recently. Survival there depended on a sharp tongue, machine-gun pacing, and the good sense to know when to duck. The shot-and-a-beer crowds couldn't care less if you knew all fifty-three different ways of producing a billiard ball barehanded.

To get booked at the Magic Oasis, you had to either be a hot, up-and-coming magician or already be one of the established magic cadre. Since I was attempting a comeback, I uncomfortably fit into both of these categories. After receiving the news of my booking, I hurriedly bought a dozen doves, seven hundred dollars' worth of silk handkerchiefs, thirty decks of extra-thin playing cards, and a hundred-and-fifty-dollar set of multiplying billiard balls. The balls were so expensive because they were cast in a special rubber that made them three times easier to palm than wooden ones. A cassette recorder purchased from a K Mart supplied my rehearsal music.

After four days of subsisting on caffeine and delivered pizza—four days of looking in the mirror at fingers that seemed to be getting clumsier instead of more dexterous—I began to lose perspective. I started to scream at my doves. I imagined that they were conspiring to get revenge for my grueling rehearsal schedule. I feared that if I turned my back on them, they would start flapping their wings in unison and fly their entire cage out of the motel room and down the highway to the Pittsburgh Zoo where they would then beg for sanctuary.

When Warner Huston called, I had just knocked over a chair while chasing one of my doves around the room. I was taking potshots at it with a blank gun, trying to scare it back into the cage. Huston explained that he was from Hartford, Connecticut, and was ghostwriting an autobiography for Arlen Roth. He said he had read an interview with me in an entertainment magazine named *Midway*. I had granted that interview because I was happy for any kind of publicity that promised not to depict me as a has-been. At the end of the article there was a brief mention of my quest for the elusive Arlen Roth and his dagger trick. Huston then told me where Roth was currently staying. He hung up before I could ask him why Roth's life merited an autobiography.

I welcomed the opportunity to get out of that cramped room filled with birdseed and cooing. With my doves loaded in the back of my van, I headed for Maylene and my long-awaited meeting with the resident magician of the Willis Café. I carefully avoided driving past any zoos during the trip. No use giving the doves false hope.

The Pritchard Hotel, having long ago dispensed with bellboys and room service, was rapidly on its way to becoming a home for transients. I didn't wait for the elevator. I raced up the fire stairs, taking the steps two at a time. Figuring on two sets of windows for every room, I counted my way down the hall on the fifth floor until I was standing outside of what I thought was Roth's room. I leaned on the wall, waiting to catch my wind. I looked down at my belt. It was drooping again, and I tightened it yet another notch. When I got my sequined tuxedo out of mothballs next week, maybe it wouldn't require a trip to the tailor after all.

Mounted on the wall next to the door was a box that said BREAK GLASS IN CASE OF FIRE. Somebody had long ago heeded the sign: the glass was all gone. The only thing inside the box was a folded newspaper. Which seemed logical. The Pritchard Hotel was such a tinderbox that if it ever caught fire, sitting down and catching up on the evening news would make as much sense as trying to escape.

The wood on Roth's door was more scarred than the lids of my high-mileage magic trunks. After I rapped on the door, I heard a bumping noise followed by scraping metal, as though someone had opened a closet door and had slid coat hangers along the hanging bar. In my mind, I saw Roth hurriedly selecting his best suit to wear when he performed his dagger trick for me. I pounded harder.

Hurried footsteps inside got louder and then stopped. I heard a muffled voice that seemed to be passing through more than one door.

I said, "What's that? I didn't hear you."

I heard someone clear his throat and then say, stronger and more distinctly, "The door is open."

It was Roth, but his voice sounded higher and dimmer than on the phone. It was the voice of a man too weak to even answer his door.

"Are you all right?" I asked.

This brought a feeble chuckle. "You didn't come all those miles to talk through a closed door, Mr. Colderwood. Please come in."

It was the second time that he had called me by name. Even a younger man with perfect vision would need binoculars to recognize me in that café from the whole way across the street, five stories up. I wondered what had frightened him so much that he'd scan the street with binoculars.

I opened the door and walked into a large living room. A darkened hallway to the right led to a closed door, probably a bedroom. Two wide brass chandeliers hung from the ceiling, and gilded sconces adorned the walls, making me think that many years ago the Pritchard had been an upscale apartment building.

Against the far wall of the living room were a sofa and two chairs with frames made of tubular metal. The sagging cushions were covered with faded black cloth and a layer of dust. A stack of books weighed down one arm of the sofa. Moving closer, I saw that they were magic books, one of them an anthology to which I had contributed a modest manipulative routine with sponge balls. In front of the sofa sat a coffee table with a scratched Plexiglas top. Atop the table a portable television silently played the same talk show as in the bar. The program was nearly over and the makeup artist was now showing off the job he had done on the show's cohost. That guy's not bad, I thought. Just goes to show how easy it is to fix yourself up. All you need is a little time, a designer wardrobe, a half-million dollars in lighting equipment, and a Hollywood makeup man.

The items lying next to the TV sent a shiver through me: a sheet of newspaper, a deck of playing cards, and a dagger with an ivory handle. Roth's tools of the trade. I regarded them with the reverence of a pilgrim visiting a shrine. A carving of a smiling devil decorated the handle of the dagger. I reached to take a closer look at it but jerked my hand back at the sound of Roth's voice. Louder now, but still indistinct.

I whirled around, unsure of its direction.

"I'm in the bedroom. I'll be out in a moment."

"But you said that you were in some kind of danger . . ."

"No, not immediate danger. I just wanted to make sure you didn't dawdle on the way up here. Make yourself at home."

"If there's one place I'm at home, it's in a hotel room."

I walked over to a low-slung wooden bookcase next to the hallway. Something about the bookcase looked familiar. Constructed of mahogany, it consisted of three shelves of books. The bottom shelf was elevated several inches off the floor by thin legs. The titles of the books ran the gamut from how-to manuals to pulp adventures. I had never heard of any of them before.

I tugged at the glass covering, but it was locked. Nice hotel, I thought. Furnishes a bookcase and then is afraid you'll read the books. The lock defied the probing of my lock picks. Probably broken, I thought. My fragile pride wouldn't admit that the lock had stymied me.

Atop the bookcase sat a framed photo of a brunette in a halter top and short skirt, daintily holding a magic wand in her fingers. The silver material of her skirt caught the light from many different angles. The picture had been carefully composed to keep the viewer's eye sliding up and down the delicate lines of her body from her forehead to her toes. The picture was dated twenty years ago and the handwriting in the lower corner said: *Arlen, hope it lasts forever. Mary.*

Of course, "it"—whatever that was—had not lasted quite forever. Otherwise, Roth wouldn't be roaming the country now, doing his small part to support the bus companies, bar owners, and hotels. Mary must have been Roth's assistant at one time.

I now realized where I had seen the bookcase before. I thumped the top of it with my knuckles and didn't like the hollow sound. I pressed my face to the glass. Although the spines of the books had a variety of thicknesses and colors, the titles were lettered in an identical style.

I tugged on the bookcase and it slid easily away from the wall. Too easily. It was built on hidden casters. Which confirmed my suspicion. Why else would a bookcase be on wheels? I slid my fingertips along the scallops and scrolls of the carvings along the sides, admiring the craftsman's attention to detail . . . all of which was needless. After all, it was only an illusion—literally. The books were phony. The bookcase was hollow.

I remembered seeing a similar bookcase onstage at a small magic convention in Minneapolis several years ago. I couldn't recall the magician's name, but I remembered him playing the role of a wealthy man puttering around in his study, smoking a pipe. After spinning the bookcase around to show it on all sides, he blew smoke at it and the books vanished. In their place was an attractive blonde lying on her side, head propped lazily on her hand. Every bookworm's dream.

I knelt down beside the bookcase and moved my fingertips along the polished wood on the side. Even this close, it was hard to see the outline of the hatch door through which the assistant could crawl in and begin her wait for the moment when the rows of fake books would drop out of sight so she could make her glamorous appearance.

I felt along the bottom and found the switch to unlock the hatch. Next to it was another switch, probably the trigger for the actual working of the illusion. A hole in the switch made it possible for an invisible nylon thread to be attached.

A familiar thrill bubbled within me. It was the same thrill that the ten-year-old Harry Colderwood used to feel whenever the mailman delivered mysterious packages postmarked New York and Chicago. Each new trick was a new riddle to explore and conquer.

As I absently toyed with the switch under the bookcase, I looked back at the coffee table and Roth's dagger and playing cards. I sighed. The bookcase could wait. It was another puzzle—the dagger—that had brought me to this room. I moved back to the table.

Leaning over the table, I reached for the dagger, but my inbred respect for a fellow magician's secret stopped me. I cleared my throat and spoke loudly. "Mr. Roth. I couldn't help but notice your dagger out here. And—uh—are you coming out soon?"

His laugh was nearly a cackle. "Can't wait, can you, son? All right, go ahead. Play with my knife all you want. But it won't help. The knife and the cards are completely ungaffed. Just be careful not to cut yourself."

That was all the invitation I needed. I pulled a chair over to the table. Amused at how damp my palms were, I picked up the deck of cards. Underneath the box of cards was a small business card. My business card. At first glance, it didn't look like a business card. There wasn't even any lettering on it. Decorating the face of the card was a fine-lined drawing of a waterfall. If you held the card at an angle, the blades of grass in the foreground magically blended together to spell a message. The encrypted message on the card read *Harry Colderwood, Magician.* Apparently Roth had been aware of my interest in him longer than I thought.

I tossed it back on the table and spread out the playing cards. I randomly picked out cards and examined them until I was satisfied that the deck had not been tampered with.

I unfolded the sheet of newspaper and held it up to the light. It was free of any double thicknesses or hidden pockets. I laughed when I saw that a faint impression of Dick Tracy had rubbed off onto my moist palm. Relax, I told myself.

I crossed my legs, leaned back, and stared at the glinting blade of the dagger. As I had done many times during the past decade, I envisioned Roth performing the trick.

First, Roth asks a volunteer to choose a card, remember it, and return it to the deck.

I selected one of the facedown cards. The card I had chosen was the special one included by the manufacturer that listed the odds of being dealt the various hands of poker. After taking sober note that the odds against a Royal Flush are 649,740 to 1, I dropped the card facedown onto the table. Using both hands, I mixed the cards around until my selected one was completely lost.

Roth covers the heap of cards with his newspaper.

I spread the paper over the heap of cards, shoving the stray ones underneath. I picked up the dagger, clutching the handle so tightly that my fingers ached.

My mind raced ahead to what the rest of the trick was supposed to look like: *Roth now slams the dagger through the newspaper and raises the knife back up, taking the whole newspaper with it. He displays the underside of the newspaper: one card has been impaled. However, it is the wrong card. Just when the audience thinks that the trick has gone hopelessly wrong, a playing card shoots out from the pile of cards. Roth chases it across the tabletop with his knife. The card hops off the table and onto the floor. Roth wildly stabs at it, sinking the knife into the floor after each miss. Finally he succeeds in sticking the card. He proudly displays the runaway card as the correct one. The card is still twitching, trying to escape from the point of the knife.*

I looked toward the bedroom and hoped that Roth would stay in there a bit longer. I didn't want him to witness the mockery I was making of his star trick.

I poised the knife over the newspaper. Moisture flowed freely down my forehead. I gripped the handle tighter, feeling the carving of the devil dig deeply into my fingers. I raised the knife higher and closed my eyes.

And heard a dripping sound.

Great, I thought. Now I'm sweating all over his newspaper. I opened my eyes and saw that the paper was indeed wet. But not with sweat. It was dotted with tiny circles of gleaming red.

The dagger clattered out of my hand and I wondered how I had cut myself. I examined my hand front and back but didn't find any cuts. Then where—?

I picked up the knife and saw a thin bead of blood seeping out of the seam where the blade entered the handle. The blade had been wiped clean, but the job had not been thorough enough.

Fresh blood, I thought. Not enough time to coagulate. But whose? I called to Roth but didn't get an answer.

It had been several minutes since he had last spoken.

"Roth. Are you all right?"

I dropped the knife on its cushion of newspaper and cards and ran down the hallway to the bedroom. I shoved the door open and stepped back. Through the doorway I could see a man sitting on the floor, his legs splayed and his back against the bed. He was wearing dark slacks and a pair of slippers, but no shirt. His head was slumped forward and his hands were flat on the floor, as if he had been trying to push himself to his feet. A bib of red covered his chest and had trickled down, soaking his trousers and part of the rug.

I ventured into the room and checked the closet and under the bed. No one else was there. Then I returned to the body. Gently touching both sides of his forehead, I pushed his head up and looked at his limp, pale face. His eyes were closed and he wasn't wearing his glasses.

"Looks like someone knew a better trick with your dagger, Roth."

His throat had been slit. He had bled quite a bit before dying.

CHAPTER THREE

The sound of a familiar melody drew me to the nightstand. I slipped my hand underneath and pulled out a telephone that was off the hook. I picked up the receiver. And heard music. It was the simpering theme song from the TV talk show that had been playing in the café.

"Hello," I said.

A familiar voice rumbled. "Are you all right? What the hell's going on? The bartender said it sounded like someone was in trouble there. We wanted to call an ambulance, but we didn't know where you are. What's your address? Hello? Hello?"

I slipped the receiver back on the cradle. The man on the phone was the owner of the Willis Café. Roth must have called again after I left the café. From the bedroom window I watched the owner hunch over the bar, fingering the button of his phone like a Morse code key.

I decided to search the bedroom. There wouldn't be much to search: just a dresser, a nightstand, and closet. I spotted a wallet, a pair of eyeglasses, and a pair of binoculars on his dresser, and I figured that was a good place to start. Even though I made a wide circle around the body, I tripped on its outstretched foot. I caught myself on the edge of the dresser, thinking for a moment that Roth was playing a monstrous joke on me. But when I looked back, his body remained in the same lifeless sprawl as before.

I found a thin collection of worn dollar bills inside the wallet. The picture section contained only one photo—another shot of Mary, his old assistant. In this picture, her costume of tassels and fringe seemed attached to her voluptuous body by mere threads. I had the feeling that Mary had once made her living by removing clothing like this.

The only other item in the plastic section of the wallet was a Pennsylvania driver's license that had expired a few years ago. The address was a room number on a street in Bethel Park. The picture on the license left no doubt in my mind that the dead man on the floor was actually Arlen Roth: the same wispy white hair, parted on the side and combed straight across . . . the same upturned nose that looked like a young boy's. In the picture he was wearing spectacles with small, round lenses that matched the ones on his dresser. I took a last look at the photo. Roth had given the photographer from the Department of Transportation one hell of a grin that day, as if he had been sitting for a high-priced portrait photographer. I clapped the wallet shut.

The sole item in the top dresser drawer was a soft leather case with a shoulder strap. The case was crammed with playing cards, dice, sponge balls, and coins—Roth's close-up magic act. An act that, according to witnesses, carried as much punch as thousands of dollars' worth of stage illusions. The other drawers contained a meager supply of clothing, mostly pullover shirts that ran from olive to brown.

What happened to your yellow shirt, Roth? The one you were wearing at the window?

I switched on the closet light and found a plastic bag stuffed with dirty clothes. I dumped them on the floor. No yellow shirt.

I checked the row of hanging shirts. Halfway down I found a bright yellow one with a cross-hatching of faint blue lines. Most of the buttons had been ripped off and the sleeves were smudged with blood. The material was slit down the center of each smudge. The killer had wiped the blade of the dagger on the shirt.

I held the shirt out in front of me and studied the stains. Perplexity begin to cancel out my fear and revulsion. It was the same perplexity I usually feel when another magician baffles me. It usually builds to an obsession that won't die until I unravel the secret.

Two main questions nagged me. I knew they had to be connected. They chased each other around in my head, like a dog trying to bite its tail.

How did the killer spirit the dagger out to the living room without my noticing? In my mind's eye I saw the animated dagger homicidally rebelling against its master and then sliding out underneath the bedroom door. Now, that would be one hell of a magic trick. Only I didn't believe in *that* kind of magic. The kind that I believed in was accomplished with wires, threads, mirrors, magnets, and other assorted forms of fakery. No wires or magnets killed Roth.

My second question was: Why did the murderer remove Roth's shirt before killing him . . . and then wipe the dagger blade on it? My head spun as impossible questions chased after even more impossible answers.

After hanging the shirt back up, I noticed a small cardboard box on the closet floor. It was an overnight express package addressed to Roth. I lifted the flaps, reached inside, and felt something smooth and long. As soon as I pulled it out, I thrust it back inside and closed the flaps hard, as though the contents might jump back out at me. The box contained a single bone. I was sure it had come from a human leg.

I switched off the light and moved out of the closet and over to the window. I tried to raise it. After resisting three attempts, it finally opened with a squeal. The window had been painted shut. I leaned outside and looked down. Most of the ledge below had crumbled away. What remained looked as substantial as an old, dry sponge. Below that was a five-story drop. There was no fire escape.

As I lowered the window I saw a flicker of red reflecting off the window of the café. My first thought was that something on the grill inside had caught fire. But then the flickering brightened into a harsh, pulsing red. It was the reflection of police-car lights.

A squad car rounded the corner and slid to a stop in the middle of the street below my window. The driver got out and un-snapped his holster. Two other squad cars converged from opposite directions and pulled curbside. Four officers rolled out of these two cars and clunked their doors shut, almost in unison. Without so much as a nod to each other, they raced into the Pritchard Hotel, leaving the driver of the first car to stand vigil in the middle of the street. I was sure they hadn't come here for lunch.

I tried to imagine the police listening sympathetically to my story and then patting me on my back, sending me on my way.

But the image kept going sour. Instead, I saw hours of interrogation and a two-bit lawyer who kept spilling coffee on his notes while he tried to plea-bargain me down to second-degree murder. I saw my name being removed, letter by letter, from the marquee in front of the Magic Oasis nightclub. I also saw my doves up for sale in the window of a sleazy skid row pet shop.

I looked at Roth's dried blood on my hand. All of a sudden, I just didn't feel like explaining anything to anybody.

Rabbits have long been the magician's stock-in-trade. I've pulled them out of hats, produced them from under peoples' coats, and even hypnotized them. But today was a first. I was going to run like one.

Heading for the hotel-room door, I suddenly remembered the dagger. My prints were all over it. Same for the phone. There wasn't time to do a thorough job of wiping off the prints, but at least I could take the knife with me. I went back and wrapped it in Roth's sheet of newspaper. Making certain there was an extra padding of paper around the blade, I stuffed it down the front of my pants and pulled my shirt down over it.

As I put my hand on the doorknob whispers out in the hall stopped me cold.

"Think he's still in there?" one voice said.

"No use taking chances," another said. I heard two hard clicks that sounded too much like hammers being pulled back on revolvers.

I scanned the room for a hiding place. I already knew that escape through the window was impossible. But even if I could have crawled outside, I would have made an easy target for the cop below. He would have had as easy a time as a poacher at a petting zoo.

Fists pounded the door. "Police!" one voice called. Then he said quietly to his partner, "What's keeping the guy with the key?"

As I made a frantic circuit of the room my elbow grazed the lamp on the end table beside the sofa. I caught it with both hands before it tipped over.

Mary, the sexy lady in the picture on the bookcase, seemed to be smirking at my predicament. "Got any ideas?" I asked. Too bad that the books below her weren't real. Maybe one of them could have been a text on outfoxing the police. I—wait a second. Of course. The bookcase.

I knelt beside the bookcase, ignoring the poking of the dagger in my ribs. I flicked the switch underneath the bookcase. Nothing happened. The cops pounded harder on the door. I flicked the switch again. Nothing.

What the hell, I thought. Feeling silly, I whispered the word "Abracadabra," and the hatch fell open. You have to be a magician to know how to talk to these things.

I dragged a living-room chair over beside the bookcase and positioned it to look like it belonged there. I crawled up onto the chair, resting my knees on the cushion so that I wouldn't leave footprints. Feetfirst, I wormed my way into the dark load chamber. I had to tuck my chin against my collarbone in order to get the door closed. If I had eaten that lunch at the café, I don't think I would have gotten the hatch shut. It was that tight a fit.

I heard the click of a key in the hotel-room door and then the smacking of the door against the wall.

Footsteps.

And the sound of smashing glass as one of the policemen knocked over the lamp that I had barely avoided breaking. Well, one less item to fingerprint.

Then I heard: "My god! Get in here, Frank."

As Frank's footsteps disappeared into the bedroom the inside of the illusion suddenly grew brighter. The hatch door of the bookcase had popped open again. I retreated even farther inside the box, my back straining against the top. I pulled the hatch shut again and this time felt the latch catch solidly. Crouched in a space that barely gave me room to breathe, I listened as more police were called to the scene.

I nurtured two hopes. One, that none of the policemen were hard-core readers and would want to browse through the "books" on the shelf. And second, that no one would accidentally trigger the mechanism of the illusion. Because then they would be treated to the damnedest magic trick they've ever seen . . . one in which a row of books is instantly transformed into a prime murder suspect.

CHAPTER FOUR

Roth's bookcase illusion was designed to conceal a petite female assistant for a maximum of five minutes . . . not a grown man for several hours. It was a such a tight squeeze, I was afraid to take a deep breath for fear that I would burst the sides. With my shoulders hunched and my legs retracted, my knees supported an inordinate proportion of my weight. They felt as flat as saucers.

The temperature inside the bookcase kept creeping higher. My nose tickled from the faint scent of perfume which I guessed had been worn by the last assistant to use the trick and somehow had permeated the wood. I clamped my teeth together and pressed the edge of my hand to my nostrils to stave off a sneeze.

For the next hour and a half the total darkness was occasionally relieved by flashes of light that flitted through the cracks of the bookcase as the police photographer went about his job. Once in a while, there was deep-throated laughter when someone made a wisecrack. But the sounds I mostly heard were footsteps and unintelligible murmuring. A few times the footsteps grew louder and the talking became more distinct. Some of the conversations centered on the murdered man in the bedroom. But most of the time the topics were mundane. For a few minutes, two officers taking a little break from their work played a little game, seeing who could name the most ways of "interrogating" prisoners without leaving any marks.

A plodding set of footsteps from out in the hall grew louder, stopped at the doorway, and then entered the room. The entire room grew silent. A man with a nasal voice said, "Nice party. Where's the host?"

"In here, Doug," a voice from the bedroom called. The footsteps faded again. Several minutes later the plodding footsteps returned, stopping in front of the bookcase. The wooden joints of the bookcase groaned, and I felt a downward pressure on my back. I jumped at the noise but quickly realized that someone was leaning on top of the case. At the same time, I felt a stinging pain stretch across my lower stomach and then subside into a dull throb. The blade of the dagger had cut through its newspaper sheath. I confined my cry to a muffled grunt.

I slid my hand across my stomach and it came away sticky. I couldn't tell how deep the cut was. Although the felt lining beneath me would easily drink up any blood, my imagination tortured me with images of red oozing through the cracks of the illusion and giving me away.

I heard Doug's voice again, talking to an officer named Jerry. Doug's voice seemed to resound from the very wood that surrounded me. As the two detectives chatted their cigarette smoke drifted inside the case and made me crave a cigarette myself. I began to plot a way to light one up: *Let's see . . . their smoke would probably cover up the smell of mine. If I put all my weight on my left hand, I could reach my pants pocket and get my matches. Then if I angle my shoulder so that the cigarettes in my pocket are— What the hell am I thinking of? My god, being cooped up in this illusion is warping my mind. No wonder my doves hate me.*

"What do you make of this goddam mess, Jerry?"

"It's a toughie. I think it's going to stay on the books."

"We've got so little to go on. I'm just thankful that the old guy was a transient. If he was a pillar of the community, it would probably mean our jobs."

"Did this Roth have many friends in town?"

"Nah, he kept to himself. The desk clerk said he was real polite. Lots of pleases and thank-yous."

"See, Jerry? It pays to be polite." Doug's laugh was slow and dry. I heard a *chhh* sound and then smelled lighter fluid mixed in with more smoke. "One of the boys told me that Roth played cards over at the café across the street."

"No, not quite," Jerry said. "He did *tricks* with cards."

"A magician, huh? No big loss. Those guys really piss me off when I can't figure out their tricks. Just once I'd like to pull out my gun and say: 'Okay, smart ass, why don't you let us all in on the secret?' Hey, maybe Roth's fancy finger-flinging got him in trouble. Maybe he got into a card game with some guys who didn't like him dealing himself a royal flush every third hand."

"It's possible, but we don't have any evidence that he gambled."

"What about robbery as a motive?"

"It doesn't look plausible. We found a small amount of cash in his wallet and a few hundred stashed in a sock in his drawer. I was thinking he might have some money hidden in these books here."

"Let's check it out," Doug said. "You know, this is a pretty impressive bookcase. I didn't know the Pritchard was so well appointed."

"Would you look at the carvings on the sides. I bet it's worth four or five hundred. They sure don't make 'em like they used to."

"I didn't know you were into antiques, Jerry."

"Not me, it's my wife's hobby. But it doesn't take an expert to see that this case is worth something. Anyway, it's not the hotel's. It's Roth's. We found receipts from several different trucking companies in one of his drawers. He apparently shipped it ahead to every city that he roamed to. It cost him a small fortune."

"What a goofball. Well, he won't have to ship it anymore. Let's take a look at these books." The entire bookshelf shook as he tried to lift the glass cover. "Dammit. It's locked. Break the glass, will you, Jerry?"

"No way, I don't want this case ruined. If there's no next of kin, I'd like to try to get it for my wife's collection. She'd love it."

Doug sighed. "Oh, all right. I'll call a locksmith to come over and open it."

"I'd really appreciate it. But, Christ, look at the time! All the lock shops in town will be closed by now. It'll have to wait."

The police photographer approached Doug and said that he had taken all the pictures he needed. Doug thanked him and sent him on his way.

Jerry said, "What do you make of that card with the picture of the waterfall on it?"

"Hard to say. Maybe he used it for a magic trick. We're going to show it to a local magician and see if he knows what it's for."

Great, I thought. Let's hope it's a magician who doesn't know how to decipher the card.

"What about this notepad they found in Roth's trousers?"

"Notepad?" Doug said. "Let me see it." I could hear him take short, shallow breaths. After a minute, he let out an uncertain whistle.

"These words don't make any sense. Looks like some kind of code. 'AT.' That could be someone's initials. And what the hell is a 'hanky-pank' and a 'flat joint'? Think they have anything to do with drugs?"

"Beats me."

"Ah, here's a name that maybe we can go on: 'Marianna.' Think this Marianna is a broad? Yeah, maybe that's what he means by 'hanky-pank.' Maybe the old fellow was screwing around with someone."

"Marianna might be the chick in the picture here. After all, it's signed 'Mary.' "

Jerry laughed, amused by the idea of a love triangle involving Roth. "That's all well and good. But how do you explain the bone?"

"The *what?*"

"The bone in the closet. Jeez, didn't they tell you?"

I heard Doug rush to the bedroom, with Jerry trailing behind. Then I heard Doug chew out his men for not telling him about the bone.

I knew that I'd have to find the killer before the police cracked the little code on the waterfall card and issued an APB for former TV magician Harry Colderwood. But I also knew that I had a substantial jump on the police: I knew the meaning of the words on Roth's notepad.

But before I could get out of this infernal box, I had to wait for the police to trudge through the rest of their investigation. My respect for magicians' assistants had deepened during the last few hours. I felt like I was hiding in a microwave set on slow cook.

It would have been fun to stick around and hear the locksmith's reaction when he realized that mere lock picks wouldn't open this bookcase, that magic words and the flick of a secret switch worked far better. But I had better things to do.

I adjusted the dagger so that it wouldn't cut me again. As I patted the carved handle I whispered: "Thanks for getting me into all this."

Thus far the magic of Roth's dagger had not impressed me at all.

CHAPTER FIVE

Fifteen minutes had gone by since I had heard any voices. I slid my fingers around the inside of the illusion, trying to figure out how to open the hatch. I discovered a small hook-and-eye assembly in a recess along the bottom. I gave the hook a flip and the hatch flopped open. The very pores of my skin seemed to absorb the rush of cool air. A chill gripped my entire body. I sneezed four times in a row and the chill departed as suddenly as it had hit. I crawled out of the bookcase, amazed at how my legs, in just a few hours, had forgotten how to move. Wanting to postpone as long as I could the pain of standing straight, I slumped down in the chair.

I pulled up the bloody front of my shirt and checked out my wound. The hours in the dark had overstimulated my imagination. My cut was long but not deep, a bit more serious than a scratch but nothing that a few Band-Aids wouldn't take care of.

I stood up and crossed to the coffee table, pushing down hard on my hips, trying to straighten my back. Roth's deck of cards still lay on the table, but my old waterfall card was gone. I thought of the day several years ago that I burned the last two thousand of those cards because I couldn't get anyone to take one. Now I wished that I had burned two thousand and one.

In the bedroom, blood still stained the carpet in front of the bed. Roth's wallet and the box containing the human bone were gone.

I dropped on all fours and crawled to the window. I raised my head enough to peer over the sill. Only one police car remained in front of the hotel. A crowd, mostly kids, milled about on the sidewalk. I could see two men in suits inside the Willis Café, talking to the owner. No doubt he was filling them in about a stranger who did card tricks and asked funny questions about Roth. I needed to make some phone calls. But the sooner I got out of this room, the better.

I wrapped the dagger in a sock from Roth's dresser drawer and stuffed it back in my pants. Then I walked out of the bedroom and over to the outside door. I flattened my ear to the door and listened for movement in the hall. Not hearing anything, I turned the knob and pushed. The door barely budged. I put my shoulder into it and, after a sharp snap, the door glided open. I had broken the police seal.

Not wanting to risk the elevators, I descended two flights of stairs and waited near the third-floor door. Although I was exhausted after being cooped up for so long, I didn't want to sit down. I leaned against the wall and lit a cigarette. I enjoyed its calming effect so much that when I finished it, I fired up another. Finally I heard what I was waiting for—a slamming door.

I stepped out into the hall and caught up to a man heading for the elevator. He was wearing a white straw hat with a flowered headband. Over thirty years older than me, he radiated a warmth that I knew would make me feel guilty for lying to him.

"Are you room three-sixty-seven?" I asked, covering the bloodstains on my shirt. "You're the guy with plumbing trouble?"

"You got the wrong man. I'm three-forty-six. Are you from maintenance? Hell, I didn't call about any plumbing, but let me tell you just the same: Nothing works right in my place. I mean nothing! Every time I turn on the hot water, it sounds like someone's beating the pipes with a crowbar. And I swear that the ceiling gets a half inch closer to the floor every day. And, oh yeah . . . while I'm thinking of it, every time I switch TV stations, the lights dim. In fact, the only thing that works good in my place is the telephone."

As I nodded in sympathy he asked, "Where are your tools?"

I laughed. "Tools? Hey, pal, you've got to remember that this isn't any multimillion-dollar condo. I have to pay for my own tools, so I keep them locked up in a storage cupboard in the basement until I actually need them. This isn't exactly a safe place to work anymore. Didn't you hear about the poor slob two floors up that got stabbed today?"

"So that's why the cops were swarming all over the place."

"Yep, you can't be too careful. Well, I've got to get back to work." I started to walk away.

"Say, wait," the man said. "After you're done in three-sixty-seven, could you take a look at my place?"

"I don't know. I'd hate to rip things up for you, particularly if the job takes me all evening."

"No problem. I'll be visiting my daughter's and won't be back until late."

"I'll see what I can do."

The man got on the elevator, and as soon as the doors closed I headed down the hall. I passed 367 and stopped in front of 346.

I had told him that I didn't have my tools with me. That had been a lie too. I had all the tools I needed. I took out my set of picks and set to work on his lock. Getting into his room was as easy as passing through a turnstile at the ballpark.

The man had been telling me the truth. His phone worked just fine. After hearing a healthy dial tone, I replaced it on the hook. I wrote down the list of words on the notepad in Roth's pocket. I thought that Roth might have been compiling some sort of glossary for his book.

I knew that a *hanky-pank* was a kind of carnival game that offered prizes that looked expensive but were really cheap.

A *flat joint* was any carnival booth that was crooked.

Marianna most likely referred to Marianna, Ohio, a town that had a reputation as a "show town"—a place where traveling shows, especially carnivals, were always welcome.

And *AT* stood for *Amusement Times*, a magazine about outdoor entertainment: fairs, amusement parks, and carnivals.

It would be a while before the police pieced together the meanings of all the words.

From directory assistance I got the number for the editorial offices of *AT*. As I dialed I thought about how superstitious carnival people were, especially about the color yellow. Roth's murderer could not bear to kill him until he had removed Roth's yellow shirt. And yet, after the deed was done, he wiped the blade clean on the shirt. Perhaps he felt so powerful afterwards that he wanted to show his disdain for this traditional color of bad luck.

A switchboard operator answered and then connected me with the routing office. I identified myself as an out-of-work ride operator who was trying to get hooked up with the carnival that had last played Marianna, Ohio. The man from the routing office punched up the data on his computer and said, "You must be talking about the Bateman Carnival."

"Bateman, eh? Tell me, what kind of an outfit is it?"

"Uh, sir . . ." The man laughed uneasily and I imagined him running his finger along the space between his collar and neck. "The purpose of the routing office is to help carnies find employment and to pass along important communications to traveling shows . . . not to give evaluations of any one show."

"Thank you. You've told me enough. Now could you tell me what city the Bateman is currently playing?"

There was more keyboard tapping and then: "They're just completing a week's engagement in Indiana." He gave me the exact location of the fairgrounds. I estimated it to be a two-and-a-half-hour drive away.

My next call was to Dr. Terry Swanson, an allergist friend of mine who knew as much about the history of magic as he did about pollen counts. He wrote a monthly question-and-answer column for *Genii* magazine. He said, "Congratulations, Harry. I just heard about your gig at the Magic Oasis. It was refreshing to receive some positive news about you for a change. I was getting tired of the kind of magic history that you've been making lately. I imagine that right now you're probably hard at work, ironing out all the last-minute kinks in your act, right?"

"Actually, Terry, I had to put my rehearsals on hold. Something's come up."

"Uh-oh. This 'something' isn't a scrape with the law, is it?"

"Well . . . ."

"And there wouldn't happen to be a dead body involved in all this, would there?"

"Are you sure this is long distance? I'd swear that you're right beside me, stewing in the very same soup as me."

"For chrissake, why can't you make my job a little easier? I'm supposed to write about people's lasting contributions to the art of magic, not their latest bizarre escapades. You won't be satisfied until I end up writing your obituary. All right, what can I do for you this time?"

"I've got a question."

"Go ahead. Just remember, I'm no forensic pathologist. My patients may wheeze and sneeze, but they're certainly not ready for any refrigerated drawer."

"This isn't a medical question, Terry. It's about magic history." I described the bookcase in Roth's room. "Do you know anything about that illusion?"

"Boy, that sounds familiar. Unless I'm mistaken, there were only a few of them made. Let me check my cross-files."

In ten minutes he was back on the line, saying, "According to a twenty-five-year-old edition of the *MUM* magazine, a similar illusion was used by the winner of the stage contest at the national convention of the Society of American Magicians that year. The article says that a prototype of the trick was first used in a small carnival called the Bates Show. It doesn't say who designed it."

"I have a feeling the author was referring to the Bateman Carnival."

"Could be. I've heard of the Bateman Carnival before, but not the Bates."

"Tell me this: Does the name Arlen Roth mean anything to you?"

"Offhand, no."

"What can you tell me about the Bateman Carnival?"

"Harry, carnivals aren't my field of expertise."

"Don't fence with me, Terry. The guy from *Amusement Times* did the same thing."

There was a long pause, and I heard Terry gasp and then sneeze.

I laughed. "What's this? An allergy doctor who won't take his own cure?"

"Not really." His voice was suddenly leaden. "Not all allergy symptoms are brought on by sensitivity to certain substances. Some are triggered by emotional upsets."

"And my mentioning the Bateman Carnival made you sneeze? Why?"

"Harry, I've heard rumors—nothing specific—that the Bateman is a rough outfit for entertainers. My advice is, don't get mixed up with them."

"I'm sorry, but I can't follow those doctor's orders."

He started to argue but thought better of it. He simply wished me luck and invited me to call if I needed his help again. I think he secretly hoped that when I called I'd have a rousing story for his next column.

After I hung up, I slid a twenty-dollar bill under the phone. I looked out the window and saw that the policeman had finally left.

I had one more call to make—a local one. I wanted to talk to the makeup man I had seen on TV.

CHAPTER SIX

The whirring air conditioner kept both the heat and music outside from invading the trailer. After sitting in the carnival office for ten minutes, I found that no amount of squirming or shifting positions could make the guest chair comfortable. Its implicit message was: State your business and get out. Well, I had stated my business, but the man behind the desk seemed in no hurry to talk. Hands clasped behind his head, he was looking placidly out the window.

I tried once again to ease the ache in my lower back. I leaned the chair back, elevating the front legs a few inches. It didn't help. My chair had only a minimum of padding and didn't have wheels on it like the big one behind the desk.

I followed the man's gaze out the window and watched the Ferris wheel turning lazily in the distance, its empty cars rocking back and forth. I could see a couple of kids with faces buried in cotton candy wander past the trailer window. A young couple, clad in matching shorts and walking hand in hand, stopped in front of a wood-framed booth with canvas walls. They listened as a man with a tight grin spoke rapidly, clapping his hands together. He pointed to the tiers of shining gifts and appliances behind him and then to a rotating plastic cylinder loaded with a half-dozen giant dice. He was leaning over his counter so far that I thought he might tumble out. After exchanging uneasy glances, the couple scurried away. The game operator rested his face on his hands, glumly waiting for new customers—an unhappy spider tending his web.

At eleven o'clock in the morning, the working day at the Bateman Carnival was just beginning.

Bill Bateman, Jr., had done his best to give his trailer the appearance of a normal business office. There was a cherry-red telephone and a Rolodex file on his desk. Next to the desk stood a top-loaded file cabinet. On the other side of the desk, against the wall, was a bookcase, filled with books about business and accounting—real books, not like the phonies in Roth's hotel room.

Overstuffed file folders lay stacked on top of the file cabinet. Bateman tried to neaten them, but papers spilled out and drifted to the floor. He retrieved them and plopped them on top of the heap, saying, "My secretary will fix them." He settled well back into his high-backed leather chair and eyed me hesitantly. "Tell you what I'm going to do." His voice was singsong, like a barker enticing me to buy a ticket to a sideshow.

Bateman was a small-boned man in his midfifties. He wore a Hawaiian print shirt tucked in at his trim waist. His hair, an artificially dark brown, was styled straight across the top of his head in an effort to mask its thinness. It would soon need another color treatment: his sideburns were turning white at the roots. He propped a foot up on his desk and retied the new white lace of his running shoe. Upon seeing me stare, he explained, "Most com-

fortable pair of shoes I've ever owned. I do a lot of walking with
my job. Also, there are certain times when I need the silent
approach."

He took a pair of squarish spectacles from a desk drawer,
inspected them for dust, and slid them on. He regarded me with
fascination, as if I were an abstract painting that defied interpretation.

In a soft drawl, he said, "So Mr. Harry Cotter wants to be a
carny, eh? Just like that"—he snapped his fingers—"you want
me to hire you green?"

I nodded and widened my eyes, trying to look naive and
determined. My fake mustache itched, but I resisted the tempta-
tion to touch it. The makeover artist, reluctant to do what he termed
"reverse work," had charged me two hundred dollars, most of
my cash reserve, to tack on a few more years to my appearance.
He had added color to the sunken areas beneath my eyes and
shaded in my temples and cheeks to make them look hollow.
Then he had whitened my hair at my widow's peak and above
my ears. He then coached me on how to apply the makeup. I was
sure that I could reasonably duplicate his work for the next few
days.

I couldn't afford to be recognized by anyone who had ever
seen me on TV. Also, if the cops came snooping, I didn't want
to match the description of the man who had been in Maylene
searching for Arlen Roth.

"Harry, you don't have any carnival experience, right?"

"Correct."

"Well, let me clue you in on a few things. Carny life ain't for
everyone. It's damn hard. I know. I grew up in this carnival. My
father built this show." He pointed to a framed picture on the
wall. I expected to see a photo of Bateman, Sr., but the photo he
was referring to was a long black-and-white picture of a cluster
of amusement rides. The trucks parked at the edge were at least
thirty years old. Dominating the foreground was a massive merry-
go-round, with horses more lifelike than on the one I had passed
on my way to Bateman's trailer. Also, the Ferris wheel in the
picture carried more cars and rose higher into the sky than the
current model.

Bateman's words poured out faster now. He must have delivered this speech many times before. "Like a lot of punk kids, I
grew up counting the days until I could escape from my old man

and his way of life. Dad had always assumed that I would take over the carnival, but I resisted all his attempts to groom me. When I told him that I wanted to go to school, he cheerfully sent me to the University of Pennsylvania, where I took a bachelor's in business. Money was never a problem in those days . . . not like now. I think he secretly dreamed that after graduation I'd come back, sheepskin in hand, and say that I had come to my senses and wanted to learn the business. But after college I landed a job with a firm on Wall Street, where I stayed for two years. I told the old man that I loved my job. Plain truth, I was miserable. Growing up in a carnival can ruin you for life. There I was, bored solid in the most exciting city in the world! After Dad's first heart attack, I took a leave of absence from my job and met up with the show in Alabama. The outfit was in chaos, and it took a week to get things running smoothly again. By the time Dad got out of the hospital, I was hopelessly hooked on the job. You see, Dad had never let me do much managing. My apprenticeship had consisted of crappy, lowlife jobs—clean this, sweep up that. I had never realized what a challenge it is to keep the wheels rolling underneath this show. There's a different crisis every day: A major ride breaks down and the closest replacement parts are in Canada . . . a church group decides to picket your gambling games . . . a new local government doesn't want to play by the old rules. Wall Street—or any street—can never beat the excitement of our midway. Hell, I still love it when I get up in the morning and sometimes have to look at my calendar to know what state I'm in.''

His phone rang, and he swiveled his chair away from me to answer it. While he talked he took in the view of the Ferris wheel as it jerkily made one revolution, loading and unloading passengers. He suddenly shot up straight in his chair. ''He's what? Well, you tell that shit Hawkins to back his truck up to the nearest dumpster and raise the bed. Tell him that if we have to, we'll buy our popcorn from the Duncan brothers. And—hold on . . .'' Bateman leaned closer to the window to watch a little girl stroll down the midway with her father. She was tottering back and forth, hugging a giant panda that stood taller than her. ''Carlson, forget the popcorn. Get your ass over to Paltrow's dice joint. Yes, I mean right now. You tell him if I ever see him roll the dice with less than three players at the counter again, he'll be reading the help wanted ads in *AT*. Yeah, he might as well be giving the pandas away. And get a whiff of his coffee. If it's got whiskey in it, kick him in the ass and keep kicking until he's off the lot. And do it loud . . . let the others hear. Might as well get some advertising out of the deal."

He hung up and watched the Ferris wheel crank into high gear. With a proud smile, he turned back to me. "I never pass up a chance to remind them who they're working for. Now, Mr. Cotter, what the hell do you do?"

"I'm a magician."

That made him laugh. "Don't need a magician. I already have enough problems. Stale popcorn and drunken game agents, for starters. Anyway, aren't you a little long in the tooth to be starting a new career? How old are you?"

"I'm only forty-four."

"You look closer to fifty to me."

I felt my shoulders sag. Just because I had paid the makeover artist to make me look ten years older didn't mean I had to feel that much older.

"What's your regular job?"

"I used to be a high school English teacher, but I resigned last June."

"Any family?"

I nodded. "I'm divorced and the kids are almost grown."

"Not wanted by the law, are you?"

"Nothing but a few outstanding traffic violations."

"How about—"

"Skip the quiz, would you? If you aren't interested in me, let me know so I can move on to another show. With the season half over, the odds are getting slim that I'll get hired anywhere. Based on what I've heard about you, I thought you'd be different than the other carnival owners. Guess I was wrong."

"How's that?"

"In a lot of ways I'm like you. My old man was a carny, only he never owned any show. Hell, as far as I know, he never owned anything."

"You never knew him?"

"Nope. When Mom and him first split up, he used to visit us during the off-season, but I was too young to remember. Ever since I was a kid, Mom always made me promise to never become a carny. So I took up the hobby of magic instead. I did pretty well locally. Last year I did more than sixty shows for banquets and parties. But I always wanted magic to be more than just a hobby. Maybe I have some of the nomad in my blood. I get restless every spring. This year I finally got tired of fighting the itch to join a traveling show. Maybe I won't be a carny for the rest of my life. But I'll never know unless I try, will I?''

He looked at me with interest. Suddenly we were just two kids trying to fill our fathers' shoes. "What show is your dad with now?"

"The last show he worked with was Nichols Amusement. Before that, he traveled with the Falcon Carnival for who knows how many seasons. They stick mostly to the South."

"What's he doing now? Retired?"

"Yeah. Permanently. He's dead."

"That's too bad."

"Four summer ago he got in an argument with a ride monkey during a crap game." A ride monkey—an amusement ride operator—is considered by some carnies to be on the lowest rung on the carnival social order. "The monkey shot him twice in the head."

"Jesus." He reached for the files, the ones he'd said his secretary would take care of later. After doing some nervous rearranging, he flipped open his file cabinet, dropped them in, and then locked it. He then went over to the air conditioner and twisted some knobs. When satisfied, he returned to the desk. The room didn't feel any different.

He said, "I hope they threw the book at the bastard that did it."

"Unfortunately, no. The police never had a clue who did it. You know how carnies are."

"Yep. Close-knit and tight-lipped."

"Exactly. They recovered the murder weapon, though. A thirty-eight snub-nosed revolver with the face of a smiling devil carved on the handle. Ever know anyone that owned a gun like that?"

"Smiling devil, eh? No, sorry. Even though hand guns are almost as plentiful as tattoos among carnies, I don't allow them on this lot." He arched his eyebrows in sympathy. "The guy that knocked off your daddy was probably a drunk. Alcohol is another thing I'm strict about. I'm not against a man having a drink now and again, but drunks get booted off my lot with no second chances." He studied my face, as though searching his memory for any carnies that bore a resemblance to me. "Was your dad a ride monkey, too?"

"No, he ran a flat store."

"Are you sure you know what a flat store is?"

"Sure. A gambling game that's so crooked no customer ever has a chance to win. I think it got its name because when you run a flat store, it's a case of flat-out robbery."

His tone grew ominous. "We run a Sunday school here . . . a real family show. I don't allow any flatties on my midway. Our games are all one hundred percent straight. Of course our odds do favor the house—just like Vegas—but we don't tolerate any rigging."

I nodded, pretending to believe him. I again asked if he had an opening for me.

"I do and I don't. The other day, one of my better performers left without any notice. The guy's name was Pitlor. A gem of a performer. He didn't do magic, but he seemed to do every other kind of novelty entertainment: paper cutting, silhouettes, lariat tossing, juggling, shadowgraphy, trick whip cracking. With him gone, there's a gaping hole in our midway."

"If you want, I'll audition. I'll get my equipment from my van and . . ."

He greeted my enthusiasm with distaste. "No need, no need. I'll tell you what. Sight unseen, I'll give you a week . . . but just a week, no more. Understand, if I hear bad things about you, I'll tell you to pack your bags. Since you're green, I'll only charge you half the rent during that first week. After that we'll iron out a new rent agreement. Deal?"

"Okay." He gave me a handshake that was loose and quick.

The door of the trailer opened and a raven-haired woman in her early forties stood uneasily in the doorway, unsure if she was interrupting something important. I recognized her right away as the woman in the photo in Roth's room. She wore an eggshell-white blouse that showed off her steep curves. Her hair refused to stay off one eye and she continually brushed it away. I smiled politely, and she returned it with such warmth that for a few delicious seconds I forgot all about Bill Bateman and his stuffy office and my new job. Even the chair I was sitting on suddenly seemed comfortable. Maybe that makeup artist had done more for me than I thought.

Bateman seemed to ignore our little exchange. "Harry Cotter, meet Mary Trunzo. She's the one that keeps the paperwork from burying me. Mary is *old* carnival." She frowned at the word "old." "My daddy hired her when she was eighteen, when we still had cootch shows. If I ever decide to front a girl show again, Mary could be the star all over again, right, Mary?"

She sighed, not from embarrassment but from having heard the same compliment too many times. She said, "Don't let Bill kid you, Harry. If he thought that I was going to take it off for a living again, he'd go through the roof. Sometimes I think he got rid of the skin shows just to get me off the stage and all to himself."

The air conditioner choked and nearly died. The lights dipped and rose. Bateman shot to his feet as though the wiring were directly connected to his body. He picked up the phone, thought better of it, and hung up. He took a walkie-talkie out of his desk. "Galloway? Galloway? Jesus, where are you?"

"Yeah," the radio squawked.

"The power just did a nice brown over here in the office. Get someone to check it out."

"Will do."

Looking over at me, Bateman said into the radio, "One more thing. We got a new guy here. Yeah, a greenie. He's does magic and he's going to take Pitlor's spot. How about setting him up? While you're at it string some juice into his tent. And tell the barker that he'll have to add another show to his schedule tonight. Treat him good, okay? He's not a carny . . . yet. But his old man was."

The radio squealed something unintelligible and Bateman put it back inside his drawer. He turned back to me and said, "What did you say that you're driving? A van?"

"That's right."

"A sleeper?"

"No. But I carry a sleeping bag in case of an emergency."

"Then you'll want to find a motel room for the few days we have left in this town. Unless, of course, one of the carnies with a trailer decides to put you up. Can you be ready to perform by six this evening? Good. Galloway will be over in a minute and show you your spot. He's our wirer and he's one of the best.''

"What's a wirer? The guy who strings your electricity?"

"Partly, but a wirer is a lot more than that. Galloway's in charge of all our maintenance and he's worth his weight in gold. A good wirer is almost as vital as a good fixer.''

"What's a fixer?"

"He's the one who takes care of the local officials so they won't interfere with us.''

"Why worry about that? I thought you said your carnival is a 'Sunday-school show'?''

"Oh, it is, but carnivals will always have an unsavory reputation, and people will always find lamebrained reasons to shut us down. It's the fixer's job to make sure that doesn't happen. It requires a lot of diplomacy. He also helps settle disputes between the carnies. Jacques Carlson is our fixer. He's the guy I was talking with on the phone about the drunk.''

Mary, now standing at the window, said, ''There's Jacques now.''

I looked out and saw a man, well over six feet, ambling up the center of the midway, staring straight ahead. His knit shirt was stretched like a second skin over his massive, chest and arms. His thin blond hair, parted in the middle, barely touched his ears on the sides but was long enough to cover his collar in the back. Carlson walked with a bowlegged gait, swaying his body from side to side.

I said, ''I thought you said that being a fixer required diplomacy. That guy doesn't look like he'd be too good with words.''

"Words are useless without the strength to back them up. For my money, Jacques Carlson is one of the most diplomatic men I know. He gets very few arguments from anyone. And he's come a long way with this carnival. Would you believe that he started out as a Bozo? Even today, he's still a performer, but he restricts himself to just one show a day. He does a lot of strong-man stuff and martial-arts tricks.''

"You said Carlson used to be a Bozo. Do you mean a clown?''

"Not exactly,'' Mary said, still at the window. ''A Bozo is a guy in a clown suit who sits above a dunking tank and insults the crowd. He tries to get them mad enough to buy baseballs to throw at the target in front of him. If they hit the target, he drops into the water.''

As Carlson strutted along the midway he glared at everyone who crossed his path. I wondered if his Bozo days were completely behind him.

Bateman noticed that Mary was still intently eyeing Carlson's bodybuilder physique. He pulled the blind down, saying that the midday glare was making it hard to see inside the office.

I stood up and shook Bateman's hand, but my attention was on the photo on the wall behind him, the one of the Bateman Carnival of days gone by. I noticed for the first time an insignia on the hub of the giant Ferris wheel. It was upside down, and I cocked my head to see it better.

It was the face of a smiling devil.

Sure, Bateman. Just a Sunday-school show.

CHAPTER SEVEN

I had to take swift, long strides to stay abreast of Walt Galloway, the wirer for the Bateman Carnival. Galloway, a ruddy-faced man with small, round ears and a wide nose, was wearing a shapeless plaid work shirt that bunched at the waist. Constant exposure to the sun had scorched his arms and faded his shirt. As we walked he periodically took off his baseball hat and scratched his balding head with the brim. A leather pouch stuffed with jangling tools hung by a strap from his shoulder. He wore an incongruously flowery after-shave. I tried not to stand too close.

The breeze floating down the midway was at my back. While insufficient to counteract the baking sun, it was still strong enough to coat the tops of my shoes with dust. Through the din of the roaring rides and the pops and bangs of the midway games, I heard a rumble of thunder. Carnies all along the dirt street leaned over their counters to pass judgment on the clouds and their threat of a profitless day. The only carny who ignored the weather was a woman in an army shirt who was intensely demonstrating how easy it was to win prizes by throwing softballs into a peach basket.

The Bateman midway was short—no longer than a city block. The crowd was still too sparse for the carnies to more than halfheartedly pitch their challenges of fun to passersby. The signs above each joint were painted with the same gaudy yellows, reds, and blues. The titles of each attraction were a combination of puns and phonetic misspellings: *Gawdfathah's Hit-Man* (a shooting gallery), *Nick-Hello-De-In* (prizes given for tossing nickels into stacked goblets), and *Wheel Spin—You Win* (a chuck-a-luck wheel). Many of the booths used music from boom boxes to liven up the atmosphere. Their disco beat blended uneasily with the ragtime calliopes of the merry-go-round and other kiddy rides.

For every three questions I asked, Galloway deigned to answer only one. As we walked he avoided looking at me. His head was in a constant pivot, keeping tabs on every operation we passed. Whenever he spotted something he disapproved of, he jotted a note on a pad from his shirt pocket.

During our journey down the midway, Galloway stopped to drive a fresh nail into a strip of colored numbers that was curling up on the counter of a dice game. He also soldered a loose wire on a faltering loudspeaker in a dart-throwing booth, and then he stabilized a wobbling horse on the merry-go-round.

After he finished with the horse, I asked, "Where are we going?"

"Pitlor's old tent is the farthest one on the left."

"Sounds like a good location."

He gave me a sidewise look. "Bateman told me you were green, but he didn't say you were stupid. Your spot is the dead worst on the whole midway."

"Which one's the best?"

He waved to a man driving past on a fork truck and said, "The best location on the midway is on the right, near the entrance to the carnival, next to the first concession stand. By the time people make it down to your end of the lot, they're usually low on money."

We stepped aside to allow a Jeep to creep past. I squinted my eyes to protect them from the dust. The driver of the Jeep was dressed similar to Galloway, but his passenger wore a blue police uniform and opaque sunglasses. The passenger said, "Stop here," and the driver obeyed. The man in uniform slid his glasses down and gave me an appraising up-and-down stare. Feeling like a piece of cattle up for auction, I waited for him to complete his inspection. Then I wet my lips and said, "Something wrong?" He smiled at me, poked his glasses back up on his nose, and signaled with his forefinger to the driver. The Jeep lurched ahead.

"What's he?" I asked. "A security man?"

"No. He's a local cop. But he's working for us this week . . . if you know what I mean." He winked but didn't smile.

"How do you mean?"

"Let's say that someone raises a fuss over losing their whole paycheck at one of the game booths. It's good to have a guy in a local uniform who can smooth things over. The mark never has a chance. He never realizes that the cop belongs to us."

"How the hell do you lose your shirt in a nickel-and-dime game?"

Galloway stopped in front of a ride called the Whip. "You really are new, aren't you?" He watched the operator push and pull on two long levers to maneuver the next car into place. When the car was completely stopped, he raised a mesh hood in front to unload and load passengers. Galloway spat on the ground, not taking his eyes off the operator.

He said, "Take the nickel-pitch game. The normal wager is five cents. But if Nick, the operator, believes that a mark has a bulging wallet, he rapidly escalates the stakes . . . up to, say, a dollar a toss. He then lets the mark win several times in a row. Get the picture? Just when the mark thinks that he's going to really clean up, Nick raises the wager again to five dollars a toss. Then he lowers the boom. In about three seconds, he can transform his booth from a game of chance into a game of no-way-in-hell-can-the-mark-win."

"Bateman tried to tell me this was a clean outfit."

For the first time, Galloway gave me a smile—tepid and brief, but a smile just the same. "We're a regular Sunday school. But we just happen to own the whole church *and* the collection plate." His eye settled again on the Whip. He didn't like what he saw. "Would you excuse me for a minute?"

He unslung his bag of tools and hung them on the fence in front of the Whip. He walked over to the operator and spoke a few quiet words with him. The operator, a whiskery man in his early thirties, wore his hair in a thin, ropelike braid down to the middle of his back. When the operator laughed at him, Galloway took a half step back and jammed a short punch into his chin. The operator wobbled back two steps before regaining his balance. His eyes widened, showing plenty of white. Though it looked for a moment as if Galloway might strike him again, the operator never raised a hand to defend himself.

Galloway pulled a long wrench out of his toolkit and stomped over to the control levers of the Whip. After a few minutes of cursing and wrench turning, he tried out the levers himself. He spoke again to the operator, thrusting his finger in his face. The operator flinched with Galloway's every movement. Then Galloway left him to continue his loading and unloading of passengers.

Resuming our walk down the midway, Galloway said, "The brakes were completely gone on that ride, and that creep was too lazy to give me a call. To stop that ride, he had to throw the whole thing in reverse every time. Ride monkeys—that name's too good for them. I think real monkeys are a damn sight easier to get along with. Bateman makes good coin off these rides, but he still insists on hiring morons like him so he can pay them substandard wages. Does it make any sense to you? For chrissake, people's lives are at stake."

"That jab of yours was pretty clean. It's a wonder you aren't the fixer for the show instead of Carlson."

"Oh, I've been fixer before. I've worn a lot of different hats in this carnival over the years. Hell, there was a time that I even made puppets for a Punch and Judy act. Even though I love just about everything about carnivals, I feel more at home working with machinery than with people. Trouble is, things have changed too damn much from when Bill Bateman, Sr., was alive. Today it's every man for himself. Back in the old days, a fixer like Carlson wouldn't have lasted long. He'll never understand the meaning of the words *light touch*. He thinks that just because he breaks boards with his bare hands in his strong-man act, everyone should automatically do his bidding. He's got some painful lessons ahead of him."

We stopped in front of a tent whose thirty-foot sign read

Mysteries of the Orient. "This is your place of business, Mr. Harry Cotter. I hope you like it."

"*Mysteries of the Orient?* You've got to be kidding. Bateman never told me this. I don't have any Far East costumes. I don't even have any equipment with Oriental decorations."

"Don't sweat it. Pitlor's show wasn't Oriental either. We've been using that same sign for years. I think they even used it for the cootch show that Mary Trunzo used to dance in. We just repaint it every few years."

"I get it. Tell me, what happened to Pitlor? How come he left?"

"Who knows? He just took off. Although there's a small, loyal group that's stuck with the carnival for years, high turnover is still a fact of life here. People join the carnival for all sorts of reasons. Some are trying to escape trouble in the real world—booze, or drugs, or a bad marriage, or a jam with the law. Sometimes that trouble catches up with them anyway."

"Do you think Pitlor was in some kind of trouble?"

He frowned at my interest in my predecessor. "Pitlor? Nah. He was too clean to be in Dutch. I think the kid just got lonesome for Mom's home-cooked meals. But, for whatever reason, he's gone and you got yourself a job. As long as you keep up your rent and stay sober—and not have too many people ask for refunds—you'll do all right here. The Bateman is the greatest carnival I've ever worked for."

He pointed at the caged booth and the platform in front of my tent. "Nice setup here. You never have to worry about talking up a crowd or taking admissions. We provide you with a roving barker and ticket girl. As soon as you start your show, they move on to the next attraction. They can service several acts that way, making the same circuit over and over. By the way, what kind of act do you do?"

"Magic."

"No kidding? Illusions or sleight of hand?"

"A little of both. Since I don't have an assistant, I'll be doing smaller tricks—standard stuff right off the magic-shop shelf. I do have a passion for the fancy stuff, but I usually stick to the tried and true. There is one trick I've been working on for a couple of years. I wish I could show it to you, but it still has bugs in it. Maybe you've seen someone else perform it before."

Step by step, I explained Roth's dagger routine, paying close attention to Galloway's reactions. At first he seemed startled by my description, but his attention seemed to lag as I went on. By the time I finished, he seemed bored. His eyes were fixed in the distance on the rigid up-and-down gallop of the merry-go-round horses. "Sounds like a great trick. Nah, I've never seen anyone do it." He shook his head. "God, would you look at that? That guy must be nuts. See how fast he's got that merry-go-round running? Those kids are terrified. Pardon me."

He briskly headed for the merry-go-round. After a few seconds, he turned and called, "It was nice meeting you. Make yourself at home."

I stood in front of the entrance to my tent. Below the *Mysteries of the Orient* sign was a platform that was just wide enough for one person to walk a few steps back and forth. Squat weatherproof speakers flanked either end, with an empty mike stand in the center. Next to the platform stood the admissions booth. A semicircular opening at the bottom of the window allowed for ticket stubs to be passed out. Before entering the tent, I turned to check on how Galloway was making out at the merry-go-round. He passed it by without giving it a second glance.

The stage inside the tent consisted of foot-high portable risers butted together. The footlights were simple white floodlamps bolted to the edge of the platform. A dusty curtain at the rear of the platform provided a place to stand before going onstage. Tiered wooden bleachers, with two rows of metal folding chairs in front, filled out the rest of the tent. The ground was littered with candy papers and soft-drink cups. I decided to do a quick cleanup job before setting up my equipment.

In the space of an hour and a half, I had driven my van to the back of the tent, unloaded my apparatus and table, set them up onstage, and changed clothes. Inside my van, I took a last-minute check in the mirror, straightening my tuxedo tie and pressing my fingers reassuringly on my phony mustache. I heard footsteps crunching on the gravel, but when I stepped outside, I didn't see anyone. Upon entering my tent, I found a man wearing a suit, standing with his back to me.

"Can I help you?" I asked.

He whirled around, facing me with fingers curled into fists that were as intimidating as two balls of dough. He was a tall man with dull gray hair that was unfashionably close-clipped. He cautiously assessed me with quivering eyes, narrowed into slits. Though he was only in his forties, his shoulders already showed signs of stooping. His necktie was rolled up and stuffed in the breast pocket of his brown suit coat. His recently polished shoes were caked with mud around the edges. When he didn't speak, I repeated my question.

He gulped, but that didn't help control the tremor in his voice. "You're not the guy who was here yesterday."

"No, I'm new here. You're a little early. My first show doesn't start until six."

"What happened to the other man?"

"Who? Chuck Pitlor? I honestly don't know."

"But he said he was going to help me."

I was familiar with the kind of urgency that drove his voice. It was the kind I usually regretted lending an ear to. Nevertheless, I asked, "What kind of help?"

He straightened his shoulders and lowered his fists. Some of the white receded from his knuckles. "The other guy was new too. Said he had been with the carnival for only a few weeks. I think that's why he was willing to help me."

He carefully cased the tent, even looking under the platform to see if anyone was hiding there. As he turned I noticed a puffy bruise on his cheekbone near his ear. "How did that happen?" I asked.

His grin was forced and threadbare. "*This*"—he gently laid a finger on the bruise—"is the price I pay for asking questions around a joint like this. As for who did it, I don't know what his name was. This outfit always seemed to get a different goon every year."

"Was he a Nordic-looking fellow with blond hair and inflated arms?"

"Yeah, that's him. He just swatted me with the back of his fist, like I was some kind of pesky insect. I guess I should be grateful it wasn't worse. He warned me not to come back, but I could tell that he was secretly hoping I would. He really wanted an excuse to take me apart."

"But you came back anyway."

"Hell, I never left. I washed up in the men's room and came right over here."

"You shouldn't tempt fate. Jacques Carlson is what the carnies call a fixer. His job is to make things right for the carnival . . . at any price. You'll never win against him. Why don't you give me your phone number, and I'll ask around about Pitlor. Maybe I can save you a lengthy stay in the hospital."

"If this man Pitlor is really gone, then he can't help me. You see, I'm the self-appointed 'fixer' for my family. We've got a problem that the law has never adequately solved for us. I'm sure the answers are hidden in this carnival."

"What kind of problem?"

"My brother is missing and I'm sure that someone in this carnival murdered him."

CHAPTER EIGHT

My visitor's name was Lee Sanders. He talked while I made last-minute adjustments on my magic equipment. He didn't seem to mind when I turned my back to load my billiard balls underneath my coat or when I ducked behind the curtain to hide my doves inside my various small box illusions.

Sanders said that he had last seen his older brother Willy twenty years ago when Willy, accompanied by a half-dozen other young men from their hometown of Milroy, Indiana, had boarded a bus, on their way to join the army.

"The group was recovering from a farewell beer bust, and the guys were full of macho pledges to set Southeast Asia on its ear. We first realized that something was wrong when army officials informed my mother that Willy had never shown up for induction. At that time, I was a freshman in college. I took a week off to look for Willy. His buddies claimed that the last time they'd seen him was in the town of Tolley.''

I said, ''How far away is Tolley from here?''

''About twenty-five miles. It's close to a place called Spanier.''

He laid his fingertips on the edge of his bruise and made gentle circular motions.

''The first thing I did after talking on the phone with Willy's buddies was to drive over to Tolley. I got very few answers there. The manager of the fleabag hotel where Willy and his buddies stayed overnight said that my brother had never checked out. When the manager didn't hear from Willy in a few days, he cleaned out his room and stored all his possessions in his office. It cost me two weeks' worth of room rent to get them back. Among his few personal effects, I found a ticket stub to the Bateman Carnival, which had been playing near Tolley all that week. None of Willy's friends had mentioned anything about attending a carnival. The last they saw Willy was at a local bar. They said that Willy had left early in the evening with a girl under his arm and a smile on his face.

''The bartender said that Willy and his friends were a loud group. He said that he had poured drinks for a lot of service-bound guys and that his experience was that the noisier they were, the more frightened they were. He said that Willy's group must have been scared witless . . . with Willy being the loudest. Much later that night, at closing time, Willy staggered into the empty bar. He was a mess. Willy said that he had been in a fight, but the bartender didn't believe him.''

''Why?''

''He said that Willy's hands and face were scratched and cut badly. He looked more like he had been dragged across broken glass rather than punched and kicked. He said that my brother's clothes were shredded and bloody. The bartender offered to drive him back to his hotel room, but Willy refused. After tossing off a few shots of whiskey, Willy left the bar. No one admitted ever seeing him again.''

I asked Sanders if he had ever located his brother's date from that night.

He shook his head. ''Yeah, but she wasn't much help. She just said that shortly after they arrived at the carnival they had a big argument and split up. She doesn't know what happened to him after that."

"Was your brother the type to pick fights with strangers?"

"Sometimes. But he rarely bit off more than he could chew. He really knew how to take care of himself. He played varsity football and wrestled heavyweight on the high school squad. He finished third in the Golden Gloves for our region. But, at the same time, he was naive about a lot of things. Particularly the war. I think he viewed the war as just another sporting event—a really big away game, minus the cheerleaders."

"Besides the ticket stub, did you find anything else of interest among his personal effects?"

"A few things. This, for instance."

He handed me a business-size envelope from his inside pocket. I opened it and slid out a folded piece of paper. I spread it out and saw it was an old handbill from the Bateman Carnival. Although the bold letters across the top advertised *The Mysteries of the Orient*, this show had nothing to do with sleight of hand. Below, a row of photos showed six buxom women in a variety of steamy poses. Each pouted sadly in a way that the photographer must have found sexy. One of the "mysteries" was named Honey, but that wasn't her real name. It was Mary Trunzo.

I said, "I can now see why you came first to this tent. They still call it *Mysteries of the Orient*, but there hasn't been a girl show with this carnival for quite some time." I stared at the lineup of beauties and could almost hear the fuzzy saxophone, punctuated by the drummer's rim shots. "Your brother probably attended this strip show after he had that argument with his date."

I went outside and came back with half a bottle of Imperial whiskey from my van and two Cokes and a cup of ice from a carnival food stand.

Sanders took a gulp of Coke and whiskey. "Starting from Tolley, I tracked the carnival to a small town sixty miles away. Without thinking about the consequences, I walked right onto the carnival lot and started asking questions. I was politely ignored. But on the second day, even though I never accused anybody of anything, things got nasty. My reception was similar to the one I received today. So I gave up and went home . . . for that year. For the next five years, whenever the Bateman Carnival came close to my hometown, I mustered up the courage and traveled out to the carnival grounds, asking questions and showing pictures of my brother. Believe me, I took my share of lumps.''

"What did the law say about your brother's disappearance?"

"They theorized that Willy probably mouthed off to the wrong person and then took a severe beating for it . . . so severe it shattered his illusions of invincibility. The police told me to expect a letter from Willy any day—postmarked Canada.''

His crooked smile told me that the Imperial was working its anesthetic wonders. He said, "Crazy how things get turned around. I had always been labeled the frail one in the family. After college, the draft board didn't want me . . . said my feet were flat. Yet for the past six years I've run ten miles a day, and my flat feet don't seem to mind at all.''

He replenished his drink with another inch of whiskey. "After a few years, the Bateman Carnival stopped touring this part of the country. Years went by without my hearing any news of it. I figured that it had gone out of business. But when I saw the recent ads in my hometown paper, I couldn't resist driving over here and asking my questions all over again . . . if only for old times' sake.''

He took another pull on his drink. "It's still the same old carnival. Some faces have changed, but the tactics remain the same.''

We both sat down on the edge of the platform and listened for a few moments to the sounds of the midway: kids screaming as their rides took unexpected dips . . . the merry-go-round ponderously cranking out a Sousa number with a tambourine and bass drum backbeat . . . .barkers shouting impossible claims.

Sanders said, "What decade is this anyway? Here we are in an age of eight-in-one movie theaters, home videos, multimillion-dollar theme parks, and legalized gambling everywhere. Why the hell do people still flock to carnivals?''

When I shrugged, he said, "Even though this place hasn't changed much in twenty years, I guess I was foolish to think I could find out about Willy all by myself.''

He thanked me for the drink and handed me his business card. His official title was Financial Planner, another of the endless euphemisms for salesman.

I said, "Tell you what. I'll keep my eyes and ears open. I can't make any promises, but I'll call you if I learn anything. Do you have a picture of your brother?''

"I did, but that goon ripped it up."

As he stood up I said, "Whoa, hold on! No way are you leaving here on foot. If Carlson sees you again, he might do you up bad enough that the only place you'd find work is in the freak show. Listen, here's what we'll do . . ."

With Sanders crouching in the back of my van, I drove off the carnival grounds, exiting through the service entrance. After I parked a safe distance away from the gate, he got out and walked to the driver's side. I saw that his tie was now neatly knotted and he had taken a comb through his hair. Stepping outside the boundaries of the carnival seemed to have restored some of his self-assurance.

"One more thing," he said. "Even though the hotel manager had already cleaned out my brother's room, he allowed me to search it. I found an empty box of medicine that had a severe poison warning on it. It's always possible that it was left there by some other guest."

"Then maybe Willy committed suicide."

"Not Willy. He was as unlikely a candidate for suicide as he was for dodging the draft."

As I watched Sanders move through the parking lot, he seemed to walk more confidently than before. I hoped I hadn't given him false hope.

I looked at my watch. Only a few minutes before my first carnival show, and I still hadn't made a final decision on my repertoire of tricks.

Successfully performing magic as Harry Cotter, amateur turned pro, would require delicate judgment. If I wasn't good enough, I might lose my job and never get to first base in finding out who killed Roth. But if I performed too well, it might make Bateman suspicious enough to order Carlson and his biceps to pay me a visit.

As I drove along the makeshift roadway behind the midway, I fought to keep the steering wheel out of the ruts. Suddenly a fifteen-foot man crossed my path. I swerved, and he took a huge side step to avoid me. The twelve-foot inseam on his trousers concealed his stilts. He had a newspaper tucked under his arm and a cigarette in his lips.

"Sorry, buddy," he yelled as I drove by. "I'm late for work."

Farther along the road, I passed the fattest man I've ever seen in my life. He was sitting in a sling chair fashioned out of three-inch pipe and steel cable. Sitting on his knee was a dwarf dressed in a pair of shorts. While carrying on a spirited conversation they passed a bottle of wine back and forth. The dwarf drank with both hands, while the fat man held the bottle by the neck between his thumb and two fingers.

Behind another tent I saw a shirtless man in his bare feet, wearing a pair of red tights. With his head tilted back and Adam's apple protruding, he held in the air a thin rod whose tip was on fire. He repeatedly lowered the flame into his mouth. Each time he licked his lips, like a child enjoying a lollipop.

Just as Lee Sanders's contact with the Bateman Carnival had eventually turned his life upside down, I, too, felt disoriented, as if I had been dropped into a foreign country. I gripped the steering wheel, but my hands refused to stop their trembling.

Stage fright before a show wasn't unusual for me. But this was the first time that I had ever feared doing *too* well.

I leaned out the window and called to the fire-eater, "Warming up, eh?"

Flames roared out of his mouth along with his words. "Why don't you stuff all your fire jokes, pal."

"No reason to get hot under the— Oh, skip it."

If people could only be more proud of their professions . . .

CHAPTER NINE

The gum-snapping admission girl popped her head into the backstage area and dropped a cloth moneybag at my feet. "See ya later," she said and was on her way. Her voice was devoid of energy, ambition, and, seemingly, any interest in life at all. I tried but couldn't imagine a conversation between her and the barker, with his joke-a-second, kibitzing style.

I peeked through the split in the curtains. The audience filled only the first few rows of bleachers. Most of the folding chairs up front were empty. Five minutes ago the barker had quit "pitching" my magic show. I could now hear his amplified voice talking up an audience for Fred's Animal Farm, farther up the midway. According to the barker, Fred had once played the White House. I took pride in outclassing Fred's singing dogs and roller-skating chimps: the barker had credited the Harry Cotter Magic Show with three royal command performances.

I stole another glance through the curtain and tried to gauge the mood of the audience. Audiences are funny creatures, each with a distinct, unpredictable personality. There were times when audiences have embraced me like a member of their family. There were other times that they seethed with a hostility that bordered on violence. And I never had a clue why.

My previous carnival experience was limited to few grandstand shows at large state fairs, usually as a warm-up for a big-name comedian or country singer. But nothing had prepared me for this audience at the Bateman Carnival. The rows of sober faces reminded me of a jury in the middle of a three-month murder trial.

The barker had billed me as the premier attraction of the carnival. Attraction, indeed. I suspected that the attraction that had drawn this audience to my tent was similar to the one that causes a drifting boat to wander into an inlet.

With no one to warm up the audience or to introduce me, I took a deep breath of air that was heavy with the scent of popcorn and french fries. I flung back the curtains and bounded onto the stage. I took a sweeping bow, head to knees.

Which earned me absolutely no applause. Just nervous coughs and the sound of someone cracking his knuckles. The audience continued to talk quietly among themselves. When I came out of my bow, two bouquets of feather flowers materialized in my hands. Still no applause. The audience intently gnawed on their popcorn and cotton candy, waiting for more magic, but not giving any indication that they were enjoying it.

A man wearing a hat that advertised dog food was the most attentive member of the audience, watching my every move with wide eyes and open mouth. I plucked a billiard ball from the air. While I continuously showed my hand empty on both sides, the ball split and multiplied until there was one between each finger.

I waved a giant playing card in front of the cluster of billiards. When I moved the card away, the balls had turned into a huge fan of regular-sized cards.

I tossed away the cards and another fan sprang out of nowhere to replace them.

I had to walk to the edge of the stage for the next trick. Suddenly the platform lurched and screeched. I shot my arms out to my sides and took two side steps to keep from falling. With a thwack that sounded like a bat hitting a baseball, the platform took a nasty tilt to the right. My magic table glided toward the edge. I intercepted it only inches from disaster.

"Get the hell off!" the man with the dog-food hat said. He jumped out of his seat, rushed over to the right corner of the platform, and crouched down. Before stepping off the stage, I jammed my magic wand under a table wheel to keep it from rolling.

After a few seconds, the man stood up and said, "There." His hat was now gone, revealing a bald scalp that had rarely seen daylight.

"That ought to hold you temporarily," he said. "Just don't make any sudden movements. You'd better get maintenance to work on that as soon as you can." He handed me a metal leg from the platform. It had been neatly cut off with a hacksaw.

I nodded my thanks and said, "Maybe the maintenance man's already been here."

I stepped back up onto the stage. Thanks to the man's make-shift shim—his hat folded over—the movement of the platform was reduced to a gentle rocking, just enough to throw off my timing.

Needing something surefire to pick up the pace, I decided on the vanishing-wine trick. I reached inside my table and discovered that someone had beat me to it. Holes drilled through the base of my plastic bottle had drained out all the wine. All the props in the bottom compartment of my table were awash in a pool of red. From the upper shelf I grabbed a handful of silk handkerchiefs which I intended to blend into one giant rainbow scarf. When I held them in front of me, I saw that they were all in shreds. Slashed with a razor blade, they had been neatly refolded to mask the damage.

My next trick was supposed to be the Fire Bird, in which a flapping dove appears from a pan of flames. Before igniting the pan, I dipped my finger in the lighter fluid in the bottom of the pan and sniffed it. My nose burned with the wrong smell. I was going to have to skip this trick, too.

I then took a quick inventory of my doves, checking all the load areas and secret hidey-holes where I had stashed them in the various pieces of apparatus. They were all gone. In a fit of wild rationalization, I thought that maybe I had forgotten to load them, that they were still inside their cage.

With a painted-on smile, I excused myself from the stage. In the corner of the backstage area, my cage lay deserted. Door open. Feeder still full of seed. The ungrateful critters hadn't even left me a farewell note thanking me for giving them their first break in show business, for introducing them to the fast-lane life of the entertainment world.

I relied on fancy improvisation to see my show through to its shaky conclusion. With no way of knowing what other equipment had been sabotaged, I restricted myself to a smattering of card tricks, before switching to magic using items borrowed from audience members.

I vanished a woman's wedding ring from her hand and later found it in the bottom of a little girl's box of popcorn. The girl's father then graciously lent me his necktie, which I snipped into a half-dozen pieces and then restored. I ended by magically passing a thick piece of rope through my neck by uttering the proper magic word. I yearned for the chance to wind the rope around the neck of whoever had vandalized my equipment. After that I would conveniently forget the magic word.

I bade the audience an embarrassed farewell and watched them silently file out of the tent. I took small comfort in the fact that while no one had applauded, at least no one had booed or asked for a refund.

The saboteur had been efficient, fouling up my entire show during the few minutes it had taken me to drive Lee Sanders off the carnival grounds. Although the culprit demonstrated a working knowledge of magic, I don't think he knew much about magicians. He obviously thought that expensive gimmicks and pretty boxes actually have something to do with the quality of a magician. If his intention was to get me to quit, he had failed. My plan was to simply alter my show strategy. Since it was impossible to baby-sit my equipment twenty-four hours a day, I decided to restrict my repertoire to tricks that I could carry in my pockets, plus those using borrowed articles from the audience.

I went outside to ask the barker and the admission girl if they had seen anyone suspicious around the tent. But they were busy two tents down, drawing a crowd for a jam auction.

A flock of pigeons were pecking their way down the edge of the midway, following a trail of popcorn. Lurking among the dirty gray of the pigeons were a half-dozen pure white birds: my doves.

I made clucking sounds with my tongue. "Here, fellows. Come on. Nice fellows. I've got some good news. You can take a few days off before we go out to California. You guys look tired. Why don't you go back into the tent and take a rest? There's plenty of seed in your cage." I clucked again, but the doves ignored me. Only the pigeons responded, crowding at my feet, scavenging through the empty peanut shells.

"Fellows, I appreciate your interest, but I don't think you're quite right for my act." I shooed them away. The pigeons flew a few feet and then dropped back to the ground, their bellies apparently too stuffed for air travel. On foot, with heads bobbing, they headed toward the crowded concession stands where the pickings were easier. My doves, delirious with their newfound freedom, joined their cousins in the migration. I called after them, "Don't say I didn't warn you. When you wake up tomorrow morning on the cold ledge of some abandoned church, don't come groveling back to me, thinking that a few pitiful coos will make me take you back."

When I went back inside my tent, I had another visitor. He had used the back entrance. And it must have been a very tight squeeze.

I had no idea of how to estimate his weight. Beyond three hundred pounds, the term *pound* begins to lose meaning. And this man hadn't seen three hundred pounds since his baby-fat years.

Once I take off my ruffled shirt, bow tie, and tuxedo coat, people are hard put to guess what I do for a living, but there was no doubt what my visitor's occupation was. He was not just any fat man. He was *the* fat man.

He wore shapeless black trousers that stopped inches above his unlaced high-top sneakers. The material from just one of his pant legs could have made three pairs of pants for me. The very act of standing erect, unaided, seemed painful for him. The massive gathering of flesh below his chin pulled his face into a frown. Sweat trickled down his forehead and was stopped by the natural dam formed by his thick black eyebrows. It was hard to get a fix on his age. His face, probably from so little exposure to daylight, looked pale and boyish, probably little different from when he was in his teens.

I offered him a seat.

"Don't mind if I do." He looked at the the puny folding chairs in the front row and began to laugh. The laughter started in some deep, hidden chamber and seemed to take an eternity to reach his lips. The ensuing chain reaction of chortles seemed unstoppable. He could not hope to control it, only give it free rein until it ran its course. Nearly losing his balance, he leaned on one of the tent poles. It bowed and creaked and the roof of the tent swayed.

I waited until he simmered down again, catching his breath. Then I lit a cigarette and offered him one. He said, "No, thanks. I don't want to endanger my health." He struggled to keep from laughing again.

After I introduced myself, he said, "My name is Delbert St. Erne. People call me Ernie. A few minutes ago I overheard some marks talking about how your magic show went haywire. Since you're new to carnivals, I thought I'd stop by just to tell you not to take the incident seriously. You'll soon learn that we carnies have a strange sense of humor." His cheeks turned rosy as his eyes settled on the folding chairs. "You did offer me a chair, didn't you?"

Still hanging on to the tent pole, he lifted his foot off the ground. After six inches, it became a mighty struggle, but he continued to raise it higher. Then he brought it down slowly onto the seat of the nearest folding chair. His foot continued on its journey back to the ground, as though the chair didn't exist. The chair squealed in protest, but within seconds it was reduced to a flat tangle of metal. This folding chair had been folded for the last time.

He said, "Kind of shoots the hell out of the theory about fat people being light on their feet, doesn't it?"

His laughter welled up again. And this time I joined in, keeping my distance so that he wouldn't pat me on the back and accidentally squash me dead. It was a relief to finally hear laughter in this tent, even coming from someone who looked as though the strain could kill him at any moment.

CHAPTER TEN

The summer heat was clearly torture for Ernie. He snapped a white handkerchief the size of a pillowcase into the air and then folded it into a more manageable size. With the studied competence of a physician applying a poultice, he daubed his moist face. To avoid needless expenditure of energy, he spoke slowly, choosing his words with care.

He said, "It's a blessing to live during the age of air-conditioning. Cool air is as essential to me as oxygen is to a scuba diver. I paid top dollar for the state-of-the-art systems in both my trailer and my automobile."

"You drive?"

"Sure. My Lincoln is completely customized. I had the back-seat removed and the front seat pushed back several feet from the dash. The steering column is twice as long as a normal one. The pedals are modified so I can comfortably reach them. It cost a fortune, but it's important to feel independent." He worked his handkerchief over to the other side of his face.

"Is it air-conditioned in the freak—I mean, uh, where you work?"

"There's no need to be timid with that word. I work in the *freak* show. When you get a chance, why don't you stop by the *freak*-show tent. I'm sure you'll enjoy meeting the other *freaks*. However, I do recommend that you wear something else. I think my coworkers would find your ruffled shirt and purple bow tie a bit outlandish. But to answer your question: Unfortunately it isn't practical to air-condition a big tent. Bill Bateman has kindly provided me with two large fans. If I sit perfectly still, I can make it through hot days like this without much discomfort. The worst part of my job is the traveling. I live in constant fear of an auto accident. How many ambulance crews would have the manpower and equipment to free me from a wreck? But that's something that I just have to live with. All in all, I like working here. At least the work is dignified.''

I raised my eyebrows, and he said, "I see that you question that. Oh, everyone in the freak show feels the same. It's the customers—not the freaks—who have lost their dignity.''

His handkerchief was now sopped to the limit. I held up my bottle of Imperial and offered him a drink.

He smiled sadly. "No thanks. What little you have left would only start to quench my thirst.'' The bottle was a bit less than half full. "From what I hear about your show tonight, you'd better save that bottle for yourself. Besides, I get plenty to drink back in my tent. Bateman gave me my very own water cooler. That's because I threatened to go on strike a few years back. After all, what's a freak show without a fat man?''

He swung out his handkerchief and shook his head at the shambles of my magic show on the stage. "The marks that I overheard said—oh, excuse me, you do know what a mark is, don't you?''

"Sure. A victim of a swindle, right?''

"Close enough. Back in the old days, carnies would single out a gullible customer by secretly drawing a chalk mark on his back. The name 'mark' stuck. Today, we call *any* customer a mark, whether he's being cheated or not. In any event, I heard some marks say that someone did a number on your equipment. Is there anything I can do?''

Seeing how uncomfortable he was in the heat, I felt grateful that Ernie had been concerned enough to venture away from his two fans and water cooler. "Thank you, but it's nothing I can't handle.'' I told him what had happened during my first show.

"Don't worry about it,'' he said. "It was probably just an initiation. Think of it as a fraternity hazing.''

A lank-haired brunette, in her early forties, hurriedly entered from the front of the tent. "There you are,'' she said to Ernie with motherly concern.

"Hi, Christine. I was just welcoming—what was your name?''

"Harry Cotter."

"I was just welcoming Harry Cotter to the carnival. It appears that someone has already done just the opposite."

My eyes darted between the cleavage revealed by her low-cut, silky black dress and her full lips, accentuated by red lipstick as thick as cake frosting. A choker of pearls encircled her neck. As she walked closer her slit dress showed plenty of long tanned leg.

She stared at me with the concentration of a person watching an old film and trying to remember the title. If there had been a mirror nearby I would have checked to make sure my makeup was intact and hadn't started to run in the heat.

Ernie squished his hankie onto the back of his neck and sighed. "Harry, Christine will have to keep you company now. I'm afraid it's show time . . . even though my 'show' consists solely of sitting on a chair and answering the marks' idiotic questions."

I asked, "What sort of questions?"

"I made up this handbill to answer the more frequent ones." He handed me a pink sheet of paper from his pocket. At the top was a photo of Ernie, dressed in a sailor's suit and standing beside an enormous bulldog. It was a parody of the picture on the front of Cracker Jack boxes. Below, the caption said: *Delbert St. Erne, the World's Fattest Man.* I figured the picture to be about five years old; Ernie's hair had been thicker and his smile more affable. The rest of the sheet contained a list of his vital statistics—height, weight, measurements—and a typical daily menu that looked like a shopping list for a banquet. A boldfaced notice at the bottom advertised glossy photos of Ernie at two prices—five and twenty-five dollars.

"Are you really the world's fattest man?"

"To my knowledge, there are currently five of us who claim that title. None of us dispute the others' claims. We figure the world's big enough for five world's fattest men."

"What's the difference between the two different prices for the photos?"

His smile was as impish as an eight-hundred-pound man's smile can get. "In the five-dollar ones I am wearing all my clothes."

Ernie waved good-bye and exited the tent in small degrees. After every step he hesitated, as if waiting to see whether he would regain his balance. For Ernie, even a minor fall could spell broken bones.

When he was gone, Christine said, "I saw you trying to keep a straight face when he was telling you about his pictures. Actually, he sells quite a few of the twenty-five-dollar ones. In fact, Ernie claims to receive an average of one wedding proposal per month. And I believe him."

I waited for her to break into a grin, to show that she was joking. But she didn't.

"Ernie must have been worried about you," she said. "I can't recall the last time he ventured away like this. He's usually either in his trailer or the freak tent."

I started to tell her what had happened during my first show, but she said that she'd already heard about it. I said, "It's hard to keep a secret around here."

"Not really. I always keep an ear open to the chatter of the marks. I never know when I'll overhear something that'll come in handy."

"What's your job here?"

"I see all and tell all." She introduced herself as Christine Sirolli, better known on the midway as Madame Sirolli—Mystic Reader and Advisor.

"Swell," I said, immediately wary. My aversion to "psychics" is exceeded only by my aversion to magicians who publicly expose secrets. For almost as long as I've been a conjurer, I've been feuding with charlatans who claim to have paranormal powers. One such feud ended in my being blackballed from network TV.

Ignoring my sarcasm, she said, "What did Ernie say about your unfortunate first show?"

"He thinks it was all a prank."

"He may be right, but I wouldn't count on it. Walking that narrow path between his trailer and the freak tent all those years has insulated Ernie from what this place is really like."

I then told her of my plan to work out of my pockets in order to avoid more sabotage. She said, "That might be wise. But if you run into trouble, give me a holler. My tent is next to the main concession stand." She also told me the name of the motel where she was staying.

"You say your tent is located at the beginning of the midway?" I asked.

"Yes."

"On the right?"

She nodded.

"That's prime territory."

She gave me an amused smile. "You learn quick."

"Quick enough to know that I need more tutoring about the ways of the carnival . . . if only to prevent further embarrassment."

"I don't want to frighten you, but embarrassment should be the least of your worries."

"What makes you say that? Has your ESP tuned in on something I should know about?"

"Sorry. I don't give free readings. In case you're interested, my fees are five dollars and twenty-five dollars."

I regretted my words as soon as I uttered them: "Do your prices also vary according to how much clothing you're wearing?"

I expected—and deserved—a slap. Instead, my remark seemed to intrigue her. "You're closer to the truth than you think. Even though I keep my clothes on, success in my line of work does depend more on *how* I say things than *what* I say. For a twenty-five-dollar reading, I put a lot more of my 'self' into it."

I had an image of her sitting with a mark at a table so tiny that their knees were touching. As her "reading" became progressively more emotional she clutched the mark's hands, leaning close enough to brush her breasts against them.

I said, "I take it that you don't really believe in ESP?"

"Of course not. I don't even claim to have ESP. If you don't believe me, check out the signs in front of my tent. The biggest one says, 'For Your Amusement Only.' If you want me to read your mind and tell you what your social security number is, or to predict next year's winner of the Kentucky Derby, I can't do it. Anyone that says he can is a liar. Yet I am still able to 'divine' startling facts out of seemingly thin air."

I was beginning to hold out hope for her. "For example."

"I'll use you as a subject." She clamped her hands to her hips and stared at me, gently grinding her teeth back and forth. "You are definitely not who you say you are. It's too much of a coincidence, your showing up precisely when there's an opening in this carnival."

"Is that all?"

"No, there's more. Don't take this as an insult, but you don't look young enough to be embarking on a new and risky career. I think you have an ulterior motive for joining this carnival. Since you handled your onstage disaster so well tonight, I also think that you know more about magic than you're letting on. Plus your equipment—particularly those bouquets of feather flowers that I spotted behind your table when I came in—is too expensive for someone on your kind of budget. I think that at one point in your career you were a lot more successful than you are now."

I gave her a slow round of applause. "Bravo! And psychic powers didn't tell you any of this?"

"That's right. My own ears, eyes, and brain are a hell of a lot more reliable than thought waves snatched out of the ether. Of course, I can't stop my customers from drawing other conclusions. People end up believing what they want to believe."

I was beginning to like her. In a grand flourish, I reached behind the table and presented her with a bouquet of feather flowers. She thanked me, but her eyes were troubled.

"What's wrong?" I asked.

"Would you turn around again? When you reached to get these flowers, I saw a white line on the back of your coat." She brushed my back with her fingers. "There, I got most of it." Her fingers were coated with white powder. "It was a streak of chalk. I think that maybe—"

A harsh voice interrupted her. The voice sounded strained, perhaps from too much shouting. "Not quite, Christine." I turned to see Jacques Carlson standing at the entrance to my tent. "That was no *streak* of chalk. I'd say it was more like a *mark* of chalk." Carlson's face was too pretty for his body, as though the head of a male model had been pasted on top of the body of a matinee wrestler. He tensed and relaxed his crossed arms, his muscles flowing like molten steel beneath his skin. If his purpose was to convince me that he could crush bones at whim, he had succeeded.

His hoarseness became a snarl. "I'd like a word with you, Christine. In private." He glared at the flowers in her hands, and then at me. She mustered a defiant stare that soon softened when she glanced over at me. Madame Sirolli, who prided herself in picking up "vibrations," had been given a silent ultimatum:

Return the flowers or the magician gets hurt. She thrust the bouquet back into my hands and tried to cut short my protest with a quick shake of her head.

I said, "Here, Jacques. Why don't you take the flowers? Seeing as how they're fake, it might be more appropriate if *you* gave them to her."

He grabbed the bouquet and then ground the flowers between his hands until they were a tiny ball of marbled color. Magicians use feather flowers because they spring back quickly after being highly compressed. When Carlson returned the bouquet to me, they remained crumpled.

He looked at me as if I should be grateful that it wasn't me he had mashed between his hands. On the way out, he said, "Magician, you and I have some business to straighten out."

Christine held her laughter in check and rolled her eyes upward. As she followed Carlson out of the tent I mouthed the word "Later?" She gave me a tiny nod.

I took the dove pan from my table and slopped some of the suspicious-smelling liquid onto the ground. I touched my flaming lighter to it and it shooshed into an explosive, short-lived flame. Someone had mixed gasoline with my original lighter fluid.

So much for the reassuring words of the fat man. "Sure, Ernie," I said to myself. "Just a harmless prank."

I wondered if this completed my initiation into the carnival fraternity. Or was it just the beginning of Hell Week?

CHAPTER ELEVEN

As the night progressed my shows got better. Nothing else fell apart or even came close to exploding. After each performance I scribbled notes on how to improve my act: new lines, new sight gags, and more efficient ways of handling the props. My goal wasn't to garner rave reviews in tomorrow's *Variety*. I just didn't want to get fired from my new job before I even got started. Because I restricted myself to props that would fit in my pockets, I was forced to do tricks that I hadn't done in years.

By the fourth show, the audience was laughing in many of the right places and even gave me sustained applause at the end. On top of that, not one spectator entered my tent with a bucket of tar or a sack of feathers.

When the tent cleared out after my final performance, I sat down on the edge of the platform and laid out all the equipment for my show: cards, rope, sponge balls, scissors, felt egg bag, silk scarfs, and billiard balls. It seemed a lot longer than six years ago that I used to be touring the country with three tractor rigs full of illusions. The props spread out beside me now would have fit easily inside the box of beginner's magic tricks that my parents gave me when I was seven years old.

I made a mental note to arrive at the tent early tomorrow for a thorough safety inspection and also to ask Walt Galloway to repair the sawed-off platform leg. I then lit a cigarette and sifted through my improvement notes.

Outside, the crowd had waned, and the cranking beat of the

merry-go-round music finally died. One by one, the ride engines wound down and quit. For a few minutes a hush fell over the midway, but that was soon broken by the shouts and laughter of workmen preparing the lot for tomorrow.

Jacques Carlson entered my tent unannounced. He was wearing a crimson sleeveless shirt with an insignia of barbells on the chest. Slung across his meaty shoulder was a leather bag the size of a mailman's. In spite of his youthful, well-proportioned body, his face showed his age. No amount of weight lifting can prevent time from taking its toll on that part of the anatomy. I figured him to be somewhere in his midforties.

As he hovered over me menacingly, I picked up a deck of cards and shuffled them. I turned over the top four cards. All of them were aces. After performing a waterfall shuffle and a quick four-stack cut, I again turned over the top four cards. Four aces again.

Carlson snapped his fingers, acting as if I knew what that signal meant. When I ignored him, he snapped again, this time rubbing his thumb vigorously back and forth across his first two fingers. I finally looked up at him and said, "Incredible! That's the loudest finger snap I've ever heard. Sounded like a gun. All those hours of pumping iron are definitely worth it."

He opened his leather bag and waited. Still unsure of what he wanted, I said, "Nice purse. If you used less makeup, you could probably get away with a smaller one."

Letting the joke roll off him like an ineffective punch, he said, "It's dues time, magic man."

"So what does that mean?"

"It means that I'm collecting rent." He took a small black book and a pen from his sack. He flipped to a back page.

"I thought I paid that by the week."

"That doesn't include your percentage."

"Percentage?"

"Yeah. Bateman gets ten percent of your take. Nightly."

"That's news to me. All he told me about was the weekly rate."

"I collect that, too. At the end of the week, along with the frontage." He consulted his black book and said, "You've got thirty-five feet at four dollars a foot. That comes to a hundred and forty dollars a week . . . on top of your rent and your nightly percentage."

The cloth moneybag beside me wasn't even half full. I'd have to sell out the tent often to keep out of the red.

He said, "I'll just settle for the ten percent for now."

I pointed to my moneybag. "Take what you need. I haven't counted it yet."

"I don't count money. You'd better have it ready tomorrow after shutdown. Or we'll shut you down. For good." There was no threat in his voice, only the cool tone of a man stating an unquestionable fact.

I stood up. His collarbone was now at my eye level. "You sure you haven't already tried to shut me down?"

His lips retracted into a sneer, revealing white, sculptured teeth. "I heard about your little problem tonight. Sounds like you're starting off on the wrong foot. Show biz is a tough life, buster. But if you start blaming all your troubles on the other carnies, it can get tougher. Maybe someone's trying to teach you that the carnival business isn't all laughs and adventure . . . and that strangers with too many questions make us nervous."

I wondered if he had seen me drive Lee Sanders off the carnival lot. "What's wrong with a few questions? I don't want to upset anyone. I'm just naturally curious. That's all part of being a magician. Take you, for an example. I'm quite curious about you. I heard that you used to be a performer, too."

His sneer softened and then disappeared. "I still am. Even though I only do one show a day, I keep trying to improve it. As a matter of fact, I have a new feature that I'll be trying out tomorrow. Maybe you should try and catch it . . . just to see what real entertainment is like."

"You really are a busy guy. On top of being a fixer and a showman, how do you find time to work out?"

"I make the time. I travel with my own set of free weights and a small Nautilus machine. It pays off too. If I want to strike a good bargain with local officials, all I have to do is make sure that I frown a lot and wear a short-sleeved shirt. Works every time."

"Did you ever compete as a bodybuilder?"

He nodded, his face thawing even more.

I asked, "So how did you end up a carny?"

"When I was a teenager in New Jersey, all I wanted was to become Mr. America. But after years of posing in front of a mirror every day, I realized that I'd never go much beyond local contests. At about that time, the Bateman Carnival rolled into my hometown. I saw a poster for a wrestling match that offered a hundred-dollar prize to any successful challenger. That's one hundred dollars more than I ever made from bodybuilding. Walt Galloway was so impressed with me that he got me a job with the carnival.''

"As a wrestler?"

He looked at me queerly. "Uh, no. I worked in maintenance for a short while, and then Galloway got me hired as a Bozo.''

"Bozo. That's a dunking clown, right?"

"Yeah. I was Bozo for most of the next season until Bill Bateman wised up and put my talents to better use and let me do a strong-man show. That's when Bateman retired the Bozo tank for good. Sometimes I miss those days. With that clown makeup on, you could say anything to anyone. The cruder the better. I think maybe Bozo helped me let off a lot of steam.''

He smiled wistfully. I wondered if his current job provided a similar release . . . only more physical.

"Why did Galloway choose the Bozo job for you?"

"The same way you got your job. The old Bozo suddenly quit and they needed someone.''

"Any idea why he left?"

"I never asked. I was just glad to get the job.''

"That's a big jump, from Bozo to carnival fixer. From what I hear, your job includes 'taking care' of the local law.''

His smile dropped away and he readjusted his bag on his shoulder. He answered my question with a wary nod.

I said, "Doesn't the local law have any power at all over the carnival?"

"Yes and no. It depends on what kind of agreement the police and I make. Most of the time, as long as we keep the carnival problems on the lot, the local cops don't hassle us. But the minute troubles spills out into the real world, all previous arrangements are null and void.''

"What about serious offenses?"

"If it involves a carny and a mark, the police want to know about it. But if it's between two carnies . . .'' His voice trailed off and he shrugged his shoulders. Even that simple movement seemed to put a strain on the seams of his shirt. "You sure ask a hell of a lot of questions, magic man. Funny, just today there was a mark going around asking weird questions too. I had to set him straight." He delicately rubbed his fingers across the ridges of his knuckles. "But your questions are different than his. They don't piss me off as much. You sort of remind me of a foreign guy that hung around the carnival about twenty-some years ago. He was making a movie and he asked a lot of questions too."

"What was the movie for?"

"Beats me, he never said. I always figured that the guy paid Bateman a bundle for permission to make it. Anyway, this guy and his camera crew roamed the midway for two weeks."

"Did he use actors?"

"No, he just took pictures of us doing our thing. And then he'd talk to us about what we thought of our jobs. Stupid stuff like that."

"It was a documentary, then."

"I suppose," he said slowly, not wanting to reveal that he didn't know the meaning of the word.

"Did you ever get to see the film?"

"No. Never heard a thing about it again, which doesn't surprise me. Who would want to watch a movie that doesn't have a story, just a lot of people talking? I don't think the damn thing ever got made. If it did, it was probably shown in another country. The director could barely talk English."

"What language did he speak?"

He puckered his lips to the side, thought for a few seconds, and said, "I think French."

He picked up my moneybag, and for a moment I thought that he was going to take the whole thing. He hefted it and then let it thump back down on the platform, satisfied with its weight. "Make sure I get your percentage tomorrow. And don't try to stiff me. We have a good idea of how much business each joint should do."

On his way out, he turned and said, "A word of warning: Be careful with your questions. They might get you into a lot more trouble than tonight. And while we're on the subject of behavior . . . let Christine Sirolli alone. She's mine."

He was gone before I could ask to see his receipt for the said purchased woman.

*　　*　　*

Apparently, most of the Bateman carnies didn't stay in motels. The far edge of the fairgrounds was a small city of trailers, vans, and motor homes. Behind me, the last lights of the midway winked and died, leaving me solely dependent on the light filtering through curtained windows of the trailers. From all directions came the muted sounds of televisions. From nearby, I heard the hiss of a beverage can being opened, followed by people laughing and someone trying to shush them.

I headed in the direction of the laughter and came upon four men in their early twenties sitting cross-legged in a tight circle on the ground. In the middle of their circle was an electric lantern. They huddled close to it, as though it were a campfire. Next to the lantern lay a modest pile of paper money, mostly coins. Each man had a paper bag sitting in front of him and a fan of playing cards in his hand. One of the cardplayers was the ride operator that Walt Galloway had slugged in the chin today. I asked him which trailer was Galloway's. He took a drink from his paper bag, discarded two cards, and then added two freshly dealt ones to his hand. He looked around at his pals, and when no one offered an objection, he pointed to his right and said, "Way down there on the end. That Winnebago." I thanked him and left him to his task of bluffing with only a pair of eights.

Galloway's motor home easily outclassed the ones surrounding it, not only in size and cost but also in upkeep. Even at night, its exterior sparkled. I knocked several times. Not getting a response, I tried the door. Locked. I glanced back at the cardplayers. They were still preoccupied with outplaying and outdrinking one another. I took out my picks, leaned close to the door, and set to work.

Once inside, using the light of the small table lamp that Galloway had left burning, I wrote on my notepad: *Your door was open. I need some work on my stage. Catch you tomorrow. Harry Cotter.* I attached the note to his refrigerator, using one of his kitchen magnets. The note was my safety device, in case Galloway caught me by surprise. If I didn't need to use it, I'd tear it up before I left.

The motor home was partitioned off into two sections. The living area reminded me of an efficiency apartment, with a kitchenette at one end and a sofa bed at the other. The neat, bright room did not reflect the strain of Galloway's long working hours and his constant traveling from city to city. The furniture, though inexpensive and functional, was new and had recently been dusted. The only signs of disarray were on the kitchen counter, where the various sections of a newspaper lay scattered beside a chipped porcelain cup containing an inch of cold coffee. The paper, from a town on the other side of the state, featured a front-page story about a man found murdered yesterday in a hotel room in Maylene, Indiana. The police were temporarily withholding the identity of the deceased.

I entered the second room of the motor home and found myself in a cramped workshop. Galloway must have spent a lot of time in here. The sweet odor of his after-shave was everywhere. The moon, filtering down through a tinted skylight, provided eerie illumination. A huge net tacked to the ceiling was intended to add a rustic, masculine air to the room. Instead, it made it look like a teenager's game room.

At the end of the shop was a small metal workbench, equipped with a vise, a grinding wheel, and a jigsaw. Spring-clamped to a Peg-Board on the wall behind it were a variety of hand tools. At first I thought that Galloway used the shop for carnival maintenance, but then I saw that the tools on the wall were meant for more delicate work. Lining the bottom of the rack was a row of knives with tiny blades that varied in width and thickness. A red toolbox on top of the bench was filled with more carving tools, in addition to several tubes of epoxy glue. I opened the middle drawer of the bench and found it crammed with canisters of nails, bolts, and screws, as well as several bundles of wire. At the back of the drawer was an envelope containing a number of narrow vials with needles sticking out of them. They resembled hypodermic syringes. I put them back in the drawer.

A closet compartment in the corner of the shop housed a modest wardrobe of work clothes: wool shirts, jeans, and cowboy boots. In the rear corner sat a steamer trunk whose padlock was so thick and ancient it would have taken me an hour to conquer it. I slid the trunk back and forth. It seemed light, not containing much.

In the other corner of the room stood a table covered with a white sheet. A floodlamp attached to the wall was focused on the table. I flicked it on and carefully lifted the sheet. The entire tabletop was populated with miniature tents, rides, and banners. "What a hobby," I said.

Galloway had constructed a minutely detailed replica of the Bateman Carnival—a tribute, I assume, to his only true love. I put my face next to one of the refreshment stands and squinted. I could see rows of candy apples, racks of cotton candy, and tubs of popcorn. I would have needed a magnifying glass to detect flaws in his model.

I flipped a toggle switch at the edge of the table, and the rides all came to life, orbiting and revolving in this miniature solar system of amusement. The ping-pang of tinny electronic music emerged from the merry-go-round.

I thought that his carnival was unpopulated until I lifted the top off the little trailer marked *Manager*. Inside was a caricature doll of Bill Bateman. His nostrils were flared and his eyes were tinted a maniacal yellow. His hair was slicked back in a satanic hairstyle. The interior of the trailer was overflowing with tiny gold coins which the mechanical Bateman was frenetically trying to count.

I lifted up the tops of all the tents and booths. Every one contained carved versions of Bateman carnies. Each likeness was hideously distorted. The Jacques Carlson doll was a puny, cowering child who sucked his thumb. Ernie was depicted as a fiendish cannibal, busily gnawing on a human leg. Mary Trunzo was shown to be performing a multipartner, multigender sex act. I looked for but didn't find a carving of Christine Sirolli. I replaced everything as I had found it and killed the power on the tabletop carnival.

As I put the cover back on Galloway's nightmarish carnival, I noticed a small wooden box under the table. I opened it and found it full of utensils and knives. All of them were used for wood carving except for one: an ivory-handled, double-edged dagger. I turned the handle around to look at the other side, and I was staring at the carving of a smiling devil.

CHAPTER TWELVE

The Gulick Motel was a five-minute drive from the fair-grounds. I didn't think any carnies were staying there: None of the cars in the parking lot showed excessive wear for its age, or had a trailer hitch on the bumper. So I checked in. Overoptimistic about my future with the carnival, I paid the clerk enough rent for the rest of the week. I then threw in an extra thirty cents for a local newspaper.

Before unpacking, I scanned the paper but found no mention of Roth. I guess a murder in a skid row hotel on the other side of the state didn't carry the same editorial weight as the election of the new Lions Club officers or a forty-seven-cent hike in cable-TV rates.

I dumped my moneybag on the bed and counted all the cash. I then raked aside Bateman's ten percent and also took out enough for tonight's portion of the weekly rent. The remaining amount would be enough for breakfast tomorrow, as long as I didn't order extra butter on my toast.

As I scooped the money back into the bag my vision began to double and my head went pleasantly slack. I rubbed my eyes and gave my head a shake, trying to override my body's demand to call it a day. I unlatched my attaché case which contained my carnival magic props. The last thing I wanted to do was rehearse. But if I were going to keep my eyes open for further sabotage attempts, I'd have to make my magic routine as automatic as possible.

I kicked off my shoes and slipped into my tux coat. The coat was still damp and the room's air conditioner wasn't helping to keep out the muggy night air.

After arranging all my props on the bed in their order of use, I loaded everything into my pockets. I then walked through all the moves of my show, without saying any of the lines. Satisfied with my handling of the props, I slowly talked my way through the entire show, consulting my notes when necessary to remember new lines. Then I practiced all the critical sleights in front of the dresser mirror to make sure I wasn't "flashing" any secrets.

My image in the mirror startled me. I had nearly forgotten my trip to the makeover artist. It was like watching a film of some other magician. When the balls and cards began to slip from my fingers, I decided to rehearse my lines one more time—minus the props—and then hit the sack.

I raised the venetian blind and drew the armchair up to the window. I rested my heels on the windowsill and intertwined my fingers behind my head. Against the horizon I could see the top half to the Bateman Carnival Ferris wheel, its cars gently swinging.

I rapidly repeated the lines from my act. Fatigue was conspiring against me. The words were there, but my mental images would no longer obey me. Instead of pulling cards out of the air, I saw daggers and flaming doves appearing in my hands . . . as an audience of carved miniature carnies clomped their wooden hands together. They clapped so loudly I could feel the vibrations the whole way down to my toes.

I woke up to blinding sunlight and the faces of two small boys who were throwing pebbles at my window. Having spotted my stocking feet pressed against the glass, they were having a grand time trying to wake me. I jerked my feet away. My legs crashed to the floor, feeling like someone else's legs until the jagged pain of restored circulation brought me back to reality. I howled in pain and the boys darted off, laughing at their mission accomplished.

A hot shower dissolved the kinks that remained from sleeping in the chair. I spread out my makeup on the bathroom sink and began the unpleasant task of aging myself in the mirror. I had asked the makeup expert if there was any way he could make me look younger instead of older. He had laughed, saying that he wasn't a magician. My hair, stiff from the dye, resisted my comb, and I took care to tear out as few strands as possible.

I decided to make a few phone calls. I called a man in Pittsburgh who raised doves for magicians and asked him to reserve a dozen for me. I told him I'd call later to give him a shipping address. He asked me what had happened to the last dozen. When I told him, he wanted to know if I was interested in a special he was running on homing pigeons.

I next phoned a magic shop in New York City and ordered replacements for my vandalized props. The owner of the shop was curious about why I was placing such a big order. After I explained what had happened, he said that I must be playing some really rough crowds. He offered to throw in a copy of Bob Orben's *Heckler Stoppers* at no extra charge.

I also got in contact again with the routing office of *Amusement Times*. I identified myself as a talent broker for a projected new theme park in Virginia. I said that I was trying to locate a young entertainer named Chuck Pitlor who had last worked for the Bateman Carnival. The clerk checked his files and consulted with fellow employees, but he couldn't come up with Pitlor's current location.

Chuck Pitlor. His departure from the Bateman Carnival so soon after the murder of Arlen Roth seemed to be too much of a coincidence. Had he quit on his own, or had he been coerced?

I then called Dr. Terry Swanson, my magic historian friend, and asked him if he knew anything about Pitlor. I told him that Pitlor wasn't a magician, but that he might have a reputation among magicians because of his skills in the allied arts—paper cutting, puppetry, etc. Swanson checked his files and said that he had never heard of him. He then added that if Pitlor was in any way connected with me, maybe he was looking in the wrong files, maybe he should be looking at the little pictures that they hang in the post office. I should have known better than to trust an allergy doctor who has a dog named Ragweed.

I was certain that each carny I had talked to so far knew more than he was saying. But thus far, there was only one person I trusted. I decided to give her a call at her motel room.

Before I could, my phone rang.

A voice said, "I know that your real name is Harry Colderwood. And that you are investigating the death of Arlen Roth. And that your life is in danger. I also know that I'd like very much to have breakfast with you today."

I said, "If you want a date with me, Madame Sirolli, you don't have to threaten me."

"I wasn't trying to threaten you. I just wanted to make sure you were awake before I asked." She named a restaurant that was a block away from my motel.

"By the way," I said, "how the hell did you know that I was just going to call you? I—" She hung up.

Jeez. Mind readers.

CHAPTER THIRTEEN

Posters advertising the carnival were stapled to utility poles along the street outside of KT's Restaurant. The gleeful man in the posters wore a straw boater hat and a candy-striped coat and was waving a cane. With his squinting eyes and pencil-thin mustache, he looked more dishonest than a used-car salesman. I reminded myself to congratulate Bateman for adhering to the code of truth in advertising.

The hostess that greeted me inside the restaurant was not as gleeful as the man on the poster. "Smoking or nonsmoking section?" she asked.

"Do you have a *heavy-smoking* section? A table with an overhead, hooded exhaust fan would be ideal."

On the way to my table we passed a crowd of customers, plates in hand, soberly huddled around a table of sizzling food. Floodlamps overhead lit the area like a boxing ring.

"Is that a breakfast buffet?"

"It's our *all-you-can-eat* breakfast buffet," she corrected.

The hostess led me to a table that had a big square ashtray in the middle. But no overhead exhaust fan. I gave her my name and told her that I was expecting a guest.

When the waitress arrived, I asked for two menus. She smiled at me patronizingly and pointed at the group of diners jostling for a better position around the table of steaming food. A woman in the crowd loudly announced to no one in particular that the vat of maple syrup had gone dry. This was met with several groans. I thanked the waitress but told her that I really wanted menus. She shrugged and walked off, saying that she wasn't sure where the breakfast menus were.

A man in a madras jacket broke away from the crowd and hustled back to his table, balancing a plate loaded with pancakes, sausages, muffins, and scrambled eggs. A busboy followed close behind, sweeping up the trail of dropped food.

When Christine arrived, she was wearing a brief beige halter top with white shorts and white sandals. Minus last night's heavy makeup and suggestive costume, she seemed younger, more energetic. She must be what they call a morning person, I thought.

I was a completely different story. Slumped over the table, a cigarette between my fingers, with eyes that looked like printed circuits, I was the picture of the night person—someone dedicated to smoky bars, alarm clocks with no AM setting, all-night movie channels, and junk-food restaurants that make late deliveries.

Christine's smile was not one of greeting but one of relief. After glancing around at the surrounding tables, she took a seat across from me.

I said, "I already checked out the place. I didn't see any other carnies. Anyway, if your friend Jacques Carlson were here, he would have already made his presence known."

"Jacques is not my friend."

"He seems to think he is . . . plus much more."

She watched intently as I lit a cigarette. Her eyes lingered on the first rush of smoke. She said, "Jacques has done a lot of favors for me, and I've done a few for him. Obviously, he has gravely overreacted to the gratitude I've shown him. Because of his 'interest' in me, none of the men in the carnival even want to come near me. Come to think of it, that may not be such a bad deal, judging by some of the crew this season."

I propped my cigarette in the ashtray. Her eyes were still

hungrily fixed on it. "If you'd rather I wouldn't . . ." I started to butt it out.

"No, it's perfectly all right. Don't mind me. I quit smoking five years ago, but sometimes it feels like only yesterday."

I moved the ashtray away from her. "Has Carlson ever given you any *real* trouble?"

She shook her head no. "Although he's run damn close to the sideline, he's never gone out of bounds . . . yet. I've tried to make it clear that his biceps and triceps and pectorals hold absolutely no interest for me. He's waiting for the day when I finally realize how sexy a man is who gets his kicks by threatening the weak. I think that what keeps Jacques at bay is that he believes I really have supernatural powers. He always acts more wary of me when I'm dressed in my Madame Sirolli clothes. Maybe he's afraid I'll put a curse on him."

"Maybe I should be wary of you too. After all, how do you know what my real name is?" I worked up the proper sneer. "Fortune-telling?"

She glanced out the window at two boys who had stopped to read one of the carnival posters. They each dug in their pockets and counted their change, seeing if they had the price of admission.

"It was quite simple," Christine said. "I already figured that you were a more experienced magician than you were letting on. So I visited a local library this morning and read some articles about magic in some old news magazines."

"How old?" I asked. "Five years?"

"More like six or seven. I found a picture of a hotshot magician levitating a lady on a float in the Macy's Thanksgiving Day Parade. His name was Harry Colderwood—that's pretty close to Harry Cotter—and he resembled you, except he was a lot healthier. What the hell happened to you?"

"I've added a few years with the aid of makeup. But it's quite possible that my life-style over the past few years has sped up the aging process too."

I could tell from the playful gleam in her blue eyes that she knew I wasn't buying her story. But she kept going anyway, filling me in on what she had learned about my recent life: my challenges to psychics, my faltering career, and my scrapes with the law.

The waitress returned with the menus. They were both dusty and cracked around the edges. Each dish on the menu was accompanied by a full-color photo. Acting on the menu's philosophy of nonverbal communication, I tapped my finger on the picture of each item I wanted: a Danish, a glass of orange juice, sunny-side-up eggs, and a cup of coffee. Christine pointed to just a cup of coffee and pancakes.

Before writing up our orders, the waitress decided to give us one last try. "I don't think you two are aware that everything you want, except the coffee, is on our buffet over there. If you ordered the buffet, it would actually cost you less."

I said, "Call me a nostalgic fool, but I don't like breakfast being turned into a scavenger hunt. Miss, uh . . ." I looked at her name tag, but it identified her only as Waitress #39. If I wanted to learn her name, I'd probably have to give her number to the manager and— Suddenly it hit me how Christine had found out so quickly who I was. Like all the wiles of fake fortune-tellers, it was simple and direct.

After the waitress wrote down our order and left, I said, "You traced my license number, didn't you?"

She smiled. "Yep. I made friends with one of the cops walking the midway beat, and he did me the favor. But first he had to promise not to blab to Carlson."

"So how do you know that I'm looking for answers to Arlen Roth's death?"

She handed me a stack of folded papers from her purse. They were photocopies of twenty typewritten pages. "This was delivered to me this morning. A note attached to it said that the new magician working in the carnival was investigating Roth's murder."

The first page was numbered 175. The heading included Roth's name and the title *Carny Years*. It was an entire chapter—called "Fortunes for Fortunes"—from Roth's autobiography. I skimmed through the twenty pages. They told of how a fortune-teller named Madame Sirolli stole money from the wallets of distraught marks.

She said, "I think that a lot of the other carnies received chapters too."

I coughed on my own smoke.

CHAPTER FOURTEEN

The waitress brought me my coffee and I took a preliminary sip. After deciding that cream and sugar would be no improvement, I began to read the manuscript chapter word for word. It was far from being a final draft. Neat proofreading symbols had been penciled in above the typewritten lines. It began by describing Christine Sirolli's physical appearance. While technically accurate—correct color of hair, eyes, et cetera—it was insulting. It described her as having "a smile that would be worth hundreds of dollars a night on any big-city street and a body to back up that advertisement."

The next several pages detailed how Christine stole from the wallets of her patrons. The description of her sleight-of-hand move sprawled out over several pages. When the narrative grew too convoluted to follow, I gave up.

"Who delivered this manuscript?" I asked Christine.

"A courier service."

"Besides the note about me, was there anything else enclosed?"

"There was also a clipping from a newspaper in Maylene, Indiana, stating that Arlen Roth had been murdered in his hotel room."

"Did you know Roth?"

"No, he was a few years before my time. Every now and then I've heard carnies speak of him, but never anything that left an impression on me. In order to write so accurately about me, Roth must have paid a secret visit to the carnival. After I received this chapter. I asked around about him. but all I got were strange looks.''

"Any idea why?''

"Like I said, I have the distinct feeling that the courier delivered more than one such package today.''

The temperature of my coffee was just right now. I drained my cup in three consecutive swallows and signaled for another. I attacked my Danish with a knife and fork, not wanting to get sticky fingers on the manuscript.

She said, "When I learned your real identity, I figured that either you were interested in solving this''—she held up the news clipping of Roth's death—"or . . .'' She looked away from me.

"Or what?''

"Or that you did it.''

"Obviously you don't believe that, or you wouldn't be sitting here.''

Even though I had already told her more than intended, I kept on talking. Perhaps it was because her wide blue eyes seemed to promise that she'd listen sympathetically to whatever I said, no matter what the topic. I told her everything I knew.

I told her that I had had nothing to do with sending her the package, but that I had been at the scene of Roth's murder. I explained about Roth's collaboration with a ghostwriter on his autobiography and about my pursuit of the secret of the dagger trick.

I asked, "How true is this description of your swindling scheme?''

"It's accurate but completely outdated. It's been a long time since I used that wallet ruse. I learned fortune-telling while I was shoveling out popcorn at a concession stand, my first job with the carnival. The woman who taught me was a single parent of three children. Financially, she lived from week to week. She's the one who showed me how to use confederates to peek the poke.''

" 'Peek the poke'?''

"That means to spot marks who are carrying fat wallets. When a likely target entered my tent, the confederate would give me the high sign to skin the poke.''

"So you used to be a pickpocket?''

"Of sorts. First I had to convince the mark that all of the problems in his life were caused by a curse that someone had put on his money. For an extra fee, I offered to remove that curse.''

"So the mark would hand over his wallet to you, just like that?"

She nodded. "Nine times out of ten. You have to remember that by this time I've delivered a convincing reading, taking full advantage of the spooky, candlelit atmosphere of my tent. After the mark's wallet was in the middle of the table, I'd wrap it in one of my 'ceremonial' handkerchiefs."

She took her wallet from her purse and folded a paper napkin around it. She demonstrated how, under cover of the napkin, she could slide out a large quantity of bills with her index and middle fingers. After folding them in half, she concealed them in her palm.

"It took me hundreds of hours to learn that move. Even after I could do it perfectly, my mentor still cautioned me to never skin the whole poke. 'Always leave something,' she said. Otherwise, it could mean a beating, jail, or even worse."

I tried to dupliate her maneuver, and it felt clumsy. I kept catching part of the napkin on my fingernails. On my first few attempts, my greedy fingers tried for too much. The folded wad of bills left a telltale bulge under the napkin. As she talked I continued to practice.

"After my teacher moved on to another carnival, I worked the wallet scam successfully for a whole year. The money was good, but the fear of getting caught began to wreck my nerves. During this time I was also honing a skill that my teacher had never taught me. I was learning how to 'read' people—to appear to know extraordinary facts about complete strangers."

"Magicians call that 'cold reading.' "

"Personally, I like to think of it as 'making two plus two equal six.' I can take an overheard conversation, a glance inside some-one's purse, and observations about a person's clothing and mannerisms . . . and when I combine them all together, it seems like a minor miracle."

I dropped the napkin-wrapped wallet onto the table and was about to declare success when I saw the corner of a hundred-dollar bill protruding from under my left thumb. I unwrapped the wallet, replaced the money, and tried again.

She said, "I got quite good at what you call cold readings. The only thing keeping me from getting better was the wallet swindle. It was interfering with my concentration. After I fired all my confederates and began to work as a single-o, my profits really took off. Except for my little demonstration just now, it's been nineteen years since I skinned a poke.''

Straightening up the manuscript pages, I said, ''What effect would the publication of Roth's book have on you?''

''It would put Madame Sirolli out of business permanently. Unlike circuses and amusement parks, there have been only a few books written about carnivals. Roth's wouldn't have to be a best-seller to capture the attention of carnival operators all around the country. After Bill Bateman bounced me off the midway, I'd never work in another carnival again.''

With a ruleful smile, I said, ''Believe me, I'm quite familar with the process of being blackballed.''

''Hey, that's right. You're still a persona non grata on TV, aren't you? How the hell did you manage that?''

I explained about how I went public with information that a network's chief entertainment executive was making multimillion-dollar programming decisions on the advice of a crystal-ball gazer. As a result, a TV magic special that I had already taped was never aired.

She looked at her watch and said, ''I've got to run. I don't give set performances like you entertainers, so if I'm going to make any money, I've got to open shop a lot earlier.''

I tried her sleight-of-hand move one last time and successfully slid the money out of her wallet and into my palm. As I gave her back her wallet and cash she seemed impressed.

''Do you think anyone else has stumbled onto my real identity?'' I asked.

She shook her head.

I said, ''Just the same, I'd better ditch my license plate whenever I drive onto the carnival grounds. If you traced me, then someone else might too.''

''But that's my job—detecting secrets.''

''Pretty much the opposite of my job, isn't it?'' I said.

''Of course I have a distinct advantage over you, particularly with male clients. It never hurts if I can make some of them—just briefly—fall in love with me.''

Her smile was solemn, with no disingenuous sweetness. I asked her to stay longer, but she said no. ''Right now there's probably a whole line of people waiting for me to tell them that they will be traveling sometime in the next year and that everything in their life is going to be fine." She stuffed the manuscript inside her purse. "By the way, do you think whoever sent me this manuscript is going to blackmail me?"

"Blackmail you for something that you haven't done in years? No, I believe that the manuscript is all a smoke screen."

"How's that?"

"Don't you see? This chapter establishes a motive for you to kill Roth. And if Roth wrote as ruthlessly about the other carnies, it'll give them motives too."

"But who would do that?"

"The real murderer. Tell me this: Where were you on the day of Roth's murder?"

"In my motel room. It rained for hours and the carnival never opened that day."

"See? There goes your alibi, along with the alibis of the whole damn carnival. The real murderer is trying to muddy the waters. I think you'd better find out—discreetly, of course—what other carnies received these special packages."

"What are you going to do?" she asked.

"First, I'm going to make a phone call to a ghost. And after that, I'm going to catch the act of a muscle man who has been flexing entirely too much muscle lately."

CHAPTER FIFTEEN

Warner Huston, the ghostwriter, seemed to be as vaporous as a real ghost. I called the number in Hartford, Connecticut, that the information operator had given me. After one and a half rings, Huston's answering machine kicked on. His voice sounded distant and hollow, as though his answering machine had been buried in manuscript papers when he had recorded his message. At the sound of the tone, I left my name and the phone number and room number of my motel. I asked Huston to call me, saying it was urgent. As an afterthought, I blurted out the number of the pay phone I was calling from, just before the second beep cut me off.

I stared across the parking lot at the manager of KT's Restaurant as he climbed up a wobbling stepladder to change the letters on his marquee. As he worked I tried to guess what the new lunch special was going to be . . . just like a TV game show. However, I failed to solve the puzzle until the end because he insisted on spelling *liver* with an *o* instead of an *i*.

As he climbed down from his perch, the manager heartily greeted a group of five snow-haired ladies as they got out of a late-model Cadillac. Judging from their easy banter, I figured they were regulars at the restaurant.

Which gave me an idea. I turned back to the phone and called the Chamber of Commerce of Hartford and asked for the names of the local newspapers. I called the first one on the list, the *Hartford Courant*, and asked for the city editor.

I told him I was an editor for a newspaper in Laguna Beach.

"I'm trying to locate a free-lance writer named Warner Huston. He isn't answering his phone." I then gave him Huston's address. "Any chance you can give me the names of any taverns in his area?" The editor laughed and reeled off five.

"That was fast," I said.

"He happens to live close to my neighborhood. Give me a few seconds and I'll even look up the phone numbers for you."

After writing them down, I hung up, checked my pockets for more coins, and realized that I had to go back inside the restaurant for change.

The woman ahead of me in the cash-register line wore her hair twisted back in an economical bun. The long sleeves of her army shirt were tightly rolled above her elbows, revealing forearms streaked with a light film of greasy dirt that had resisted soap and water. Her baggy camouflage trousers were turned up at the cuff. The heels of her muddied work boots were worn down at a steep angle.

When it was her turn at the cash register, she gave the manager her check and a twenty-dollar bill. While waiting to be rung up, she began to idly leaf through a local shoppers' tabloid. Her check totaled less than a dollar. Probably just a cup of coffee. The manager counted out her change onto the counter with practiced snapping motions. As he started to close the cash drawer she said, "No, wait." The crowd behind me started to shuffle and groan restlessly. I found myself shuffling and groaning restlessly too. The manager smiled politely.

"Sorry. I forgot that I need some cigarettes. A pack of Newports, please." She counted out the exact amount, using some of the coins she had just received from the manager. As the manager handed her the cigarettes and took her coins, the woman pulled a one-dollar bill from her purse. "Would you look at that. I went and broke that twenty when I had a one-dollar bill on me all the time. Tell you what, how about if I give you this dollar, along with nine of the dollars that I just received in change? Then you can give me a ten back."

The manager shrugged and handed her a ten from his drawer. As the woman walked away the manager said, "Oh, miss, you gave me too much. You must have gotten a ten mixed up with that extra one-dollar bill that you found. You gave me nineteen dollars instead of ten." He held up the fan of bills to show her the mistake.

"Now, there's something you don't see every day—an honest man. Thank you very much. That would have messed up my budget for the whole week. Tell you what, since you may need the change later on, let me give you another one-dollar bill. With the nineteen you already have in your hand, that makes twenty, right? Good. You can just give me a twenty-dollar bill back."

The manager adjusted his tie, gave her a customer-is-always-right smile through gritted teeth, and slapped her twenty-dollar bill onto the carpeted mat in front of the register. She thanked him and quickly moved away from the counter. Needless to say, the manager did not give her a complimentary breakfast coupon.

As I took out a ten-dollar bill, ready to try the manager's patience by also asking for change, I glanced back at the lady as she headed for the exit. I realized where I had seen her before. She was the operator of the softball-in-the-basket game at the carnival.

In my mind I replayed her seemingly simple transaction at the restaurant cash register and realized that it was anything but simple. I had never seen that kind of dodge executed with such glib confidence.

I stepped away from the counter and caught up with her just before she reached the door. I shot out my arm, locking my fingers around her wrist. She stopped with a jerk, and her pocketbook flopped up against my hip. I brushed it away with my free hand. I smiled and said, "Hello," in a sardonically pleasant voice. "I'm Harry Cotter, the new magician with the carnival. I didn't recognize you without your peach baskets."

She struggled to slide out of my grasp. Her gray eyes revealed the relaxed cunning of a cat. Her lined, stark-white face reminded me of an old-time daguerreotype.

When she finally stopped trying to escape, I relaxed my grip. She said, "I'm Amelia Halfhill. Nice to meet you." Her voice had taken on a down-home drawl that I hadn't detected during her conversation with the restaurant manager.

In a tight-lipped, low voice, I said, "Watch out. This almost slipped out of your purse."

I raised my right hand and displayed her billfold. "It's none of my business, but I think you should know that there's ten dollars in here that rightfully belongs to the restaurant.''

She frantically rooted her hands through her purse but then realized the improbability of my carrying around a duplicate billfold. A dazed look settled over her face, as though she thought that she was somehow immune to deception.

I dropped her wallet back inside her pocketbook. With indignation, she jerked down the cover of her purse and snapped the buckle shut.

''You're smooth,'' I said. ''The manager never suspected a thing. You've really got style. Part of the fun of magic is pulling the wool over people's eyes, but somehow I get the feeling that your brand of fooling people is a little more profitable than mine.''

She nervously fixed her eyes on the door. ''Maybe we can talk later.''

''I'm sure we will,'' I said, smiling in anticipation. ''While I'm thinking about it I'd like to ask you a question. Do you read much?''

''Some. Why?'' Her lack of makeup seemed to amplify the fright spreading across her face.

''I received a package this morning that really has me baffled. I think it's some kind of promotion for a new book. It's not a whole book, only part of one—in manuscript form. I don't know what to make of it. Since the subject of the book is carnivals. I thought that maybe other people in the carnival received one. Did you?''

''Now I *know* we're going to have to talk. By the way, I don't run just the peach-basket game. I own nine other joints on the midway. And every one of them is a money-maker.'' She retreated out the door, her work boots scuffling on the floor.

Amid loud protests from those behind me, I squeezed back in front of the line. I leaned on the counter, palms down. ''Ah, sir?'' I said to the manager. ''That lady who just left is every bit as honest as you are. She said that you gave her ten dollars too much change. Here.'' I turned my hand over to reveal the ten-dollar bill that Amelia Halfhill had shortchanged the restaurant. The manager smiled in thanks and gave me a complimentary breakfast coupon.

Christine would have been proud of me. I was getting good at "skinning the poke." So good, in fact, I could even do it one-handed now. Amelia Halfhill had never noticed.

With a pocketful of coins, I returned to the pay phone outside. It was ringing. I picked it up and a voice said, "Colderwood? Christ, you're hard to get hold of."

It was the ghost I had been trying to catch.

CHAPTER SIXTEEN

Warner Huston told me that he had just called home and he had used his remote control to play back my message on his answering machine. Huston's voice sounded slurred and he talked more slowly than the recording on his answering machine.

He said, "I suppose you're interested in the fate of Arlen Roth's autobiography."

"What? Oh yeah. I was wondering how his death will affect your plans to complete the book."

"Needless to say, it's going to complicate matters legally, but I intend to stick with it until the end. Ever since hearing of Roth's tragedy, I've acquired an incredible thirst for solitude."

"Have the police been around to question you yet?"

"Not yet."

"How far along is the manuscript?"

"I've just completed the second draft."

"Do you have it with you right now?"

"Of course not." Underneath his voice, I could hear recorded music mixed in with a clatter of glasses and the murmuring of many male voices. "Are you in a bar?"

"Yeah."

He told me the name of the bar. It was one of the ones on the
list that the newspaper editor had given me.

"Funny you should ask about the manuscript," he said. "I
don't work at home. I rent space in an old office building. I
stopped into the office for a few minutes this morning and
discovered that the door had been jimmied. There were all kinds
of things that the burglar could have stolen—including a seven-
hundred-dollar typewriter. But instead, he ripped off a copy of
Roth's manuscript."

"A copy?"

"Sure. I keep copies of all my writing. It's only smart. In case
the whole office building burns down, my work can still go on.
The original manuscript is at home right now, locked in a fire-
proof safe."

I told him that a portion of his manuscript had been sent to
Christine Sirolli and also that other chapters might have surfaced
at the carnival.

"Wow. I really feel uncomfortable about her reading it. That
chapter on her was pretty heavy stuff. I kept trying to tell Roth
that we should tone down some of his personal attacks, but he
insisted that I write it the way he wanted. So you think that the
fortune-teller's chapter is just the tip of the iceberg?"

"There's a good possibility. Is there any way you could give
me a list of the other carnies that Roth tramped on in his book?"

A voice in the background tried to hurry Huston off the phone.
The noise of the bar grew faint as he covered the mouthpiece. I
gathered that he was buying a drink for the man waiting to use
the phone.

After a few seconds, Huston came back on the line and said,
"Much of Roth's book is a heartwarming, nostalgic look at
carnival life in America. He didn't need to sling any mud."

"Did he ever say why he wanted to write all that vicious
stuff?"

"Nope. He never wanted to discuss that subject. Maybe he
thought that all the barbs would spice up his book and make it
more commercial."

He then gave me the names of all the Bateman carnies that
Roth mentioned in his book. I had met all of them, except for a
man named Zig Mulvaney. Huston told me that Mulvaney ran a
mug joint, where carnivalgoers get their pictures taken. Of every-

one on the list, Huston said, there was only one that Roth said anything nice about: Mary Trunzo.

I said, "He didn't write anything about a young performer named Chuck Pitlor?"

"No, I don't think so. Wait, come to think of it, he did make brief mention of a Pitlor once. At one time Roth had an assistant named Blanche Paloma. That was her stage name. Her real last name was Pitlor."

"She was with the Bateman Carnival?"

"Just briefly. This was right after Roth dumped his other assistant."

"And what was this other assistant's name?"

"Mary Trunzo."

"Did Blanche Pitlor part with Roth on good terms?"

"Roth was vague about that. I got the feeling she left suddenly, perhaps in a fit of jealousy. Roth had a continuing love affair with Mary Trunzo, even after she was no longer his assistant. In spite of his being fifteen years older, they were very serious about each other."

"Is Blanche Pitlor still in show business?"

"I'm afraid I have no idea."

I started to say good-bye when Huston interrupted me. "I think I've given you the wrong impression about the theft of the manuscript. Actually, the *entire* manuscript wasn't stolen. That would have been quite impossible."

"I don't understand."

"Roth wrote the last chapter himself. He was still revising it at the time of death and he never let me see a copy of it."

"What was so special about that chapter?"

"He never discussed it with me, although he did continually refer to it as his 'catharsis.' I always figured that his phantom last chapter dealt with why he left the Bateman Carnival. That was one subject that Roth refused to touch on."

I asked him if he knew the exact date that Roth quit the carnival. I had to wait while Huston inserted additional money into his phone. When the chiming stopped, he said that Roth had quit twenty years ago, on July 12. The anniversary of the end of Roth's carnival career was only a few days away.

I said, "I need to ask you a big favor. It won't be long before the police come around to question you. Any chance that you could conveniently forget about our conversation?"

"That's no problem. I'm not in any mood to talk to the cops anyway. Even though my relationship with Roth was mostly over the phone, I can't tell you how devastating it is to work with him all these months and then for him to be gone, just like that. For the next several days, the only time I'll be home is to pick up the mail. I intend to spend most of my time here in the dark solitude of the barroom."

"Sounds inviting. Wish I could join you."

"You know, ever since I heard of Roth's murder, I've been afflicted with a writer's block—I mean a *serious* block. So far, I haven't found the proper mix of alcohol to dissolve it. But I'm working on it."

"Perhaps in a few days I'll have a story for you that'll make a whale of a final chapter for Roth's book."

"Hey, that sounds good. Keep in touch."

"In the meantime, though, don't try to wash away that writer's block all at once."

"Yeah, sure. And you take it easy yourself, okay? I've already lost one coauthor. Don't let me lose another. It's bad for my image."

CHAPTER SEVENTEEN

The aroma of hot sausage and french fries blanketed the grandstand area of the fairgrounds. The bleachers were half full, a good crowd for so early in the afternoon. Blaring from two six-foot speakers onstage was the overture for Jacques Carlson's act—a medley of theme music from every schmaltzy sports movie of the past decade.

Apparently Carlson had invited other members of the carnival to catch his new act. Standing by the entrance to the grandstand was Amelia Halfhill, master of the carnival game and the art of the shortchange. Next to her were Bill Bateman and Mary Trunzo. A pair of binoculars hung from Bateman's neck. Mary was relaxing in a folding lounge chair. She was wearing a pair of clinging shorts that nicely displayed her legs. While Mary seemed annoyed that Bateman was engaged in such intense conversation with Halfhill, she was also basking in the admiring glances from the males in the grandstand.

A truck with Carlson's name painted on the side rumbled through the back gate of the grandstand grounds and backed up against the rear of the platform. It's corrugated-steel door rose slowly and a paunchy Walt Galloway—looking just the opposite of a hero in his short-sleeved khaki shirt and high-laced boots— schlepped out onto the platform. Under his direction, two men wheeled out a long, tarp-covered cylinder. After clearing the truck, they took a few moments to catch their breath. The two crew members then hopped back inside and roared off the field at a considerably faster pace than they had entered.

The handbill I had been given at the gate described Carlson as "An Adonis of iron and stone, able to do the work of five men . . ." Then why, I wondered, did he need a stage crew? Let's see, counting Galloway, Carlson still had the strength of two more men than they did.

As the tempo of the music increased, the crowd clapped rhythmically and whistled in impatience. The show was now fifteen minutes late. Apparently Carlson also had the tardiness of five men.

After the truck cleared the back gate, a black Lincoln Continental with dark amber windows eased through and parked beside the wooden fence lining the rear of the grandstand area. No one got out or wound down any windows.

Mary nudged Bateman and pointed at the Lincoln. They both waved, and the driver beeped back. Halfhill shoved her hands into her pockets and turned her face away in disgust. She seemed revolted by even the thought of being friendly toward fat man Delbert "Ernie" St. Erne. Ernie mustn't have been thinking of

Halfhill when he had told me that carnies were a tight-knit community, blind to physical anomalies.

A man and a woman sitting in front of me took out a pair of binoculars and began to pass them back and forth. The music quickly faded and was replaced by a voice that had an artificial echo. Since I didn't see any announcer, I assumed it was a recording. The voice told the audience about the Atlas-like feats that Carlson had performed over the years: pulling railroad cars with his teeth, changing tires on cars without using a jack, and swimming five miles while towing a professional football team in a chain of rowboats. He said that Carlson once won a thousand-dollar bet by putting a nail between his lips and spitting it through a two-by-four. My god, I thought, chewing tobacco would be a lethal weapon in this man's hands.

I started to hear the words of the announcer coming behind me. I turned and saw Christine Sirolli sitting on the bleacher above me, softly reciting the announcer's lines, word for word. She nodded and gave my shoulder a squeeze. Christine was now dressed for work. Her midnight-blue, low-cut gown accentuated the swell of her breasts. Clinging to her neck was a sapphire-blue choker. Professional pride kept me from asking how she had sat down behind me without my noticing.

Many admiring eyes in the audience were now dividing their time between Mary Trunzo and the darker, more subtle beauty of Christine. I said, "In case you didn't notice, there seems to be quite a contest going on between you and Mary."

She shook her head. "There's only one beauty contest going on today. Shhh! It's about to begin."

As the announcer cued the audience to applaud, Carlson, wearing only a cape and burnt orange bikini shorts, bounded up the back steps of the platform. He looked like a comic-book superhero dressed for a day at the beach. As the announcer continued, Carlson embarked on a series of strong-man feats.

The announcer said, "Ladies and gentleman: push-ups . . . the hard way." Carlson stood on his hands and then lowered himself to the stage, touching his forehead to the platform. Showing no strain, he pushed himself back up and down again several times, looking like a human piston. I felt the nudge of Christine's knee in my back.

She said, "I haven't done much fortune-telling so far today. I've been busy doing some checking."

"And?"

"I was right. Chapters of Roth's book were delivered to several carnies."

"And the reviews?"

"Not so good."

"Did you talk to everyone who received a chapter?"

"All but one."

As two stagehands trundled a cartload of steel bars to the center of the platform, Carlson invited six spectators to join him onstage. Each volunteer was more mountainous and fierce-looking than the last. Carlson passed out the steel bars and challenged the volunteers to bend them. Each tried a different strategy, some stepping on the bars, others putting them behind their necks. All grimaced and grunted under the strain. After a few seconds, it was obvious they would fail. Carlson then walked past the row of volunteers, taking their bars. He bent them like pipe cleaners.

Christine rested her fingertips on my shoulder, tensing and relaxing them as he dropped the twisted metal onto the platform.

After telling her about my conversation with Warner Huston and about the missing last chapter of Roth's book, I asked, "What did the carnies think of the manuscript?"

"Most are playing it close to the vest. There was only one who didn't hide his anger."

"How angry was he?"

"Full-tilt-ready-to-kill angry."

I looked down at Carlson strutting about the stage, striking as many different bodybuilding poses as possible. "Him?" I asked.

"Sure. Who else?" She leaned closer, planting her knees in my back.

"You said there's one carny you haven't talked to yet. Who?"

"Do you see the gentleman with camera down there?"

To the right of the stage stood a short, wiry man wearing a black derby and a black pin-striped suit. In sharp contrast to his Gay Nineties costume was the thirty-five-millimeter camera around his neck.

"Is that Zig Mulvaney?"

"Right. He runs the mug-shot booth."

Mulvaney moved closer to the stage as Carlson donned a karate outfit and launched into a series of quick stunts. "His grand finale will be coming up after this," Christine said.

Most of Carlson's stunts were valid feats of strength, like his one-armed presses with dumbbells too heavy for two ordinary men to budge with both hands. But some of his stunts were variations on old magic tricks, such as ripping a deck of cards in half with his bare hands, running an eighteen-inch needle through his arm without injury, and swallowing a length of thread and several razor blades. When he pulled the thread back out of his mouth, all the blades were strung in a row.

"Did someone have to read aloud the manuscript for Carlson, or did he figure it all out himself?"

When Christine didn't answer, I turned and saw that she was devoting her full attention to Carlson's feats of lifting, bending, and breaking.

Finally she said, "I think you have the wrong impression of Jacques. He's more sensitive than he looks. I had to prod him for a while, but he finally admitted that Roth had depicted him as an impotent wimp who had enveloped himself in layers of muscles in order to mask his lack of manliness."

The kids in the audience thrilled to Carlson's act, particularly when he began to break things with his bare hands. He moved to the edge of the stage, where a stack of flat, wide boards waited atop a pair of cinder blocks. He hammered at the wood with the rigid edge of his hand until all the boards were split in half. He then drove his forehead into one of the cinder blocks, crumbling it to pieces. Doing a war whoop, he jumped back to prevent the chunks of cement from hitting his toes.

Only now was Carlson starting to work up a sweat.

Assuming that Roth's theory about Carlson was correct, I wondered what had frightened him badly enough to construct such a gruesome armor of muscles.

I asked, "Did Carlson show you his chapter?"

"No. He said he ripped it to shreds."

"More likely he put sugar and milk on it and ate it for breakfast."

Carlson now instructed the same volunteers to sit atop a long wooden table in the center of the stage. He crawled under the table, jammed his massive shoulders up against the bottom, and then steadily rose to a standing position, taking the table and its human cargo with him. After a pause to acknowledge the audience's cheers, he eased everyone back down again.

The recorded voice thanked the crowd for its kindness and invited everyone to meet personally with Jacques Carlson . . . and to share his secret of success—a product called Ener-Charge. Which was on sale. At $19.95 per bottle. (Today only: three for $50.00.)

I said, "Is that stuff safe?"

"Jacques bought the formula from a snake-oil salesman who used to tour with another carnival. A few years back a state health agency, looking to grab publicity, confiscated several bottles of the elixir."

"What was the verdict?"

"Their tests found it to be a harmless combination of herbs. The elixir's only active ingredient produced a mild sedative effect, no more powerful than some over-the-counter sleep aids. They concluded that the most that Ener-Charge can do is give you a warm feeling of well-being. As long as Jacques promised to tone down his claims for the elixir, he was allowed to peddle it."

Many in the audience were now moving down front, some clutching money in their hands. Carlson held up his hand to stop them. A stagehand passed him a microphone, and for the first time Carlson spoke to the group. As his voice quaked and cracked with nervousness, I could see why he relied on a recorded announcer. He invited the crowd to return to their seats and watch a special premiere performance of a new feature of his act.

From beneath the platform, two stagehands rolled out a circular frame, about eight feet in diameter. Because of a fine mesh netting that stretched across the metal frame, it resembled a trampoline. Carlson then asked an audience volunteer to pick out any spot on the expansive grounds surrounding the stage. Following the directions of the volunteer, the crew wheeled the frame of netting to a spot one hundred feet away.

After the crew returned to the stage, they whisked away the tarp covering the cylindrical shape they had wheeled out of the truck earlier. It was a giant cannon, painted with red stripes and silver glitter.

Carlson said, "This cannon is going to shoot me into the air at a speed of over eighty miles per hour. No human cannonball has ever attempted to hit as small a target as that little trampoline out in the middle of the field. The positioning of the cannon must be precise, taking into consideration the speed and direction of the wind. There is no room for error. An out-of-shape, untrained person would have only a one-in-ten chance of surviving this attempt. I hope my odds will be considerably better."

"Is this really the first time he's ever tried this?" I asked. Christine gave me a curt nod, keeping her gaze fixed on Walt Galloway as he steadied a ladder against the mouth of the cannon. Carlson inserted a pair of plugs in his ears, scaled the ladder, and then saluted the audience. He wriggled his way down into the mouth of the cannon.

Galloway peered into an instrument that looked like a surveyor's sextant mounted at the rear of the cannon. He pulled out a pocket calculator, hit a few buttons, and then looked through the viewfinder again. Without taking his eye off the lens, he made hand signals to the rest of the crew. Grabbing on to handles at the base of the cannon, they began to rotate the big gun. Trembling under the strain, they exerted themselves more than Carlson had during his entire act. Once the cannon was pointing in the general direction of the trampoline, Galloway turned two large wheels at the rear of the cannon, changing its position slowly, almost imperceptibly. Satisfied that the big gun was on target, he removed the sextant and put it away in a plush storage case.

Galloway did a slow countdown, starting from ten. When he reached zero, he pulled a stubby lever on the side of the cannon. Nothing happened. He pulled it again, and this time the cannon recoiled and made a woofing sound that caused my eardrums to waver.

The blur that hurled out of the mouth of the cannon was Jacques Carlson, his body ramrod stiff. As he shot skyward he stretched his arms out in front of him, his hands forming a wedge to cut through the air. As he reached the pinnacle of his arc he tucked in his head and raised his knees. He began to rapidly spin head over heels.

For a moment it appeared that Carlson had overshot the net. But then his body stopped its dizzying somersaults and headed straight for the trampoline. He hit the net dead center, feetfirst. It bowed downward, nearly touching the ground. When it sprang back, it flung him several feet into the air. He did a full flip and landed on the ground, taking only a half step to regain balance.

Carlson turned to the grandstand and took a full bow.

Although it earned an instant ovation from the audience, I was more acutely aware of Christine's reaction. She sighed in relief and then broke into uncontrollable, giddy laughter. Her hands slid down my shoulders, her fingernails biting the middle of my back.

"He did it. He did it!" she cried.

She pulled me back and planted a kiss on my lips. The kiss lasted longer than a kiss of mere friendship but was shy of being truly passionate. It made me wish that Carlson would crawl into his cannon and do it all over again.

Still standing in the spot where he had landed, Carlson was promptly attended to by his assistants. One pumped his hands in congratulations, and another draped his cape over his shoulders. Carlson seemed in a fog, as though—in his mind—he were still tumbling through the air. I asked the couple in front of me to lend me their binoculars.

I fingered the focus knob until the image of Carlson came in sharp . . . so sharp that I could see the individual veins bugging out of his arms and chest, looking like overheated, faulty wiring. Carlson looked up into the grandstands. From all that distance, and only moments after risking his life, he had spotted Christine kissing me. While he angrily spewed out expletives I noticed that even his jaw muscles had the same chiseled, well-defined look of the rest of his body.

I lowered the binoculars and saw that a few rows down from us a boy was proudly showing his parents pieces of broken wood that he had retrieved from the stage—a souvenir from Carlson's orgy of smashing. The boy said, "Look at the writing on this board, Daddy. What's it mean?"

"Darned if I know, Matt," his father said.

I focused the binoculars on the two pieces of wood in the boy's hands. Something was written on them in Magic Marker. The boy's father took the boards, turned them around, and put them back together again. The lettering spelled out *Harry Cotter*. Apparently Carlson had found it easier to shatter boards when my name was written on them. A warm glow spread throughout me. It was gratifying to be an inspiration to a fellow showman.

I settled back in the bleachers and watched the line swell in front of the booth that was peddling Jacques Carlson's health elixir.

The black Lincoln was still parked, engine running, at the far edge of the grandstand area. Condensation from its overworked air conditioner formed a large puddle under the car. The amber windows made it hard to see inside. I tapped on the driver's window. No response. I tried again.

With a gentle churring, the electric window glided down to reveal a huge face that seemed to fill the whole opening. Chilled air, the smell of pizza, and the high decibels of symphonic music rushed out at me. Ernie hadn't exaggerated. His car had no backseat and the front seat was set a foot and a half farther back than normal. Ernie had paid a fortune for his on-the-road autonomy.

I said, "Carlson's act was really something, eh?"

Ernie shrugged, sending ripples throughout his face and neck. "It was adequate. Oh, I grant you, the guys does put out a lot of energy. And maybe he does face *some* danger, but why bother when there are easier ways to earn a living? He'd have to go a long way to beat my job. I don't have to zoom through the air like a punted football and risk scrambling my brains. Hell, I could sit around all day and read newspapers, and the marks would still pay money to see me."

I motioned for him to turn down his tape player. I heard a scrunching sound as he batted aside several empty pizza boxes to reach the proper knob.

I said, "Maybe fascination with the Carnival Fat Man is not as universal as you think, Ernie. Did you ever wonder what Arlen Roth thought of you?"

His hand darted for the window button, but he changed his mind.

"What nasty things did he write about you in his book, Ernie?"

He sighed. "Sorry, Harry. I really have to get to work. If I may paraphrase an old saying: The freak show ain't over until the fat man shows up, sits on his ass, and does absolutely nothing."

When I didn't laugh, Ernie turned off his tape player. The

corners of his eyes were moist. He put his hands on the steering wheel, leaned forward, and rubbed his forehead on the back of his hand. He finally looked up and said, "Roth was such a decent guy when he worked here. What the hell happens to some people, Harry?"

"If you want, we'll talk about it later, Ernie. You'd better get going." I pulled a slip of paper from my pocket and handed it to him. "Here. The treat's on me." When Ernie started to protest, I said, "Don't worry about it. This place is dying for publicity."

I had handed him a coupon for the all-you-can-eat breakfast buffet at KT's Restaurant. Judging from his wide grin, you would have thought I had just given him a five-hundred-dollar bill.

Come to think of it, maybe I had.

CHAPTER EIGHTEEN

An envelope with my name on it lay in the middle of the platform in my tent. Written with a ballpoint pen that skipped badly, it reminded me of a child's connect-the-dots drawing. I opened it and pulled out a carnival ticket stub. On the back, in the same pen, were the words: *I need your help. Go to the duck pond at 2:30.* There was no signature, only the initials *A.H.*

If A.H. was Amelia Halfhill, it was an abrupt change of tune for her. My sleight-of-hand trick with the ten-dollar bill at the restaurant this morning must have made her sore. If so, it was partly her fault. She had violated one of the cardinal rules of flimflam men: Always count your stolen change before leaving the counter.

*   *   *

On the way to the duck pond, I passed the Ferris wheel. The big wheel was motionless, all its cars empty. Near the top of the wheel, a man swung nimbly among the struts, using his hands and feet with equal grace. He wore a golf hat, a jangling bag of tools, and a pair of welding goggles. He moved so swiftly, his tool bag threatened to tangle up in the metal skeleton. I shielded my eyes from the sun but still didn't recognize this man moving with such apelike finesse.

From nearby, I heard a rhythmic hissing and spitting. Thinking there was a leak in the Ferris wheel engine, I walked to the other side of the ride and found that the sound was coming from inside a steel cage. The door to the cage was open, exposing a mass of gears, belts, and shafts. Just inside the cage, slumped in a lawn chair, was a man in his early twenties, wearing a snap-brim hat pulled low on his forehead, almost covering his eyes. Every time he exhaled, his snore made the off-and-on hissing sound that I had heard. Thick green rubber gloves encased his hands, and greasy rags lay heaped at his feet. His legs were crossed at the ankles, and his body looked so slack that if I had shaken his chair, he would have rolled off, like jelly on hot toast.

I started to walk away, but my foot clanged into an empty bucket in my path. With a grunt and a "What the—?" the man snatched up a rag in each hand and jumped to his feet.

He straightened his hat, focused his glazed eyes at me, and then relaxed, throwing down his rags in embarrassment. He said, "Christ, I thought you were Galloway."

I introduced myself as the new carnival magician, and he told me his name was Gabe. He removed his hat and wiped his sleeve across his forehead. After stretching and yawning, he stooped down and removed a sopping rag from a bucket full of black liquid. He wrung it out and began to wipe off a long axle that lay across a wide board on the ground. The grease bubbled and rolled off the axle, leaving behind a path of glistening metal.

"Pretty strong stuff, huh?" I asked, pointing to the bucket.

"You bet. It sure saves me a lot of rubbing. Better than any solvent or acid I've ever used. It's so good, Galloway won't let us fool with the undiluted stuff. He mixes this solution up for us."

"Does the carnival regularly shut the rides down to service them?"

That gave Gabe a good laugh. "Sure. We service them regularly . . . whenever they break down. And that's pretty regular. Galloway says that as long as there are customers in line and as long as the Ferris wheel can turn at least once without falling off its hub and rolling down the midway, we're supposed to run it. But I ain't complaining. Maintenance is such a pain in the ass, I'd rather just sit back and let the machine run."

Before dipping his rag into the bucket again, he made sure that the cuff of his glove was pulled back tight, protecting his wrist. Trying not to make even a small splash, he carefully wrung out his rag. Dissolved grease ran back into his bucket, turning the liquid even blacker. He whistled as he finished wiping down the rest of the axle. The fumes from the rag and bucket made me wrinkle my nose, and I stepped back. But they didn't seem to bother the ride operator. In fact, he seemed to thrive on them: The more he rubbed, the louder he whistled and sang. When Gabe broke into the first verse of "Palisades Park," I waved good-bye and walked around the base of the Ferris wheel, ready to continue on to the duck pond.

I looked up to check the progress of the worker atop the big wheel, but I never knew if I spotted him or not. My memory of the next moments is lost.

Something thudded nearby and the ground trembled. My legs were suddenly robbed of all sensation and power. I found myself facedown, several feet forward from where I'd been an instant before. My forearms felt raw and scratched, and I tasted gravel. Although my vision was blurred, I could see dust clouds settling around me.

I couldn't breathe. I tried to exhale. And couldn't. I tried to inhale. And couldn't. For ten seconds, I was in a panic, wondering what to do about this no-breathing thing. Just when a pleasant warmth began to descend over my body and I began to enjoy being finally relieved of my illogical dependence on air, I choked and sputtered and began taking in shallow gulps of air. As regular breathing returned I felt the same satisfaction as a mechanic who has just revived a doomed car engine.

What the hell exploded? I thought. As my vision cleared, my legs began to throb and sting.

The words of the ride operator ran through my mind: "Maintenance is such a pain in the ass." I began to laugh. *Shut 'er down,*

I thought. *Something's broken.* My laughter was cut short by the increasing throb in my legs. "Burns like acid," I said aloud.

I twisted my head around and saw Gabe hugging my legs. Farther back was a dent in the ground where I had been standing. A few feet to my side lay the remains of a Ferris wheel car. The fall from the top of the big wheel had reduced it to a shapeless heap of metal.

Gabe let go of my legs and stood up. He had saved my life. When he had tackled me, slamming me out of the path of the falling car, he was still wearing his acid-soaked gloves. That's why my legs were stinging.

"So much for carnival tradition," I said.

Gabe shucked off his gloves and dusted himself off. "What are you talking about?"

"The carnival has a tradition of special words for everything and everybody: ride monkey, wirer, fixer, and joint store. Right?"

"So?"

"And if I yell 'Hey, Rube!' you know what that means, don't you?"

"Sure. That means there's a fight on the midway."

"Then why don't carnies have a word for when a crummy, ill-maintained ride falls apart and almost kills someone? I would have settled for something similar to, say, the lumberjack's 'Timber!' "

"Beats me. Guess we'll have to invent one, won't we?" He took my hand and pulled me to my feet.

I looked up. The man who had been crawling in the framework of the Ferris wheel was gone. "Who was that guy up there?"

"What guy?" Gabe said. "I was working here alone. I didn't see anyone."

Christine and I sat at the small round table in the center of her tent. She drank tea from a Styrofoam cup. Her table was so small that the toe of her shoe kept brushing against my ankle. Just as my smoking cigarette in her ashtray was burning itself out, I was waiting for my anger to consume itself. The process was excruciatingly slow. "The hell with it," I said. I took one long drag on the cigarette and ground it into the dirt with my heel.

When I had showed up limping at Christine's tent, I told her of my near miss. She reacted with resignation, as if this kind of thing were a regular occurrence. She hung an out-to-lunch sign in front of her tent and got a cup of water from a concession stand to sponge off my legs. This relieved most of the stinging. The scratches at the bottoms of my forearms turned out to be minor. My tux coat would cover up the small tears and dirt on my shirt sleeves. I gave Christine the keys to my van, and she came back with a spare pair of trousers.

A low-wattage bulb swinging above the table barely provided enough light for me to see the expressions on her face. The red beads on her choker sparkled like rubies. While her costume and makeup seemed gaudy and cheap in the light of day, inside the tent they heightened her aura of mysticism. "It's dark in here," I said.

"It's all the light I need—just enough to read the denominations on paper money. If I need more, I set up candles. Atmosphere is everything here, Harry." She bobbed her tea bag up and down. "What were you doing over by the Ferris wheel?"

I showed her the note written on the ticket stub. "I was on my way to meet Amelia Halfhill. Now I'm beginning to wonder if she even wrote this."

Christine shook her head at the note. "I can't help you. I don't know if this is her handwriting or not." She finished her tea and went to the corner of the tent, where a metal TV tray held a little pot connected to an extension cord. She put another tea bag and some sugar in her cup and then poured hot water from the pot.

When she returned, she said, "After Jacques Carlson's show today, I talked to Galloway and wheedled out of him what Roth said about him in his manuscript. He said that Galloway's safety practices were shoddy, making the carnival rides dangerous, a menace to the public."

"Dangerous? Hell, the rides aren't dangerous . . . as long as you don't ride them. Or walk underneath them."

I looked at my watch. There was still enough time to meet with Amelia Halfhill before my first show. I planned to take the long way around, walking behind the tents. Far away from the amusement rides that I no longer found so amusing.

CHAPTER NINETEEN

Amelia Halfhill wasn't at the duck pond when I arrived. The man working the game booth asked if I was Harry Cotter and then said that Halfhill wanted to see me in her office trailer. Office trailer? Something told me that Halfhill wasn't any ordinary game operator. He gave me directions.

Her trailer was nestled in between Bateman's office and the hospitality trailer reserved for members of the local fair board that was sponsoring the carnival this week. When I knocked, a voice said, "Door's open." Inside, Halfhill offered me a seat by her desk and said she'd only be a minute. She went back to busily tapping at her computer keyboard.

Her computer and printer took up most of her desk space. A wide ribbon of paper extended out of the printer and down to the floor. The paper was crowded with columns of numbers. Squeezed in among the numbers were lots of dollar signs.

I suspected that Amelia Halfhill lived here in her office. A portable television set was bolted to a wall shelf in front of a sofa bed. A sliding door beside the sofa revealed a closet hung with mostly jeans and denim shirts.

After only a few seconds, my forehead and the back of my neck went moist. I looked around for an air conditioner, but there was none.

Packages of cigarettes—mostly half full—lay everywhere. I wondered if each one represented a victory for her shortchange scam. She brushed aside the butts in her ashtray to make room for the one she had just finished. She picked up the nearest pack and gently shook it until a cigarette popped into view. She clamped her lips on the filter and drew the pack away. Leaning close to a large butane lighter on her desk, she pressed a button and a flame popped up. She sucked on the cigarette with such vigor that the tiny flame nearly died.

She offered me one. Usually just the sight of another person smoking makes me reach for one of my own. But the dull yellow spot on the ceiling above her desk chair, a result of her nicotine habit, canceled out that desire.

Noticing that I was staring at the discolored ceiling, she said, "I own ten game booths in this carnival. To keep things running smoothly, I spend endless hours out on the midway. I have a rule that no one—including myself—can smoke on the job. Personally, I think a game operator with a butt hanging from his lips looks too sleazy. I guess, when I get in the office here, I try to make up for lost time."

She shifted her cigarette to the corner of her mouth and punched more keys on her computer, watching the screen fill with numbers. The computer beeped once and the screen went blank.

I said, "It seems strange that you'd keep records on what is essentially an off-the-books, cash business."

"Not really." She laid her cigarette on the edge of the ashtray, just in time to avoid dripping ash on her keyboard. "I have to keep *some* kind of records. The government dicks aren't stupid enough to believe that all ten of my joints are losing dough. After all, how much overhead can there be in a game of tossing softballs into a peach basket? The way I figure, if I'm going to keep phony books, I might as well keep a set of accurate ones, too. That way, I can keep score of how well I'm doing. It also helps me figure out which of my employees are ripping me off. The 'real' books—the ones the feds will never see—are on a special computer disk. I'm the only one that knows the password to access it."

"You say you run ten joints? That's a lot."

"Hell, with the frontage and the PC I pay Bateman, some weeks I damn near keep this whole carnival afloat."

"PC?"

"Percentage. I pay Bateman a percentage of my take, just like you. The only difference is that my PC varies each week, depending on how much of a fix Carlson has in with the local cops. My extra PC helps defray Bateman's under-the-table payments to the lawmen's 'favorite charity.' The bigger the 'contribution,' the more they look the other way. Every once in a while my PC takes a ferocious jump, but it's usually worth it. In those cases, Carlson has negotiated so well that he declares a town wide open."

"What's that mean?"

"Anything goes. In a wide-open town, the cops don't care how much we bilk the marks, as long as we keep all trouble on the lot."

I laughed. "You mean you worry about the police busting a kiddy game like your duck pond?"

She smiled at me through a cloud of smoke and sat back in her chair, putting her hands behind her head. "That 'kiddy game' normally brings in over three grand a week. But in a wide-open town, the sky's the limit."

"The duck pond is rigged? How the hell do you do that?"

"You're too green to be asking questions like that."

In my mind, I saw the swirling tub full of floating ducks. At the rear of the tub was a fake cavern where the circling ducks floated in and out. Each duck had a letter on the bottom: S, M, or L. The shelves at the back of the booth were full of glitzy prizes, also labeled with one of the three letters, depending on whether the value of the prize was small, medium, or large. For a dollar, the mark got to choose any three ducks he wanted and then pick prizes from the corresponding category. The S prizes were mostly slum—cheap goods bought in large quantity . . . combs, baseball hats, et cetera. The M prizes weren't much more impressive. But the L prizes were gems. They included television sets, cameras, luggage, and compact disk players.

During the few minutes that I had watched the duck pond in operation, I didn't see anyone pick an L duck. Yet I knew there were L ducks in that tub. Sometimes, to show how easy it was to win, the attendant would pick up a duck and display a big L printed on the bottom. After he mixed the L duck back in with the others, the marks were never able to relocate it.

I slapped the top of Amelia's desk. Her ashtray took a hop and the sudden breeze fanned ash particles into the air. "Magnets," I announced triumphantly.

"Come again?"

"The duck pond is rigged with magnets. It's the only answer. I thought that maybe the lettering on the bottom of the ducks was done with a special paint that would rub on and off, but that's too elaborate. Like a good magic trick, the answer has to be simple. And magnets are definitely simple."

She smiled just enough to keep the cigarette from tumbling from her lips. She tore the stream of paper from her printer and started to fold it. "Go ahead."

"A small but powerful magnet is stuck to the outside bottom of the tub, underneath the little cave the ducks float through. All the L ducks have little strips of metal glued to the inside bottom. As long as the magnet is attached to the bottom of the tub, the one or two L ducks stay hidden in the cave, out of sight. If a mark gets suspicious and claims that there aren't any L ducks, then the booth operator casually palms off the magnet. Voilà! The L ducks float out with all the others. Since they're probably specially marked on top, the operator has no trouble picking them out, thus silencing the wise guy."

Halfhill rested her elbows on the folded stack of computer paper on her desk. She smiled as though she had just spotted a new car that she was dying to buy. "I was right about you. That's why I think we should talk."

"Then you did send me this?" I laid the ticket stub on her desk.

"Of course. Why would anyone—" She stared at the dirt and snags on the elbows of my shirt. "Harry, I see that you're already learning that the carnival can be a goddam tough place to work. But let me tell you, there's a lot of money here if you're willing to pay the price, willing to face that toughness head-on. So far, it doesn't look like you're doing a very good job."

I shrugged. "This isn't the only job in the world."

She lowered her chair with a bump and leaned across the desk. "Like hell it isn't. Once you get a taste of carny life, you'll never settle for anything else."

I thought of the dingy interior of my carnival tent, and then I thought of the Magic Oasis nightclub, with its candlelit tables, handwritten menus, and dressing rooms serviced by uniformed valets. I also thought of the handsome money the club paid its entertainers . . . always on time, always in full. And no PC.

"I think you're a true carny," Halfhill said. "Newcomers usually don't last long. But I think you're an exception."

My imagination lifted the curtain on a pleasant daydream. In my mind's eye I saw myself on the Magic Oasis stage, the rays of the quarter-million-dollar lighting system filling me with power and confidence. The audience's welcoming applause was just dying down and I was about to perform my first trick. I reached up in the air, but instead of a fluttering white dove, a yellow rubber duck appeared in my hand. It had a big *S* on the bottom. Even though my act was supposed to be silent, I began to talk to the audience, speaking lines from my carnival act, but with slight differences. Because of some subtle changes, my lines were suddenly brighter and funnier than before.

I reached for my notepad but realized that I had left it in my acid-damaged trousers. I asked Halfhill for a pen and hurriedly transcribed my new, improved lines onto the carnival ticket stub.

"What are you writing?" she asked.

"Improvements for my act. If I don't write them down, I'll forget them." I reread my notes, crossing some words out and making new additions. The audience that I'd be facing twenty minutes from now would tell me whether these new lines worked. By evening's end, after five shows, the improvements either would be a permanent part of my act or would be crumpled up in the bottom of a waste can. Either way, I realized that I could never do this at the Magic Oasis. It was too dangerous to try out material there.

"Why bother trying to improve your act?" she said. "Is it going to make any difference in your nightly take? When I said that the carnival could get into your blood, I didn't mean as a performer. I was talking about using your talents for broader applications. To be frank, you showed me a thing or two at that restaurant this morning."

"The restaurant—?" Oh yeah. Her shortchange scam.

"I haven't figured out your exact maneuver. I asked a couple of my boys, but they didn't know either. Care to show me?"

I shook my head. "Sorry, I don't want to think of the hundreds of dollars you'd swindle people out of by using it. When I fool people, at least I do it up front. The marks know it before-hand. They know what they're paying for.''

"Come off it. This is a carnival, for chrissake. Everyone here sells some kind of excitement. You think it really matters to a mark whether or not he wins a stuffed bear that probably won't fit inside his Toyota anyway? He's paying for the thrill of winning and losing, not the merchandise. And if he happens to lose a little more than he wins, he's still happy. And so are we.''

"But what if the town's wide open and two of your stooges double-team a mark into losing his whole paycheck in fifteen minutes? How happy is he then?''

"That rarely happens.''

"Oh, I'm sure it's a rare occurrence,'' I said. "So rare that you need several grand worth of computer hardware to keep track of the dough pouring in. On the way over here, I saw a mark who obviously had too much to drink. He was playing a game where he had to toss rubber rings around clothespins with num-bers on the back. The number of the clothespin determined the number of the prize he won.''

"We call that a peek joint, Harry, because the operator peeks at the numbers.''

"The wagers kept escalating after each throw, and the mark was too drunk to notice how much money he was losing. Half the time the operator miscalled the numbers by holding his fingers over one of the digits. The mark shelled out eighty-five dollars in just a few minutes. And all he had to show for it were a few warped record albums and a two-dollar sewing kit . . . and—oh yes—the 'thrill' of playing.''

She blew smoke in my direction and pointed a triumphant finger at me. "The man running that ring toss is the best peek man I have. He's smooth. No one's ever caught him holding his finger on the numbers. *That* is why I wanted to talk to you. With me, you could earn more in one week than during a whole season of your rickety tent shows.''

"But I—''

"I know. You don't want to work out front. Okay. You don't have to. All you have to do is teach some of my boys what you know. And maybe do a little finger flinging every so often. You'll work hard during the season, but I guarantee that you'll live like a king all winter.''

"Sorry." I waved the ticket stub containing my one-liners. "I like making people laugh. Not cry."

I stood up and she did the same, running her fingers through her tangled hair. "I've heard about your 'troubles' in adjusting to this place. But you haven't seen anything yet."

"Is that a threat?"

"No, just an honest assessment of your situation. I wish you'd reconsider my offer. If you don't want to coach any of my operators, then how about teaching me? All I want is a few ideas to make my games more profitable."

She took a computer disk from her desk and placed it in the computer's drive. After she hit a few switches and keys, the printer began to chatter, jerkily spewing out more paper covered with numbers. She looked over at me and shook her head with pity. "You don't know what you're passing up, do you? If someone had made an offer like that to me when I was starting out in carnivals, God only knows how far ahead I'd be today."

"How did you get started?"

"A little more than twenty years ago, I was just a seventeen-year-old farm kid from Iowa who thought her mom and dad were the worst people on earth. When the carnival came to town, I fell in love with a ride monkey and went on the road with him. Our romance lasted two weeks, long enough for him to find another naive farm girl to replace me. There I was: three hundred miles from home and penniless. But a nice gentleman took me under his wing and taught me enough about this business to get started. Without him . . . well, who knows what would have happened?"

"Was that guy a magician too?"

"Yes, but he knew a lot about carnival games and how to gimmick them."

"Is he still with the show?"

"Nah, he's long gone."

"What happened to him?"

"Damned if I know. One day he's working the midway, and the next day his tent is empty, already drawing cobwebs. This is a funny business. People come and go."

"Obviously, you're thankful to him for giving you your start. What if someone did just the opposite? What if someone went public with all your trade secrets . . . your duck pond, peek joints, game wheels—and wrote a book about them? What do you think would happen?"

She curled her lips, exposing crooked, dulled teeth. "Nothing, at first. But if the book was popular, it could cause trouble for all carnival joint stores in the whole country. The owners would all be scrambling to replace their exposed games with new ones. Until the new games were established, there would be a lot of money lost. As for myself, if I were mentioned in this book, then I wouldn't be too popular—or too safe, for that matter—in the carny world. But of course this is all hypothetical, isn't it?" She broke into a devious smile that took a few moments to expand to its fullest. "There are too many fail-safes to prevent that kind of wholesale exposure."

I turned around to see who she was smiling at. A man's head disappeared from the window of her door, too fast for me to recognize him.

She said, "I think you have too much sympathy for the marks. You know the old saying about not being able to cheat an honest man."

"Yeah, I've heard that before. If that saying is true, then why was it so easy for me to clip you for ten dollars this morning?"

I had touched a sore spot. She opened a side drawer on her desk, allowing me to glimpse several bound stacks of money. Next to the money was a small pile of white paper. The top page was covered with typewriting. Roth's manuscript?

As I headed for the door she said, "Keep my offer in mind, especially at the end of the week when you see how little you have left after all your payments to Bateman."

Keys jangled in her hand as she reached the door ahead of me. She wriggled the doorknob, and I heard more jangling. She had locked the door during our little conference.

Outside, a man stood beside the doorway, his back to the wall. Arms folded, he wore a sleeveless shirt with a number on front. His arms were as big as Carlson's, though not as well shaped or tanned. There was an unhealthy pallor to his face, as though his skin were made of clay, malleable to the touch. His round, tight stomach made it evident that beer was his main source of nourishment. I recognized him as the operator of Amelia Halfhill's chuck-a-luck wheel.

As soon as Halfhill's door clicked shut behind me, he stepped into my path. I started around him, but his flabby arm darted out with surprising speed, his fingers curling around my collar. As his knuckles dug into the bottom of my jaw, I felt my shirttail pull out. When I talked, I sounded like I'd had a bad day at the dentist.

"Whoa, hold on," I said. "You don't have to treat me like some mark trying to win a TV set. I already had one employment interview today. Can't Amelia Halfhill take no for an answer?"

He pulled my face close to his. His chin sparkled with the blue of two shaveless days. "This ain't no interview," he said. "I'm here to settle a matter of ten bucks."

"Wow, Amelia really hates to lose, doesn't she? If you'd be kind enough to release me, I'll see what I can do."

When he did that, I put my hands behind my back and tugged on my shirt until the tail draped over my waist. "I was wondering when your boss would get around to collecting her due. She was beginning to disappoint me. Actually, I had planned on giving these to her personally."

I brought my hands out from behind my back and presented him with what was left of the bouquet that Carlson had ruined the night before. I had cut off all the crushed feathers and hung ten one-dollar bills on the skeleton that remained. As he took them I spun around him, out of reach.

I was thirty feet away when I heard him start to curse. I turned and saw a group of kids pointing and laughing at him. His pants were down around his ankles, revealing a pair of red bikini briefs that tightly hugged his chubby thighs, making him look like an aging TV wrestler. He clutched the little money tree in one hand as he tried to hoist his trousers with the other. His fingers fumbled in search of his belt buckle.

I called to him, waving his belt in the air. Then I tossed it. As he tried to catch it he leaned too far and fell face forward. As he struggled to his feet passersby chuckled, thinking he was part of the midway entertainment. People began to pluck dollar bills from his bouquet.

I didn't find the sight as amusing as the midway crowd did. Since Halfhill had used muscle to get back a measly ten bucks, I wondered what she might do if someone threatened to blow the whistle on her whole operation. Someone like Arlen Roth.

I paused long enough at the duck pond to see the operator

"accidentally" drop some coins on the ground behind the water tank. A few seconds later, he plucked a duck out of the water and displayed the large *L* on its bottom. The mark nodded at the duck, shrugged, and dug deeper into his wallet.

I felt as though I were floating in a duck pond too. Only I had no idea who was controlling the magnets that were pulling me this way and that.

CHAPTER TWENTY

Trying to get back to my tent on time, I zigzagged through the midway crowd, offering weak apologies every time I bumped into someone. The side of my arm was sticky from some kid's candy apple.

Action was heavy at every joint in the carnival. Except mine. No crowd. No noise. Just an empty, quiet space that people had to walk past in order to get to the freak-show tent and other attractions farther up the midway.

The barker and the admissions girl were sitting in the ticket booth, silently flipping through magazines. When Eddie, the barker, caught sight of me, he closed his magazine, shut his eyes, and took a deep breath. When he opened his eyes, they were bright and alert. His smile was sharp and wide, and his cheeks were dimpled. Even before he got to his feet he was talking, his voice cutting through the murmur of the passing parade of people. He wasn't even close to the microphone yet and his canyon voice was stopping the marks in their tracks, making them want to hear more about "the great Harry Cotter and his seven wonders of magic.'' Hell, I even felt like shelling out a few bucks to see the show myself.

Though the stream of people filing into my tent was growing, it was too close to show time for the audience to be as big as usual. As Betty, the admissions girl, rapidly exchanged money for ticket stubs, I asked her, ''Why the delay? I'm going to lose money on this show.''

''Carnival policy.'' Her voice was as bland as the barker's was enthusiastic. ''If the performer ain't in the tent, then Eddie don't bally him,'' she said, sounding as though she were quoting from international law.

''Why? You know my show only takes a few moments to set up. You could have started without me. I would have made it here on time.''

''There's nothing we can do about it. Bateman doesn't want anyone working if they've been . . .'' She pantomimed taking a drink from a bottle. ''Eddie and I are left holding the bag if your tent's full of customers and you don't show . . . or if you do show up, but with a snoot full. An angry mob can do a lot of damage quick. Believe me, I've seen it. When you showed up—and you were walking straight—Eddie knew it was okay to begin barking.''

I sighed and went inside to clean the candy apple off my arm.

I retrieved my briefcase from my locked van and carried it backstage (if the four-foot space between the curtain and the back wall of my tent can be called a backstage). I quickly loaded the props from my case into my pockets. Shortly after Eddie stopped barking, a hand with painted nails thrust a moneybag through the split in the curtain. The hand dropped the bag and gave a quick wave good-bye. I walked out and greeted the audience.

I was getting better at this work and was now including children's tricks. It had been so long since I had worked with children, I was rusty at doing the kind of jokes they liked. After only a few seconds into my act, I was feeling loose. The ad-libs were flowing so fast that I was tempted to interrupt the show and write them down on my notepad.

I closed the performance by rapidly constructing a giant paper hat for a girl in the audience. Every time I folded the paper, the hat got bigger and the colors got brighter. By the end, the hat was so big, it hung down to her waist. It was a souvenir she would keep for a long time.

The audience—all smiles—wanted still more. I patted my pockets, but they were empty. I had used up all my tricks, including the ones reserved for emergencies. In addition to running out of magic, I had also run out of time. Eddie and the ticket girl would soon be back for another round. Yet I didn't want to see those smiles in the audience leave. They weren't at all like the smiles on nightclub audiences.

Come to think of it, I wasn't sure if my nightclub audiences ever really smiled. Sure, they laughed at jokes, but usually because I had said something wickedly unexpected, something that caught them with their guard of sophistication down. Yet when the laughter died out, the hardness always returned to their faces and once again they were challenging me to catch them unawares, daring my hand to be quicker than their eyes and my tongue sharper than their minds. This battle would continue until the final seconds ticked away on my ten-minute act.

Of course, the nightclub audiences would be bored by my carnival show, with its leisurely pace, corny asides, and kid tricks. But at least I didn't feel that carnival audiences were my adversaries. When they liked something, they didn't feel too hip to let me know.

As the tent emptied out, some in the audience stopped and chatted. One woman said that the carnival fortune-teller had advised her to catch my show. The father of the girl with the paper hat told me that the fat man had recommended me.

I was beginning to like this job.

When the audience had all gone, I parted the two sections of the backstage curtains and decided to sneak a peak at how much was in the moneybag. As I reached for it there was a cracking sound, like strong wood breaking. The moneybag danced away. I tried again. There came another crack—earsplitting this time—accompanied by a ripping noise. The bag tumbled away from me. There was a big rip down the middle, and coins and wads of dollar bills poured out of the rupture.

I turned in time to see a hoop of rope sail through the air toward me, wobbling round and round. I tried to sidestep it, but was too late. As though I were a clothespin in one of Amelia Halfhill's games, the ring of rope settled down around me. When it reached waist level, it suddenly shrank, pinning my arms to my sides. I struggled, but the rope grew tighter. I felt myself being towed out onto the stage. The taut rope extended the length of the tent and out through the rear exit. I couldn't see who was pulling it.

Then I heard a sneering, squeaking voice say, "Good-bye, Harry. Nice knowing you."

The voice seemed to be coming from the moneybag.

As the rope pulled me across the stage to the edge, I relaxed and said, "Okay, Pitlor. I'm impressed. Now cut this goddam rope off."

I hoped Chuck Pitlor wasn't mad about my taking his job.

CHAPTER TWENTY-ONE

Fifteen cigarettes—all sliced in half—lay at my feet. I positioned another one between my lips, gripping it as near to the end as possible. I tried unsuccessfully to control its quivering. When I laughed, it fell out of my mouth. I replaced it with another.

"You actually want me to do it again?" Chuck Pitlor said. "Okay. Better set your coffee down."

He stood at the opposite end of the platform, bullwhip in one hand and a paper cup of coffee in the other. I set my own cup on the floor. I vowed to keep my eyes open this time, but fear clamped them shut.

A whistling sound preceded the crack of his whip. A puff of air disturbed my hair. I opened my eyes. Again I was left with half a cigarette in my mouth. Shredded tobacco hung out the end. When I spoke, I let the butt drop on the floor with the others.

"Where did you learn to do that?" I asked.

"Same way I learned everything else in my act. An uncle taught me."

Pitlor's talents covered a wide span of novelty entertainment: balloon sculpturing, paper tearing, juggling, trick lariat tossing, and precision whip cracking. "Your uncle must be quite talented."

He took another swallow of coffee and whirled his whip in the air. It made smaller and faster circles until it was tightly coiled around his hand. "I had a lot of uncles. I never knew my real mom and dad. I called most of the people that raised me aunt and uncle."

Pitlor, a short, compact man in his midtwenties, wore a faded brown sweatshirt. The slit sleeves extended only two inches over his shoulders, revealing lean, tight muscles. His hair was clipped close on the sides, making no attempt to cover oversized ears that rose to rounded points. His hairline was uneven, even ragged in places. In a few years, baldness would claim what remained of it.

Pitlor was self-conscious about talking. When he spoke more than a few sentences at a time, he scowled into the distance, as though reading from cue cards a script that he thoroughly disliked.

Each time I asked him why he had left the carnival, he changed the subject, preferring to quiz me on my magic and to ask me to do tricks. He seemed to enjoy my magic but was too embarrassed to compliment me, preferring to nod in appreciation and then show me stunts of his own. Of all his skills, he seemed to enjoy whip cracking the most.

Pitlor finished his coffee and tossed his cup into the air. He snapped his whip, and the cup exploded into confetti. He then stepped off the platform and sat down on one of the folding chairs. I moved to the edge of the stage and sat facing him. Our little performances were now over, yet we were still expecting encores from each other. Deciding to let him go first, I asked, "With all your dexterity and showmanship, you don't perform magic. How come?"

He slid his hand thoughtfully along the side of his head. "It's hard to put it in words. All the people that raised me—my 'aunts and uncles'—were former entertainers, mostly carnies. They taught me a lot of my novelty tricks. But all of them refused to teach me any magic. In fact, from an early age I was conditioned to dislike magic. It seemed that every time I learned a little conjuring trick, they gave me a cold response. No one ever said why. I always figured they knew something I didn't. Turned out I was right.''

I took out a cigarette and lit it, this time not waiting for him to slash it in half.

He continued. ''As I grew older I started asking tough questions about who my mom was. From fragments of information, I eventually pieced together most of her story. For many years she was an assistant for various magicians. In fact, she died as a result of the negligence of a magician. It wasn't until recently that I learned that the Bateman was the last carnival that she had worked for. That was about twenty years ago, when she was an assistant to a magician named Arlen Roth. That's why I hired on with this outfit, to find out where she went after here. Since I'd already worked for several other carnivals, it wasn't hard to get a job here.''

''Why exactly did she leave?''

''It was Roth's fault. He took off without any notice, leaving her high and dry.''

''Do you know where she went next?''

''At first nobody here would say. It was strange how just the mention of the name Arlen Roth raised eyebrows.''

''Do you know that Roth is dead?''

His grip on the whip went limp. It uncoiled out of his hand like an escaping snake.

''He was murdered,'' I said.

He pounded his thigh once with his fist. ''Hell, now it all makes sense. You see, I made it clear to everyone that I'd move on when I got a solid lead on where my mother went after here. I guess that explains this.''

From his pocket he handed me a stack of paper, folded in quarters.

''I think it's some kind of manuscript,'' he said.

I unfolded it. It was pages 145–157 of Roth's autobiography. Like the section that Christine had shown me, this one was covered with pencil marks and erasures.

''It arrived by special delivery the other day.''

''Mind if I read it?''

''Be my guest.''

The gist of this chapter was that Pitlor's mother, after leaving the Bateman Carnival, went to work for a magician who toured the country under the auspices of charities that were raising funds. Later that year, during a show in Texas, his mother met a nasty fate. Her boss, whose stage name was Winko, the Happy Magician, performed a spectacular magic trick that made him forever unhappy: His buzz-saw illusion *functioned*. That's right. It functioned, not malfunctioned. Instead of only appearing to sever his pretty assistant in two, it did the real thing.

A court of law eventually found Winko not guilty of criminal negligence. The death of his assistant was ruled accidental. There was no evidence of tampering or carelessness. Since Pitlor's mother had worked under so many different names, the news of her death was slow in reaching her relatives. By that time, it was too late for them to file suit against Winko. He had hung up his magic wand for good. The incident had destroyed him, both emotionally and financially. I wondered why Warner Huston hadn't told me this story.

I said, "After reading this, you set out after Winko, didn't you?"

Pitlor nodded. "That manuscript said that the buzz-saw accident occurred in Collins, Texas. I thought it was a logical place to start. I took a plane down to Texas and had no trouble picking up Winko's trail. He had made himself a prisoner of that town, never once leaving it after the accident. Collins had adopted him as a local eccentric. Winko spent his nights sleeping in parks and abandoned houses. Everyone knew about the incident that had driven him over the brink. I found him sitting on a park bench, wearing a tattered tuxedo and warped top hat. He was talking to an invisible audience."

I stared at Pitlor's whip. "You didn't hurt him, did you?"

"No, I just wanted to ask him a few questions. I never told him who I was. I think that would have been too much for him. Some of what he told me made sense, but mostly he talked gibberish."

"What kind of gibberish?"

"For example, he told me a story about my mother and him driving on a road near Spanier, Indiana, while they were on one of their tours. He said that as they passed the walls of an abandoned prison she demanded that he stop the car. She got out and walked through a wooded area to a clearing near the prison. She just stood silently in this clearing, refusing to talk. He said she looked sad and lost, and that for the rest of the day she was in a dark mood. She never said why."

"Spanier? Isn't that—?"

He nodded and flipped through the stapled manuscript. He folded back the page he was looking for. "Here. Second paragraph. See? Spanier was the name of the town the Bateman Carnival was playing when Roth deserted both my mother and the carnival."

"Do you think there's a connection between that clearing in Spanier and Roth's death?"

"I don't give a damn if there is." He folded up the manuscript and jammed it into his back pocket. I had a feeling it would end up in the nearest litter can. "I've already found what I was looking for. For a long time I was suspicious that Arlen Roth was responsible for my mother's death. Now that I know he wasn't, I'm no longer interested in him. I really don't care how he died."

"Suppose it hadn't worked out that way? Suppose you had found out that the faulty buzz saw was really Roth's doing?"

The knuckles on his whip hand turned bleach white. "Oh, I see what you're driving at. Believe me, I wasn't harboring any deep-seated vengeance for Roth. Until I learned what happened to my mother, there were certain avenues in my life that were blocked. Now that most of my questions are answered, I can move on. You're looking at a free man." He did his best to broaden his tight, forced smile.

"Chuck, I think you'd make a natural magician. Since your mother died at the hands of a magician, maybe learning to do magic was one of those 'blocked avenues.'"

He shrugged off my compliment and said, "Who knows?"

I wrote some names, phone numbers, and addresses on my notepad. "If you ever decide to take up magic, these people will be glad to get you started on the right foot. Tell them a broken-down carny magician named Harry sent you. They'll know who you mean."

As he thanked me a young couple with a three-year-old daughter shuffled into the tent. Feeling awkward about being the first of the new audience to enter, they took seats in the back. I heard the voice of the barker outside again drumming up an audience.

I invited Pitlor to stay for the show, and he took a seat on the side. With Pitlor in the audience, I tried extra hard to do a bang-up job, and the audience responded kindly to my efforts. At the end of the snow, I invited Pitlor onstage to demonstrate his abilities with a lariat. The audience heartily enjoyed the extra surprise.

When the tent was again empty, I asked Pitlor what had brought him back to the carnival today.

"Some unfinished business. A couple of months ago I bought a used ventriloquist's doll, but the controls on the head needed a lot of work. I paid Walt Galloway to repair it, and I came back today to pick it up. Boy, that doll looks great. That man does quality work."

"When he wants to," I said, thinking of the Ferris wheel with the loose cars. "So you do ventriloquism, too. I've got to hand it to you, that talking moneybag really had me going."

"Well, I'm just learning. I've had some good teachers, but I'm not good enough to add it to my act yet."

"Where are you going to next?"

"Oh, you don't have to worry about me trying to get my old job back here. I'm finished with this carnival. I might even take some time off and follow up on your suggestion to learn magic." As he turned to leave he said, "Don't let this place fool you. These carnies may seem like a weird bunch, but I really learned a lot here."

A few seconds after he was gone, a shrill voice laughed and said, "And I'm still learning." The voice seemed to be coming from my empty coffee cup on the platform. I heard a car door slam and an engine start up. And the coffee cup fell silent.

I looked at the specks of white on the stage, a result of Pitlor's repeatedly slashing paper cups with his whip. I picked up a handful of the confetti and let it sift through my fingers. Something about Pitlor's portion of the manuscript differs from the others, I thought.

Unlike the chapters sent to the other carnies, his manuscript hadn't been sent to establish a motive for him to kill Roth. In fact, his chapter did the opposite: It absolved him of motive. Instead of being angry, Pitlor was happy to read it. It gave him a clue that led to his learning the cause of his mother's death. Although Pitlor was angry that Roth had deserted his mother, he wasn't mad enough to kill over it. Whoever had sent Pitlor the manuscript had wanted him out of the carnival. Fast.

As I started setting up for my next show I found that my hands were sluggish, only going through the motions. My mind kept wandering to Winko the Magician and how he lost his assistant. I had lost assistants too, but never that abruptly or that completely. There was even one assistant that I had been in love with. After we had parted ways, I had lost track of her. As I continued to reset my show I tried to convince myself that I had no feeling left for her. My hands slipped and a dozen billiard balls fell to the stage, bouncing in all directions.

The new audience began to trickle in. I tried to psych myself up for the next show, vowing to give them my all.

But the magic had gone out of it.

CHAPTER TWENTY-TWO

While driving past KT's Restaurant the next morning, I saw in the parking lot a station wagon bearing TV call letters. A man with a microphone was chatting with the manager, who was nervously shuffling back and forth, unhappy with the interview. Perched on a stepladder, a restaurant employee was removing the letters from the sign advertising their all-you-can-eat breakfast buffet. I spotted a black Lincoln with no backseat, parked near the entrance. *Bon appétit*, Ernie.

As I headed down the midway toward my tent I passed a sallow-faced, breathless Bill Bateman coming in the opposite direction. As he rushed past, with the shoelaces of his running shoes flapping, I tried to tell him about Ernie's free publicity for the carnival. But he brushed me off without even a polite smile and disappeared around the corner of the skee ball booth.

Christine emerged from her tent, wearing her costume and

usual beaded necklace. "What's up?" I said. "Bateman just ran by like it was the end of the world."

"When it concerns money, it's always the end of the world for him."

"What happened? Wholesale price of popcorn go up?"

"Worse than that. He's missing a big chunk of change."

"How big?"

"He tried to hush it up, but Mary Trunzo couldn't keep it under her hat. He's missing about fifty thousand."

"In cash?"

"Of course. And he's steamed. He's offering a five-thousand-dollar reward for the crook. No questions asked."

"Is he angry at Mary for talking?"

"I think so, but that never lasts long." She smiled to herself. "They have quite an interesting relationship."

"There's something I wanted to ask you about. Those two have been together for a long time. Have they ever been serious about marriage?"

Christine laughed. "I think *not* getting married is what keeps them together. She wants to get married, but Bateman doesn't. He's never totally ruled out the possibility, but for him that prospect is always in the distant future. Mary and Bill complement each other in lots of ways. For instance, Mary has an insatiable desire for jewelry and clothes. She loves Bateman to lavish her with gifts . . . even though his implied price for those gifts is to stop pressuring him to marry."

"Expensive gifts?"

"Yeah."

"Expensive enough for him to siphon money out of the carnival and then fake a robbery to cover it up?"

Christine raised her eyebrows and shrugged, telling me that my guess was as good as hers. "Mary told me that Roth covered that subject in his chapter about Bateman. He accused Bateman of mishandling carnival money, grossly swindling both the carnies and the government."

"So publication of Roth's book could mean jail for Bateman."

Christine nodded. She turned to watch a lady, with a bandanna covering her head full of hair curlers, hover hesitantly at the entrance to Christine's tent. With wide eyes, the lady was reading the sign that proclaimed that Madame Sirolli knew all and told all. When the woman opened her purse, Christine said, "Gotta run." Her smile turned heavy and sultry and her eyes grew hooded as she slipped into her character of the omniscient seer. She followed the lady into her tent.

Violent shouting came from the other side of Christine's tent. As I rounded the corner I saw a lanky man in a tank top and baggy Hawaiian shorts, sandwiched between two policemen. The cops' uniforms seemed tailor-made, adding inches to their chests and subtracting inches from their waists. They both wore opaque aviator sunglasses that accentuated their cold expressions. I couldn't imagine the deep lines on their faces rearranging themselves into anything remotely resembling smiles. Only one policeman was doing the talking. The other stood with his feet apart, nodding periodically and keeping a relaxed hand on his nightstick.

The policeman said, "Let's get this straight: You say you've been swindled?"

"Damn right. Are you going to do something about it?"

All three heads turned when they heard my feet crunch on the gravel. I retreated around the corner a few feet and then put my back to the wall of Madame Sirolli's tent. And listened.

"Of course we'll do something about it. We're the police, aren't we? But if you want your charges to stick, you've got to be more specific. First of all, how much did you lose?"

The mark's voice wavered like he'd had a few drinks too many. "How the hell should I know? I didn't bring an accountant with me. I just got paid today and . . . wait, let's see how much is left. God, is that all? I lost between three and four hundred dollars."

"Four hundred dollars! Where do you think you are—Las Vegas? I don't see any slot machines around here. What game were you playing?"

"The one where you knock down those little dolls with baseballs."

The policeman laughed out loud, and the other one snorted as he tried to keep from laughing. "How do you lose that kind of money on a kiddy game with baseballs and dolls?"

"It happened gradually. I was trying to win a portable TV set for my girlfriend. I even had the guy plug in the TV to make sure it worked. Just when I was getting close to knocking down the right number of dolls, the operator started to whine about what a jerk his boss was. Well, I can identify with that. I hate my boss too. He said that in special cases he was allowed to take side bets on his game and that he was just dying to give away some of his boss's money . . . really stick it to the bastard good. He said that he would let me win big—enough to buy five TV sets—as long as I didn't tell anyone. Since it was his boss's money, I said, 'Why not?' I began to win right away. After racking up over a thousand dollars, I tried to quit. But by then a crowd had gathered, and every time I tried to walk away, I got booed. Pretty soon I began to lose. I secretly tried to get the attention of the game operator, but he ignored me. After five minutes, I was completely wiped out. You know what? I think he was lying about getting revenge against his boss.''

''Now, that's a real sad story. You have my sympathy, son. But it sounds to me like you just froze under pressure and now you want to blame it on that game operator. You don't need a policeman. You just need more time in the bullpen. Tell me, how the hell could that guy cheat you?''

''First of all, just knocking the dolls down isn't good enough to score. You have to knock them completely off the shelf. What tipped me off was that after he showed me that television set, he put it back crooked on the shelf. I could see the reflection of the back of the dolls in the screen. The shelf holding the dolls was really made of two boards, not one. Every time the operator leaned on the counter, the board at the rear moved backwards a few inches. That made the shelf so wide that no matter how hard I threw, I could never knock any dolls the whole way off the shelf.''

There was a long pause. I imagined the officers looking at each other, silently exchanging glances on how to handle the mark. Finally: ''So what do you want us to do?''

''I'll show you where the secret lever is. If you catch him in the act, you can arrest him and get my money back.''

''We can do that,'' the policeman said tentatively. ''But we can't play it exactly the way you want.''

''Huh?''

''For one thing, the minute you stopped trying to win that TV set and started making bets, you were wagering. That's illegal. The judge will charge you both with gambling. After paying your fine, you *might* get some of your money back.

But not all of it. The judge won't believe that you lost that much on a simple carnival game. If you're lucky, you'll get back enough money to cover your fine."

For the first time, the other policeman spoke up. "Of course, you might have to spend time in the jug. And after the game operator makes bail, he'll probably skip town, leaving you holding the bag."

"That's right," the other cop chimed in. "It— Hey, where are you going? Come back. We wanna help you. . . ."

After a few seconds of silence, one of the cops let out a high-pitched chuckle. He said, "That was too close, Mike. You'd better find Carlson. Tell him that the jerk operating the doll game is getting too greedy . . . and that he's got a TV set on his prize shelf that needs straightening. Also tell Carlson that we'll handle more marks like that, but only if it's worth our while."

So the fix is in, I thought. The lot is wide open. On top of that, Carlson was "burning the lot"—letting Halfhill and the other game operators rip off the marks so badly that the carnival won't dare return here next year.

It looked like Bateman was trying to get back his missing dough the quick—and dangerous—way. Because extra pocket money was being rapidly siphoned from the customers, I didn't expect big audiences tonight. And I didn't expect many smiling faces.

I decided it was time to pay a visit to the freak show. Where people never get swindled. Where they get exactly what they pay for.

CHAPTER TWENTY-THREE

The lurid paintings on the front of the freak-show tent advertised a wide spectrum of human oddities, including a tattooed woman, an alligator man, and a man who ate glass and metal. The fat man was depicted as a jolly fellow with little feet, skinny arms, and a small head. He looked like an ordinary man whose limbs and head had been attached to an inflated weather balloon and who had then dressed in a giant suit of clothes. The picture didn't look at all like Ernie, and I suspected that none of the other members of the troupe matched their billings either.

Since there was no beginning or end to the show, the freak tent didn't need a barker. You paid your money and took all the time you wanted to gawk at the "less fortunates," as the sign called them. Hunched on a stool inside the admissions cage was a small-eyed girl, leafing through a magazine filled with photos of celebrities in evening wear. She was dressed in a hospital smock, perhaps to add a scientific atmosphere to the show. That way, customers could kid themselves that they were here to enhance their knowledge of science, not to satisfy a dark curiosity.

"Three bucks," the admissions girl said. Not wanting to explain that I was a member of the carnival, I grabbed a handful of quarters and slid them across the counter. Without counting them, she raked them into a cash drawer. Her magazine was opened to a two-page spread of a TV actor and his date getting out of a car even bigger than Ernie's Lincoln. Both their smiles looked touched up. Nothing could be *that* white.

The girl tore my ticket in half and slid it across to me. I walked into the tent, leaving her to her worship of the physically perfect.

Inside, there was no central lighting, just a few spotlights above the walkway and one or two floodlights on each exhibit. Each "performer" had his own dais that stood a few inches off the floor. Padded rope in front of the exhibits kept the curious from becoming too curious.

For now, I was the only visitor in the tent. After hearing someone clear his throat—probably a secret signal to the others—I saw slight movements on each dais as each "exhibit" readied himself for display. The first man I saw was called the Fireman, even though he wasn't carrying a hose or wearing a red hat. Emaciated, he had skin the color of eggshell and wore his hair shoulder length. From a crystal vase he withdrew a metal rod with soft tips that looked like a cat-o'-nine-tails. He reached inside his pocket.

"Allow me," I said, producing a flaming match out of the air. He touched the end of his rod to my match and I stepped back from the rush of heat. The Fireman laughed and licked his lips. He held his flame close to my face and said, "Ahh, I thought you looked familiar." Then he announced to everyone: "It's the magic man."

An air of relaxation spread throughout the tent, as though it were a classroom and the teacher had just walked out. The Fireman said, "So, magic man, are you here to find out how the other half earns their bread and butter? I hope we won't disappoint you."

He raised his flaming stick in the air and leaned back. But then he realized his bad manners and offered me a taste. I said, "No, thanks. Too early in the day. My personal rule is never do fire and swords before five."

He nodded sympathetically and took a long taste of fire. Sighing with satisfaction, he blew out his flame.

I applauded lightly and said, "As talented as you are, I'm afraid I didn't come here for entertainment. I'm looking for Ernie."

"Ahh, our star. He's the last exhibit on the right."

I passed a man billed as the Human Pretzel, but he was so plump he should have been called the Human Bagel. He was sitting on a stool, legs crossed, reading a *TV Guide*. As I passed, his leg flipped in the air and bobbed up and down. He looked up from his magazine and pushed his glasses up on his nose with his toe. He bobbed his foot up and down again, more insistently. I waved back.

Next was Gladdy, the Tattooed Woman. She wore a bikini, and—except for her pale face—no area of skin was untouched by her whorls and splashes of color. She looked like she had wrapped herself in a horrific version of the Sunday comics. Like an optical illusion, the conflicting designs hurt my eyes. Yet I couldn't take my eyes off her. Gladdy didn't even look up when I passed. She was knitting a sweater.

I next said hello to the Man Who Will Eat Anything. The table in front of him looked like a bargain bin at a hardware store: springs, screws, bolts and nails and light bulbs. He had a sorrowful, undernourished face with protuberant eyes. "You a carny?" he asked.

I nodded.

"Good." He reached underneath his table, brought out a half-eaten jumbo burger, and ripped a bite out of it. "Dinnertime's too far off. I need a little pick-me-up."

I looked at the assortment of junk on his table. I asked, "Have you ever eaten fire?"

He shook his head and smiled mischievously. "Are you kidding? The union would never hear of it."

The next exhibits reminded me of B-movie titles: the Alligator Man, the Man with Two Faces, and the Wolf Girl. I was sure that none of these three used makeup to simulate their conditions. They weren't as friendly as the others, perhaps because their "oddities" were a matter of birth and not choice. Even though I was a carny, they didn't know me and still regarded me with the suspicion reserved for outsiders.

Next to the Wolf Girl was an empty platform twice as big as the others. It contained a giant chair, a water cooler, and two rotating fans. There was no sign in front of this platform. Ernie wouldn't need one to explain what he was.

I asked the Wolf Girl where Ernie was. She tugged at her beard, a fierce brown and gray that contrasted with her teeth, giving them a sinister gleam. She said in a contralto voice, "Hey, anyone see Ernie?"

The tent erupted into raucous laughter.

"Anyone see Ernie?"

"Maybe he's hiding behind this chair."

"Is that him over there?"

"Holy shit, I think we lost the fat man!"

The Wolf Girl smiled and said, "He'll be back soon. Why don't you wait?"

I ducked under the rope and sat on Ernie's chair. It resembled an office chair, but its wheels were eight inches wide and its cushion was twice as thick as a mattress. I sat on the edge and leaned forward so the giant chair wouldn't swallow me up.

The tent suddenly grew quiet. An invisible signal must have passed down the line of exhibits. The Man Who Will Eat Anything put away his hamburger and the Tattooed Woman stopped her knitting.

A mother and her young son entered the tent. She patted him on the head, and he fearfully clutched her hand with both of his. He pulled his hat down over his forehead, shielding his eyes from all the scary people. The cartoon character on the front of the boy's hat was half man and half robot.

As they walked along the exhibits his mother said, "See? If you keep it up, you're going to look like *that* someday." I wasn't sure which exhibit she was talking about, or what bad habit of her son's she was referring to.

As they passed from platform to platform the boy hid behind his mother's skirt, venturing out only when curiosity got the best of him. When they got to Ernie's platform, they paused. The mother moved close to the padded rope, looking for a sign. She peered at me through appraising eyes. After years of performing, I've gotten used to the hard challenge on the faces of audiences, but I'd never seen a stare like hers before. Her narrow-eyed look of superiority unnerved me. She eyed me up and down until I began to feel like something under plastic wrap inside a grocer's cooler. Her son tugged at her, and she bent down so he could whisper to her.

She looked at me and said, "My son wants to know what's wrong with you."

I glanced at the Wolf Girl, and she was biting her lip to keep from smiling. "There's plenty wrong with me," I said. "For one thing, I smoke too much. Also, I'm not as ambitious as I used to be. And I have a compulsion to ask nosy questions. Plus, I fall in love too easily. I used to have an assistant named Cate that I was crazy about. I can't get her out of my mind—"

With horror in her eyes, the mother pulled her son away and headed for the exit. He said, "Boy, he's weird, Mom."

When they reached the exit, they stepped aside to let Ernie enter. Mopping his forehead with his handkerchief, he bellowed at the lineup of exhibits: "I thought this was supposed to be the freak show. You people don't look strange to me."

He looked at the lady and her son. "Pardon me, do you work here?"

The boy giggled as his mother dragged him outside. The rest of the tent broke into laughter.

Ernie, puffing and swaying from side to side, walked the length of the tent. He stopped in front of me, red-faced and blowing hard. In between breaths, he said, "I wish I was the first exhibit in line. It's such a long walk back here. I guess that's the price of stardom."

He lifted the rope, crossing the no-man's-land into the world of freaks. He adjusted his fans until they pointed where he wanted, and then he drew water from his cooler into a quart cup. I stood to give him his seat. He flopped down on it so hard, it rolled back two feet.

"Harry, thanks so much for the free breakfast. However, I'm afraid I broke that poor manager's heart." He took a long draft of water. His face grew serious. "I talked to Christine today. She told me exactly who you are and why you're here—*Mr. Harry Colderwood*. Please don't be angry with her. She didn't think she was doing any harm. You have to understand that she and I are fast friends."

He finished his drink, pouring the remaining drops over his head. "Yet Christine doesn't know me as well as she thinks. You see, I'd gladly have *paid* for the chance to kill Arlen Roth. I am genuinely sorry that someone else did it first."

CHAPTER TWENTY-FOUR

My conversation with Ernie progressed haltingly. Every time a customer entered, he stopped talking until the tent was empty again. At Ernie's suggestion, I stood on the "mark side" of the rope, as he called it. "Otherwise," he said, "people might think we're some kind of David and Goliath act."

When the latest visitors left the freak show, Ernie said, "The people working in this tent are the ones that benefit the most from the camaraderie of the carnival. You don't find the Alligator Man straying far from the lot during his time off. Everybody here accepts each other for what they are. That's why I'm so shocked by Arlen Roth's smarmy book."

He handed me a stack of perspiration-soaked paper from his

back pocket, apologizing for its condition. I began reading it, laying each page on the edge of his dais as I finished.

The first few pages summarized Ernie's early years, starting with his upbringing in a circus family. By some genetic quirk, he was the only overweight person in his family. Numerous pediatricians agreed that Ernie's condition was untreatable. By the time he was nine, he weighed more than most adults. It was out of the question for Ernie to play any role in the family's high-wire act. Because he was too enormous to even be a circus clown, his parents treated him as if he were worthless. After suffering years of rejection, Ernie ran away from the circus to join the carnival. Because his parents considered carnies to be low caste, they disowned him.

The next several pages told of how Ernie joined the freak show and, for the first time in his life, felt like part of a family. It was not until the last page that Roth drew blood. Again playing amateur psychologist, he said that Ernie was afraid to undergo a thorough, modern medical exam to make absolutely certain that his obesity was due to a glandular disorder and not gross overeating. He claimed that Ernie deliberately stayed fat so he could isolate himself from the everyday problems of "normal" life. He said that Ernie used his hugeness to avoid working for a living and even to avoid dealing with the opposite sex.

Roth was particularly vicious regarding the last subject. He wrote that Ernie was afraid of women, almost to the point of hating them. He said that Ernie favored enormous desserts over any sexual contact.

I put all the pages back in order and then watched Ernie count change for a middle-aged man buying one of his autographed pictures. After the man left, Ernie handed me one of the photos. The picture showed Ernie in a vested suit, sitting in a jumbo wingback chair. The top button of his shirt was open and the loose flesh of his neck nearly covered the knot of his necktie. The necktie looked like it had been cut from a bath towel. Ernie's heavy lips were parted in a gracious smile and a column of smoke rose from the half-finished cigarette between his fingers.

"My only objection is the cigarette," he said. "It's a bad example for the kids, but Zig thought it would add atmosphere and help 'frame the piece' . . . whatever that means. I wanted it to look like I spent my winters living in a big mansion, instead of being a virtual prisoner in a constantly air-conditioned trailer parked in Florida. And, by god, he did it! I've sold a ton of these in the last five years. Even though I'm fifty pounds heavier now, I have no desire to update the picture.''

''You say Zig Mulvaney took this?''

''Yeah. He's a lot better than your average mug-shot man. If he hadn't fallen in love with the carny life, he could have been a great photographer. If you need publicity photos, he's the man. His pictures are worth their weight in gold.''

''Did Zig Mulvaney know Roth?''

Ernie nodded and said, ''They were actually good friends, but I don't hold that against Zig.'' I handed back his picture and the manuscript pages. ''I'm not saying that Roth is completely wrong in his theory about me. Who knows? Perhaps everyone in this whole carnival—yourself included—is hiding from something. What really bugs me is what he says about women and me. It's infuriating, humiliating, and goddam untrue. No real carny—even a former one—would do that to another carny.''

He stomped his foot, shaking the platform so hard that his fans swayed and the water in his cooler frothed back and forth.

''Shhh,'' the Wolf Girl said, running a quick comb through her beard. ''We got marks.''

Ernie looked up to see a slender woman in heels and a calf-length skirt move serenely along the roped aisle. Her blond hair was styled short, emphasizing her aristocratic features. Ernie beckoned me closer and spoke in a low voice. ''Everyone in this show has a better grip on reality than Roth thought. And the same goes for our customers. Like I said before, the marks have a fairly good idea of what to expect for their money.''

The blond woman stopped in front of the fire-eater and gazed at the curling flames that disappeared down his throat. The reflection of the yellow-and-red fire danced in her eyes and in the crystal of her earrings. She moved on.

As I turned to leave, Ernie said, ''Don't worry. Your secret's safe with me, Harry. It could be fatal if the wrong people find out who you are.''

As the blonde drew closer Ernie wheeled his chair over to his water cooler. In the reflection in the glass, he adjusted his hair with his hands.

He wheeled himself back to the center and said, ''Christine

also told me about the scene of the murder. I freely admit I was angry with Roth . . . angry enough to kill. But that doesn't mean that I did it. Just think about it: Do you really think I could have sneaked into Roth's room, murdered him, and escaped without anyone seeing me? While you were waiting in the next room? Tell me, do you remember seeing an eight-hundred-pound man tiptoe by? If I had so much as walked into the lobby of that hotel, it would have caused vibrations the whole way up to the top floor. I've never been a sneaky person. In fact, at an early age I developed other aspects of my personality to make up for it.''

''Such as?''

His only answer was a long chuckle. His eyes darted over to the approaching blond woman.

I nodded and said, ''One more thing I need to know: Does Bateman have a VCR in his motor home?''

''Yeah. What are you going to do? Watch some movies during all your free time?''

''No. There's just one movie I'm dying to see. In fact, if I'm going to rent it, I'd better make a phone call tonight.''

When I reached the exit, the blonde had moved to Ernie's dais. She was talking quietly to him, all the while rubbing her fingers back and forth on the plush rope that separated them. After signing a picture for her, he shook his head when she tried to pay for it. It looked like their conversation was going to last for a long time.

Maybe Ernie was right in saying that publicity pictures were worth their weight in gold. In between magic shows tonight, I'd have to pay a visit to the mug-shot booth.

CHAPTER TWENTY-FIVE

After my first show of the evening, I headed down the midway for Zig Mulvaney's tent. The midway was in a more impatient mood than earlier. The barkers' amplifiers were cranked up higher. The crowd was flowing faster. More people bumped into me than before and fewer said excuse me. The marks seemed to be spending money faster, trying too hard to have a good time. Even the wheel on Amelia Halfhill's chuck-a-luck game seemed to spin with extra zip.

As I approached the Ferris wheel I couldn't bring myself to walk underneath it. I ducked between two game booths and walked behind the row of tents lining the left side of the midway. The tents provided a baffle to the cacophony of the carnival, toning down the blend of high-pressure pitchmen, merry-go-round music, and earsplitting bells and horns. Even though I had to tread carefully to avoid the ropes and tent stakes, unimpeded by the crowd I made faster progress than on the midway.

As I neared Mulvaney's tent I heard a voice inside: "Just one more. That's nice. Come back in thirty minutes and they'll be ready." In the distance, I saw the mass of trailers and motor homes in the makeshift carnival trailer court. Because the night's work was in full swing, the area was deserted. In the dimness ahead, I thought I saw the flutter of a familiar black dress. I walked past Mulvaney's mug-shot tent and headed straight for the trailer lot.

A pair of men emerged from a squat, blue-trimmed trailer. Both bald, they wore western shirts and bolo string ties and carried slim briefcases of rich leather. I recognized them as the two brothers who operated the carnival's "poppers"—joints that sold popcorn and cotton candy. They walked silently in step. In suits and ties, they would have looked like commuters heading for office jobs.

At the sight of me, they drew close together. As I passed, one brother recognized me and whispered to the other. They both nodded at me courteously.

I reached the intersection of trailers where the ride operators had been playing poker the other night. To my left I saw Christine Sirolli, checking her makeup in the reflection in the window of the motor home beside Walt Galloway's. Satisfied, she went to Galloway's door and knocked.

I ducked behind a red van and listened to Galloway's unctuous voice greet her. After a few moments, his door clicked shut and their voices faded away. I took a slow walk around the motor home.

All the curtains were drawn. The only sound from inside was an occasional rumbling voice. I wasn't sure if it was Galloway or just a radio.

I put my ear to the wall of the motor home and heard a scraping sound followed by loud creaking. Probably someone pulling up a chair. I heard the bump-thump of someone walking across the floor.

"Whatchadoin'?"

I stiffened and withdrew my ear from the trailer well. I rubbed my ear. It felt gritty and cold. I turned around.

The boy couldn't have been older than six. He wore a straw cowboy hat and a denim vest with white embroidered galloping horses. His too-large hat covered his entire head, except for a lick of springy blond hair in front.

"Where'd you come from?" I asked.

He pointed in the direction of the midway and asked, "And where'd you come from?"

I pointed in the same direction and said, "I bet you're looking for your mom."

He nodded sharply and his hat slid to the back of his head.

I thought I heard a high-pitched giggle from inside the motor home.

"Pretty," the boy said.

"Huh?"

"Pretty music," he said, pointing to the lights of the Ferris wheel above the midway.

"Think you'll be able to find your way back to your mom all by yourself?"

He stared at me blankly.

I said, "Do you like popcorn?"

He gave me a wide smile and I could see his tongue through the gaps in his teeth.

"Tell you what, let's get some popcorn while we find your mommy. As for now . . ." I reached behind his hat and pulled out a purple lollipop as big around as his face.

He unwrapped it and started licking it.

"Come on," I said, starting toward the midway.

I walked slowly so he could keep up. He was delighted with the lollipop and didn't seem amazed that I had pulled it out of the air. I suppose that he was so overwhelmed by the magical sights and sounds of the carnival that anything seemed possible to him tonight.

I said, "Yeah, I think you're right, kid. The minute you walk in that carnival gate, anything's possible." I stared back at the curtained windows of the motor home and heard more laughter from inside. "Anything."

CHAPTER TWENTY-SIX

"Hold it right there. Raise the cards a little higher. That's it. We're getting a glare. Tilt the cards forward. Give me that smile again. No, too big, it'll jump off the picture. Good. Now hold that."

Click.

"Another."

Click.

"That's it. Good enough."

After I introduced myself to Zig Mulvaney, he had insisted on taking my picture, saying it was a free service he offered all new carnies. I relaxed, glad to finally stop all that smiling. I didn't feel like smiling tonight. Nor did I feel like doing any more magic.

Before entering his tent, I had looked over his photo display out front. They were mostly of teenagers and their dates, but there were also several portraits—new and old—of people on the outskirts of society: beatniks, hippies, bikers, and punks.

Mulvaney's tent was cramped. Metal folding chairs lined one wall. Three lights on tripods were pointed at a lone stool in front of a screen with gray clouds painted on it. The air reeked of the fumes of both photographic chemicals and whiskey.

I crossed my legs and slid forward on the stool. With the photo session over, I began to absently play with the fan of playing cards in my hands. I cut them and riffle-shuffled one block of cards into the other. Instead of squaring the two interlaced blocks, I fanned them, creating a giant fan.

I said, "I checked out your display outside. I like your work."

"Thank you." He took off his thick spectacles and laid them on the desk, moving slowly because of the gnarled, swollen joints in his fingers. He wore a black clip-on bow tie and a loose-fitting checkered vest. "If I was running a normal photo studio, my work would be all routine; yearbook pictures, family portraits, baby pictures, and publicity shots for politicians. But in the carnival, I never know who's going to walk in next. When the show hits town and word gets around that there's a mug-shot man, I get all sorts of requests—stuff that I wouldn't dare tack up on the front of my booth."

"Fantasy stuff?"

"Yeah, you might say that. A lot of housewives and a few workaday guys who think they've dug the trenches of their daily lives too deep. They come to me, put on a costume that they think is sexy or macho, and for a few minutes they can be someone else."

"What do they do with the pictures?"

"Beats me. I never ask."

"Do you keep copies of your pictures?"

He smiled quizzically and said, "Why would I do that?"

He flipped open his camera and removed the packet of film. "Your picture will be ready in an hour."

As he busied himself, fishing out another film packet from his desk and loading it up, I said, "How did you pick up this trade?"

"Young man, I've been a photographer as long as I can remember. When I was four years old I found an old box camera in my father's closet. I've had an itchy shutter finger ever since."

His seriousness surprised me. "You've never wanted to be anything in the carnival other than a mug-shot man?"

"You make it sound like I'm wasting my time here. To answer your question: No. I'm a photographer first and a carny second. I can't imagine myself doing anything else here. I'm no jack-of-all-trades like, say, Walt Galloway. That man's done it all. He should write a book . . . but it looks like someone's already beat him to it."

He disappeared through a curtained doorway. He returned several minutes later, drying his hands on a towel with the thoroughness of a doctor prepping for surgery. "Your pictures are developing now."

The smell of whiskey was stronger now, and the smile on his face seemed more permanent and his eyes less focused. He stumbled while pulling a chair over to my stool.

"How long have you been doing mug shots?"

"It's been about thirty years. Before that I was a college student, believe it or not. Oh, I was so dedicated in those days . . . constantly scrounging for money for film. My family thought I was nuts. To them, photography was just a matter of pointing the camera and clicking the shutter. They never thought it was an art."

The light directly in front of me was beginning to bother my eyes. Mulvaney snapped it off and said, "The parents of a college buddy of mine ran a cookhouse for the Bateman Carnival. They said that the mug-shot man needed a summer helper and asked if I wanted the job. I said, what the hell. It would sure beat sweating in some factory for three months. As luck had it, the old mug-shot man died of a coronary in July and Bill Bateman, Sr., asked me to take over the whole operation. I told him I'd do it only until school resumed." He put his glasses back on and then shifted their thick lenses up and down, trying to sharpen his image of me. Without remorse, he said, "I've been here ever since."

"What made you stay?"

"It's hard to say. Maybe all the freedom here spoiled me. Maybe I fooled myself into thinking I could be a serious photographer and still handle this job. Some might even say I'm hiding here because I'm afraid to find out how good I really am."

I had a feeling that the "some" he was referring to was really Arlen Roth. And that Roth had expressed those opinions in a chapter of his book.

"I know what you mean," I said. "I could learn to like it here. Traveling in a small community like this would certainly take some of the loneliness out of the road. It's going to be hard to leave."

"*If* you ever leave," he said with a haunting half-smile. He stared at my hands. I was still manipulating my cards, doing fancy slip cuts and one-handed steals. Realizing that these moves were too advanced for the caliber of magician I was pretending to be, I dropped the cards on the floor. After sloppily restacking them, I put them away.

I said, "Have there been many magicians in the carnival since you joined?"

"A few. Only one was any good—a fellow named Arlen Roth. Haven't seen him for years, though. I heard that he died recently. Murder. I also heard that they don't know who did it."

"Zig, I heard about Roth long before I joined up with the carnival. In fact, he's one of the reasons I wanted to work here. I was hoping that someone could tell me about one of his tricks. It's a card-stabbing trick done with a dagger. I really want to learn how to do it."

Mulvaney chuckled in recognition. He went into the back room and returned with a knife in his hand. "Is this the kind he used?" The dagger had a smiling devil carved on the handle.

"Hey, that's it! What's that smiling devil mean?"

"Oh, that was a brainstorm of Bill Bateman's father. He was hoping to use it as a trademark for the carnival. He wanted it to appear on all the tickets and circulars. Fortunately, he chucked the idea before it got off the ground. It would have driven me batty looking at this hideous face all day. While Roth was still developing his stabbing trick he had a few daggers like these made up. He gave me one as a present."

"You guys were buddies?"

"I thought we were. Roth was a good guy in those days. My only beef with him was his addiction to practical jokes. Whenever he'd buy magic tricks, he always loaded up on joke items . . . stuff like itching powder or soap that turns your hands black. I was always checking my back to make sure he hadn't taped a sign on it."

All accounts I'd heard of Roth in his later years depicted him as a somber man. I wondered what had killed his sense of fun.

Mulvaney continued. "In the end I had to wonder whether we were such good friends. Twenty years ago Roth suddenly upped and left the carnival, with no good-byes. I never saw him again."

He fell silent, smiling at a reminiscence. Then he said, "I remember one time when Roth showed up at one of Amelia Halfhill's game booths disguised in a fake beard, hat, and sunglasses. He broke the bank before she figured out who he was. It was easy for him to cheat her, since he's the one that got her started in the game racket. But in spite of his pranks, Roth was as good a magician as I've seen, particularly when he was giving his whiskey bottle a rest. Also, he protected his secrets with a vengeance.''

''Including the dagger trick?''

''Particularly that one. I don't know where he learned it. Maybe he invented it. The first time he showed it to me, it didn't impress me. But just one week later, he did it again. Suddenly it was a knockout. I took some pictures of him performing it, but he later requested that I destroy the prints and negatives. He was that afraid of exposure.''

''How do you account for his rapid improvement?''

''There's a good chance that somebody tutored him. Roth was an excellent student . . . not a high compliment in his case. Part of the price Roth paid for his amazing ability to soak up knowledge was that he was highly sensitive to what people thought. He'd go to any lengths to please people. In short, he was easily led.'' Mulvaney paused to laugh at some private joke. ''Apparently Roth finally rid himself of that bad trait. I'll always wonder what I did to piss him off.''

I heard a soft chiming, similar to an elevator bell, coming from Mulvaney's darkroom. He excused himself and walked through the curtained doorway.

I picked up a magazine from a stack on Mulvaney's desk. It was a twenty-five-year-old photography magazine. Handling it with care, I flipped through it, looking for photos credited to Zig Mulvaney. I didn't see any.

Several minutes later, Mulvaney returned, holding in his shaking hand a wet eight-by-ten glossy of me. As I stared at the picture he said, ''Something wrong?''

The image of the grinning man with the fan of playing cards caught me off guard. I had forgotten my altered appearance: unkempt mustache, gray intruding on my hairline, pronounced creases on my face, five o'clock shadow, and darkened rings beneath my narrowed, sinister eyes. I didn't like this older, more worn version of Harry Colderwood. He seemed too much at home here at the Bateman Carnival. I worried that this stranger in the photo was not entirely a product of makeup, that maybe my new role was rubbing off on me.

''No,'' I assured him. ''It's fine. You do excellent work.'' I pointed to the magazines. "Any of your stuff ever get printed in them?"

He shook his head. "I used to submit a lot of pictures to those magazines. I had a scrapbook full of rejection slips. One night Roth and I got drunk and we burned it, proclaiming that those magazines would regret passing me up. Funny how things change. I heard that at the time of Roth's death he was working on a book about carnivals. And that he made mention of me in that book, calling me 'the resident failed artist of the carnival.' He did a cruel thing: He actually sent copies of my earlier photographs—gifts from me—to some photography critics. They passed judgment on my pictures. Roth was actually going to print their opinions in his book."

"What did the critics say?"

"They creamed me. They said I showed no promise, that my work was pretentious, and that I had the artistic eye of a housepainter. Although their specific opinions varied, they all agreed that I stunk."

"You didn't let it bother you much, did you?"

"Hell, no. Like I said, I'm no stranger to rejection. Don't get me wrong. Roth's betrayal hurt plenty, but you have to remember I haven't seen him in years. It's not the same as having a current friend turn against you. I certainly wasn't angry enough to, uh, do anything about it, if that's what you mean."

"Zig, when the police eventually trace Roth back to this carnival, they won't see things that way. Do you have an alibi?"

"Unfortunately, no. You see, the day that Roth was killed was a mud day. The carnival was closed. I spent most of the day in the darkroom, catching up on personal work. Of course, Harry, since you're new here, the police will question you, too. Do you have an alibi?" His smile exuded slippery cunning.

"Me? I was out job hunting. In fact, I've been to so many carnivals, I'll be damned if I can remember which one I was applying to that day."

"How convenient. It looks like you and me will both me in a fix if the police want to finger us. Maybe we should collaborate on a mutually beneficial story."

"Thanks for the offer, but for now I think I'll just settle for the free picture. We'll both have to stick to our stories, lame as they are."

Standing to leave, I said, "You said I could come back later for the photo?"

He nodded.

"One other thing I've been wondering about," I said. "Do you know why Roth left the carnival?"

Mulvaney's lips tightened in a grimace. "I'm not sure. He took off, leaving behind most of his equipment and clothing. A week or two later, he sent for his bookcase illusion and a few small tricks. Did you know that his bookcase illusion was his pride and joy? And that he used to perform it with Mary Trunzo as his assistant?"

"I heard. She never told you why Roth left?"

"No. At the time that Roth quit, she was just starting to get involved with Bill Bateman. She used to have a thing for Roth, but he dropped her all of a sudden. Maybe she pressed him too hard to get married."

I'm not sure what Mulvaney said next. My mind was on a file cabinet in Bateman's office, one with a rusted lock that looked like a piece of cake to pick. My thoughts were in a state of flux. I needed specific dates and times to bring the blur of possibilities into focus.

A young couple, holding hands, entered the mug-shot tent as I left. The boy's hair was multicolored, as though he had dyed it in a vat of melted crayons. He wore a T-shirt with an unpopular political slogan on the front. His girlfriend was dressed in a cheerleader's costume and a blue felt hat with a huge yellow feather. They had come to challenge the lens of Zig Mulvaney's camera. But I was sure that old Zig and his camera would win, despite Roth's opinion that he was a loser.

Before visiting the office of the carnival owner, I decided to check back on the wirer and the seer.

CHAPTER TWENTY-SEVEN

The old man's name was Buzz, and he and I were sitting under a tree about forty feet from Galloway's motor home. We were playing a game that used three quarters, the rules of which I barely understood. All I knew was that Buzz was using a double-headed quarter and that he was cheating me every chance he got.

While I was snooping around the trailer court Buzz had come up behind me and asked if I wanted to play a game with quarters. Because I wanted to stick close by Galloway's without drawing suspicion, I said okay.

Buzz was a member of the carnival maintenance crew. He told me he didn't work regular hours, that he was needed only when something needed fixing. Some days were easy, but there were some that he worked twenty hours straight. Tonight Buzz was taking advantage of his free time by taking a new carny to the cleaners.

Because I kept looking up every few seconds at Galloway's motor home, it was hard to concentrate on the quarters jingling inside Buzz's hands. I made another bet and lost. I was now fifteen dollars down. My wait for Christine was getting expensive. It would have been cheaper to sit in a taxi with the meter running.

Buzz noticed my impatience, let me win a few more rounds, and then suggested that we up the stakes. I said I didn't feel like playing anymore and asked him if he had any beer. With a sly smile, he told me that alcohol on the carnival grounds was against the rules.

"No," I said. "I just want the bottle."

"What for?"

"I thought you were interested in upping the stakes."

Buzz rubbed his knuckles against his chin. He knew I wouldn't explain anything until he got the bottle. "Okay."

"And get a glass of water, too. I'm thirsty." He nodded and walked under the dirty awning of his tiny trailer and on inside. His trailer, having been on the short end of too many scrapes and sideswipes, didn't look like it would last another season. It rocked back and forth as he moved about inside.

When he returned with the beer bottle and water, he asked what kind of work I did. He thought that he'd seen me at one of the "grab stands"—concession stands without seats.

I shrugged and said, "Yeah, I've spent some time there." I thanked him for the glass of water and drank some of it. "Buzz, do you have a penknife I could borrow?"

"What the—? Okay, here," he said, reaching into his pocket.

I held his penknife, point up, and let it drop to the ground a few times. Each time it did a one-eighty, sticking point first. Perfect. I then slid the casing of the knife halfway into the bottle. It just fit.

I looked up at the tree we were standing under. I usually used the ceilings in barrooms, but the thick limb fifteen feet above would have to suffice. Feeling like a pirate, I clinched his knife between my teeth and jumped up, grabbing the lowest branch. I made pedaling motions with my legs until my feet found traction against the tree trunk. I wrestled my way upward, branch after branch. When I reached my target branch, I jabbed the knife into the bottom of it, leaving the knife hanging straight up and down. As I carefully descended, the knife swayed but remained stuck in the bark. I hoped that a sudden breeze wouldn't dislodge it prematurely.

Back on the ground, I brushed the dirt and bark from my hands. "Buzz, that knife won't stay up there long. I barely pierced the bark. Now, how much will you bet that I can't position your beer bottle in the precise spot on the ground so that when that knife falls, it'll land inside? You already saw that it barely fits through the mouth of the bottle."

Buzz looked at me as if I were mad. He squatted underneath the branch and looked up. In the dim light it took several seconds before he could even spot the knife. Suddenly he cried, "What the hell am I doing under here?" He rolled away, afraid of getting stuck by his own knife. "Pal, if that knife lands in this bottle, I'll give you all your money back."

"Big deal," I said, starting to walk away.

"Wait, dammit. Now you got me intrigued. I'll double your money."

I kept walking.

"Okay, okay," he said. "How about double your money . . . plus another hundred?"

"That's more like it."

I climbed the tree again, but more cautiously this time, not wanting to disturb the branches. When I was within reach of the wobbling knife, I asked Buzz to hand me the glass of water.

"The what? Oh, I forgot all about that. Wait a minute, you suckered me, didn't you? Hey, now I know who you are. You don't work in no grab stand. I bet you're that new goddam magician."

Although he sounded crestfallen, when I looked down he was smiling shrewdly. He held the glass over his head and I twisted my back, leaning down far enough to grasp the top of it. I then reached up and dunked the knife handle into the water. After drinking the rest of the water, I said "Catch," letting the glass drop into Buzz's hands. Moving lightly, I climbed down a few branches and then jumped. There was no time to lose.

By now Buzz had already counted my money into a neat stack. He said, "I should have known there'd be some kind of hocus-pocus in this. Here you go."

I pushed the bills away. "Whoa, not yet." I hurriedly located the damp spot on the ground where water had dripped from the knife handle. I was glad that a few drops were still falling. I then slid the beer bottle until the drops hit the edge of the mouth. I nudged it. A drop plunked into the bottle without touching the mouth. I then gave the bottle one final little twist. The next drop entered dead center of the mouth.

Now it was just a matter of waiting. Every time a breeze rustled the tree, the knife swayed a bit more freely. Buzz kept his eyes fixed on the knife, as though it might purposely fall when he was looking away. He took out a stick of gum, unwrapped it, chewed it, and then did the same with another stick, all without letting his gaze waver from the knife.

The leaves and branches of trees on the other side of the trailer court told me that a gust of wind was on its way. Buzz stopped chewing his gum when the wind hit our tree. The knife wiggled, and I was afraid that the movement of the tree would alter the trajectory too much. But then the wind died and the knife hung motionless for a few seconds . . . and finally dropped away. Buzz jumped back, as if the knife might change its mind and seek him as a target. But that didn't happen. The knife obeyed the laws of physics, not the laws of magic that Buzz so feared.

The knife did a graceful half turn and headed for the beer bottle. It clacked against the mouth, rocking the bottle, and then disappeared inside.

Buzz snatched it up and shook it. The knife clinked inside. The bottle now had a spiderweb crack on the bottom. He tried to dump the knife out, but it kept getting caught in the narrow neck. To retrieve his knife, he broke the bottle on a rock. After examining the blade for damage, he folded it and pocketed it.

He rolled the stack of money into a tight cylinder, and for a moment I thought he was going to stiff me. But he winked and shoved it inside my shirt pocket. I thanked him.

"No need for thanks," he said. "Just tell me this: Did a carny show you that stunt?"

"No."

"Did you show it to anyone else in the carnival?"

I shook my head again. He rubbed his hands together, chewing his gum in earnest. "Great! It'll earn me a bundle before the night's over. I consider *that*"—he pointed to the wad of bills in my pocket—"an investment. You won't show that trick to anyone else, will you?"

"No, I—"

Galloway's door popped open and Galloway stepped out. He tried to look casual, but his movements were stilted. Looking back inside, he nodded, and Christine Sirolli joined him in the doorway. As she adjusted her necklace Galloway stepped behind to lend a hand. She smiled and kissed him on the cheek. He backed off as though the kiss were painful. He looked up and down the crooked street of mobile homes, making sure that no one was watching. She laughed as he awkwardly retreated inside.

As she slowly made her way back to the midway, I heard a hiss behind me that I thought was another breeze in the trees. But it was followed by rapidly retreating footsteps. That sound wasn't the wind. It was somebody gasping . . . in surprise.

I looked at Buzz. He had taken out his knife again and was wiping the blade with a handkerchief. His years as a carny had taught him when to look the other way. Unfortunately, I didn't have the benefit of such training. He gathered up the broken glass, thanked me again, and went inside his trailer.

As I started to leave, Galloway's door sprang open, crashing against the side of his motor home. While talking into a walkie-talkie held between his hunched shoulder and cheek, he locked his door.

His radio squawked unintelligibly and he said a few quiet words into it. After strapping it to his belt, he took off at a fast clip toward the midway.

I followed, about to learn how much of a jack-of-all-trades Galloway really was.

CHAPTER TWENTY-EIGHT

The crowd in front of Fred's Animal Farm wailed in laughter. I looked up to see what everyone was pointing at. Perched atop the highest peak of Fred's tent was a small monkey, clutching a woman's purse to its chest. A heavyset lady in a bold polka-dotted sack dress stood in the front of the crowd, screaming about how much money was in her purse.

It wasn't hard to figure out who Fred was: a man in a tan safari jacket and pith helmet was trying to reassure the big lady that he'd get her purse back. When she continued her hysterics, Fred moved closer to his tent. He cupped his hands and shouted, "Mickey! Get down! Now!"

His stentorian voice echoed up and down the midway, and the crowd became hushed. Mickey bared his teeth, reared back his head, and screeched defiantly. With the handles of the purse looped around his neck, he began foraging through it. Whatever didn't meet his fancy he tossed into the crowd—lipstick, comb, keys, and a plastic rain bonnet. No billfold yet.

By the time Galloway pushed his way through to talk to Fred, Mickey was making faces in the mirror of the lady's compact. He let loose with a long, chittering laugh. It was answered by a chorus of roaring and growling and barking from inside the Animal Farm tent. Mickey's former cellmates were cheering him on in his bid for freedom.

I moved closer to Galloway and Fred.

"Fred, what's his name again? Mickey?"

Fred's chin was quivering. The crowd was now cheering on Mickey's antics. Galloway had to repeat his question.

Fred said, "Yeah. I bought him last year from the Clouser Carnival in Canada. You remember the Clouser show, don't you? They had—"

Galloway patted him on the back and said, "That's okay, Fred. We'll talk about it later." He pointed to the lady in the polka-dot dress. "I'll see what I can do with Mickey. Why don't you try to calm her down? I'll— Jesus, duck!"

Galloway covered his eyes with his arm, and the makeup mirror bounced off his elbow. The crowd backed off a few steps.

Galloway edged toward the animal tent, calling out softly to Mickey. The monkey answered with a mocking giggle. What Galloway shouted next didn't sound like English. It didn't even sound human. He let out a long shriek that duplicated the monkey's, only lower in pitch. Mickey immediately quieted. Galloway snapped his fingers and repeated his shriek.

Mickey looked around for an escape route, but there was no place higher to climb. Lowering his head to avoid Galloway's reproving stare, Mickey began to creep down the back side of the tent.

Galloway seized two of the guy wires of the tent and pulled himself off the ground, wrapping his legs around one of the poles that supported the sign in front of the animal tent. He shrieked again, this time with such ferocity that Mickey could have no doubt that Galloway would pursue him to any corner of the carnival lot.

The monkey's eyes grew wide with respect. Then he bared his teeth, let out a subdued laugh, and ambled down the maze of wires and poles. Galloway dropped back to the ground, and the monkey sprang after him. A few members of the crowd gasped, thinking that Mickey was attacking him.

But when Galloway turned around, Mickey had flattened himself against Galloway's chest, his arms wrapped around the man's neck and his legs digging lovingly into his sides. Galloway held the woman's purse in his hand.

When Fred retrieved it from him, Galloway said in a low voice, ''Compensate her for the stuff that Mickey destroyed. And if she claims there's money missing, give her whatever amount she wants.''

''But where—?''

''Take it out of your till. And make sure that she gets a long strip of free ride and refreshment tickets.''

Fred tried to pet and talk to Mickey. Like a protective mother, Galloway shielded the animal from Fred. Barely containing his anger, Galloway said, ''Don't you think your mistreatment of this animal has caused enough trouble? What the hell are you going to do if one of your Bengal tigers gets loose someday? Huh?''

Speechless, Fred pulled his pith helmet over his eyes and shuffled over to return the lady's purse. Galloway disappeared into the animal tent, speaking soothingly to the monkey. I moved closer and looked into the entrance of the tent. Galloway was still stroking and cooing to the monkey. The monkey looked into his eyes with the fascination of a child listening to a bedtime story.

The crowd dispersed, disappointed at the anticlimax to the monkey's high jinks. I watched for several minutes as Galloway and his little friend continued their conversation.

After finding Christine inside her tent, I had asked her to do me a favor—a dangerous one—and she agreed.

We were now standing outside the entrance to Bateman's office trailer. I knocked again, and there was still no answer. I had been knocking for the past two minutes. The shades were drawn and it was dark inside.

"Ready?" I said.

She swallowed her fear and nodded. I hadn't asked her about her rendezvous with Galloway. Her personal life was none of my business. She was nothing to me. Just someone whose confidence I had won so she could help with little chores like gathering information. At least that's what I told myself.

I said, "Remember, if someone comes, knock twice on the side of the trailer. If I have to, I can squeeze through the window on the other side."

She said something and motioned me closer.

"What?" I said.

She motioned me still closer. She gazed in my eyes and kissed me. I looked around, hoping that no one saw us. I was confused. Why was I edgier about someone seeing us kiss than about someone seeing me pick Bateman's lock? Maybe Carlson's muscles intimidated me more than I cared to admit.

She winked and turned away, leaving me to the task of manipulating the tumblers of the lock. And also wondering if her kiss was intended for more than just good luck. I tried to tune in on Madame Sirolli's thought waves. Damn. This ESP stuff never works when you need it.

The lock yielded easily to my efforts.

Using my penlight, I prowled around the office, not sure where to start. A door to the right of Bateman's desk opened into a small conference room, containing just a table, some chairs, and a sofa. Nothing of interest in there.

I decided to pick my way into the file cabinets first. But after getting the drawers open, I soon grew bored of flipping through the reams of computerized breakdowns of the dough that the carnival was raking in.

I opened a narrow sliding door behind Bateman's desk, using a celluloid strip to trip the spring lock. I was looking into a small storage closet. Arranged in neat rows were stacks of cardboard boxes, each with a different year printed on the lid. I opened the box dated for the carnival season of twenty years ago. It was filled with file folders containing financial statements, receipts, letters, employee records, memos, and purchase orders. Trying to read using just the meager illumination of my penlight was slowing me down. And there were too many papers to take them all with me.

Taking a chance, I switched on the overhead light and knelt down in front of the box. I hurriedly rustled through all the papers, pulling out any that were even remotely interesting.

The door of the trailer slammed shut. I hoped it was just the wind. But then I saw a pair of burgundy Aigner shoes on the rug in front of me. I looked up to see Mary Trunzo towering over me, frowning. So much for Christine Sirolli and her warning knock. Maybe her kiss hadn't been for luck. Maybe it had been a good-bye kiss.

With cold wonder, Mary asked, "Wasn't the fifty thousand enough? Did you have to come back for more?"

CHAPTER TWENTY-NINE

I breathed as deeply and as quickly as I could. But my gasping sounded like hiccups and wasn't convincing. I had to make do with the situation as it was: Shortly after a theft of fifty thousand dollars, I had been caught red-handed in the carnival manager's office, holding files that had been stored under lock and key.

I got to my feet and staggered forward, holding the back of my head. Mary caught me in her arms. "Did you see him?" I asked.

"See who?"

After enjoying her closeness for a few moments, I stood up on my own. I rubbed my head and groaned.

"Are you all right?" she asked.

"It's nothing. The guy gave me a shot to the head."

"Let me see." She reached for my head and I drew away, as though fearing escalation of the pain. "What guy?" she asked.

I knelt down and tried to square up some of the file folders. Papers slid out the sides. I scooped up a handful of them and dropped them on Bateman's desk. Then I leaned on the edge of the desk, trying to steady myself.

I said, "Christine Sirolli and I were walking past when we saw the door here wide open. I thought that I'd drop in to say hello to Bill. The first time I knocked, I heard what sounded like a stack of papers falling on the floor." I pointed to the files. "I knocked again but didn't hear anything else. I knew someone in here was waiting for me to leave, and it sure as hell wasn't Bill Bateman. I told Christine to wait outside and get help if she didn't hear from me. When I entered the office, I found this mess on the floor. Then someone clouted me from behind." I touched my head again and winced. Don't overdo it, I thought.

I continued. "While I was regaining my equilibrium whoever slugged me took off. I checked outside, and Christine was gone too. I couldn't resist taking a quick look at these files to see why they were so important. That's when you came in."

I picked up a handful of paper. "This stuff is twenty years old. July twelfth. Does that date mean anything to you?"

Mary shook her head but averted her eyes from mine.

"And how about this name?" I read from a letter in my hand which was dated June 30, twenty years ago. "Arlen C. Roth. Hey, I've heard of him. He was a magician. Did you know him?"

Her fingers tugged at her lip. Perhaps she hadn't bought my story, but I could tell she wanted to talk to someone—even a suspected burglar—about Roth. She said, "Yes. As a matter of fact, I used to work for him. It was so long ago." She stepped over the rubble of papers to sit on the desk chair. My mention of Roth seemed to have robbed her of strength. "After I gave up exotic dancing, I was his assistant. I suppose you could say that Roth was the reason I quit taking off my clothes in front of people." She seemed numbed, as though her words had been kicking around inside for too long a time without anyone to tell them to. "He left without any good-bye. And you say you knew him?"

"No, but I knew of his reputation. I heard he did a card trick with a dagger that was a real knockout. At one time, I hoped to learn that trick. Now I doubt if that day will ever come." I allowed wistfulness to creep into my voice. It didn't impress her.

"You magicians and your precious secrets," she said caustically. "Sorry, I can't help you. That dagger trick was one of the few that Arlen wouldn't let me in on. You'd think that after I nearly suffocated every night inside his illusion boxes, he'd at least give me a hint."

She tried to smile, but her cheeks were lined with tears. She said, "Like a true magician, Arlen Roth's death was clouded in secrecy. He was murdered. And they don't even know who did it. He was killed with his own knife. Some magician Roth turned out to be!"

"How did you find out about his death?"

She found a tissue in a desk drawer and touched it to her face. "Some writer phoned a day or so after it happened. Bill thought he was joking, until he made some calls to check it out. Bill wanted to go to the funeral, but he can't leave the carnival even for a day."

Allowing her time to dry her eyes, I spread out some of the papers on the desk. "This is fascinating," I said. "Here's a memo from Bill Bateman dated July twelfth. He talks about Roth suddenly leaving the carnival and his having to find a replacement. In fact, most of these papers are dated for the week before and the week after July twelfth. And would you look at this." I waved a pencil-drawn map of the midway, two decades old. Some of the attractions were still running, but many had gone by the boards.

"What the hell was *Wrestle-Challenge*?" I asked.

"What?" She was still lost in her memories. "Oh, that was a wrestling match where a chimpanzee took on challengers. Anyone that could pin the chimp's shoulders to the mat for three seconds received one hundred dollars."

"That doesn't sound too hard."

"Then you've never seen a chimpanzee wrestle. They can be vicious. Once they latch on to the sides of the cage and start pummeling you with their feet, it's all over. But the days of chimp wrestling are over . . . too much flak from the humane societies. Hell, it was the poor marks that deserved their sympathy, considering all the bloody noses and black eyes that were doled out over the years."

Looking at another handbill, I said, "I take it that *Mysteries of the Orient* was a girl show back then?"

"Yep, a genuine skin show."

"Why did Bateman drop the girlie shows?"

Still dabbing her eyes, she managed a mischievous smile. "I convinced Bill he could make more money without the sleaze associated with that kind of entertainment."

"Of course, with the dancers gone, that made less competition for you, right?"

"The thought crossed my mind."

"While we're on the subject of former carnival acts, here's something else I find puzzling: The Bozo dunking clown is a standard attraction for other carnivals. Why did Bateman dump it?"

She gnawed on the thought for a while, then said, "I really don't know. I think he stopped using a Bozo about a year after he dropped the strip shows. Did I tell you that Jacques Carlson was the last Bozo we had? Maybe Jacques did such a good job, Bill thought he could never be replaced. It worked out fine, though. Jacques really came into his own with his strong-man act, and then later on became one hell of a fixer. Sometimes I think that there's no situation he can't fix. He's made the carnival thousands— probably hundreds of thousands—with his special 'techniques.' "

I began to stack the files back in the box. "There's something funny going on around here, Mary. And I think it concerns more than just a missing fifty thousand dollars. Roth's name cropping up on these papers is awful fishy. I think we'd better talk to Bill Bateman. Where is he?"

She shook her head. "Bill would just delegate the matter to Jacques Carlson anyway. It'll be simpler if we just give Jacques a call. I'll check with the main gate so they can raise him on the walkie-talkie."

She picked up the phone and dialed three numbers. She let it ring a long time and then hung up. Thumping her fingers impatiently on the desk, she said, "Something's wrong. There's always someone at that gate."

I heard shouts from outside and the sound of running feet. A man rushed into the trailer without knocking. He wore a baseball hat with the bill bent straight up. I recognized him as the merry-go-round operator.

"What's wrong?" Mary said.

"There's been a murder," the man said.

"Oh, Christ!" Mary snatched up the phone and dialed the three numbers again. This time someone answered immediately. "This is Mary Trunzo. Could you hold on a second?" She glanced up at the merry-go-round operator. "Where did this happen?"

"Over in the trailer park. It's—"

Into the phone, she said, "Get hold of Carlson and tell him to report to the office trailer immediately."

She banged the phone down.

"He can't," the ride operator said. "Carlson's the one that's dead."

You were wrong, Mary, I thought. That was the one thing your fixer couldn't fix.

CHAPTER THIRTY

Outside the trailer, I watched Mary struggle with her keys as she locked up. I didn't tell her I could have done it faster—without the keys.

Only the most astute of marks would have noticed that something was amiss on the midway. Most wouldn't have paid any attention to the operator of the chuck-a-luck wheel miscalling several numbers, or the crew of the sausage sandwich booth huddling close together and talking in hushed voices, or the man running the Ferris wheel wandering away from his post to peer down the midway.

But to me, the carnies' fear was palpable. If Jacques Carlson, with all his muscles and martial-arts skills, could not defend himself, was anyone really safe?

As Mary disappeared around the corner with the merry-go-round man, I tapped my hand on my backside. The papers I had taken from Bateman's office were still there, stuffed down my pants. I headed toward my tent. There'd be plenty of time later to find out what had happened to Carlson. Despite these unpleasant developments, I still had magic shows to do . . . in addition to a lot of reading.

Two uniformed policemen passed me in a dead run.

As I walked by the mug-shot booth Zig Mulvaney stepped out in front of me. He was aiming something shiny in his hand at me. Out of reflex, I ducked, weaving to the right.

Mulvaney was fighting a losing battle: for every step he took, he had to take two more in the other direction to keep his balance. His tongue seemed too lazy to form his words. I could smell his whiskey breath from several feet away. He said, "Say cheese!" and clicked the shutter of his double-lens reflex camera. I doubted that there was any film in the camera, that they even made film for old cameras like that anymore.

Obliging him, I said cheese and he clicked the shutter again. I moved close enough to let his arm encircle me. "Your pictures are done, Harry. They're in an envelope on the desk inside."

I guided him back to his booth. I didn't want him to lose his job tonight.

Inside, I sat him down on the stool in front of his big camera. I switched on the kettle-shaped lamps, bathing him in light. I lifted up the cloth behind the camera and stuck my head in, watching the focused image of Mulvaney as he squinted into the lens of the camera.

"Zig, old buddy, I have a feeling you've been fibbing."

"The camera never lies, Harry. Never. It's impartial."

"That impartiality is exactly what I'm counting on. You know, I bet you have such respect for your art that you've saved copies of all your work. Am I right?"

"Harry, if my keeping a file copy of your picture makes you uncomfortable, I'll gladly give it to you. What's wrong? You're not wanted by the law, are you?"

"No, you can keep the copy. What I'm really interested in is a picture from about twenty years ago. How good is your filing system?"

"Ah, it's nice to see a young man who believes in preserving history. You know what they say about learning from past mistakes. In my case, however, the only thing I've learned is how to make the same mistakes over again, but with less effort and more speed. Go ahead, be my guest. Look through my files, if you think you can learn anything from the ten thousand ways that people stare into ground glass and pray that I can make them look like someone they aren't. Everything's stored in my van behind this tent. I have a box for each year. And each contains smaller boxes for each month. I am quite efficient for—what did Roth call me?—a failed artist."

Before leaving Mulvaney's booth, I slipped the papers from Bateman's office into the clasp envelope that contained the photos of me and also the twenty-year-old photos I had taken from Mulvaney's archives. I looked up the midway and saw Ernie and Christine strolling toward me. His comforting arm was draped around her shoulder, and he was taking care not to crush her.

When they spotted me, Ernie had quiet words with her. Then he bought her a cherry snow cone from a nearby grab stand and left her standing by the counter while he joined me. Seeing him outside the confines of the freak show, passersby regarded Ernie with awe. A few young people made jokes under their breath. But no one looked him in the eye. They all took the long way around when passing him.

The simple act of walking down the midway with Christine had placed a strain on him. I had to wait for his breathing to settle down to normal. Then he said, "Needless to say, Christine doesn't feel like talking at a time like this." He watched a young couple saunter by, each taking bites off opposite ends of a hot dog. "Funny. For the first time in my life, I'm not hungry."

I nodded with understanding, and Ernie said, "Christine tells me that you two were involved in some shady business when she got the word about Carlson's death. She says she's sorry that she deserted her post. She hopes it didn't cause you difficulty."

"No. It worked out okay. I figured that's what happened. Tell her I'm glad she's all right. And, just to keep our stories straight, tell her that Mary Trunzo thinks that someone else broke into Bateman's office."

He nodded and looked over at Christine. She was leaning on the counter of the concession stand, her back to us.

"Of course, Carlson's death is a shock to us all," I said, "but I'm surprised at how hard Christine is taking it."

Ernie sighed. "Like the rest of us, she despised Carlson. But she can't forget that the man was in love with her—at least according to his own definition of love. She's feeling guilty for giving him the cold shoulder. Even though snubbing Carlson, in my opinion, was the healthy thing for *anyone* to do."

He rubbed his finger across his wet upper lip. I thought Ernie should get in front of one of his fans as soon as possible.

"So what happened to Carlson?" I asked.

"One of Galloway's assistants found him strangled in his trailer. They figure it happened sometime between nine and nine-thirty."

"The police have any idea who did it?"

Ernie shook his head. "The police? I almost forgot about them. Oh, I guess they're doing their share of meddling. But so far the only clue is an odd ring on one of Carlson's fingers. It looks like some kind of primitive tribal jewelry—little beads threaded on a piece of elastic. The funny thing is, it's well known that Carlson hated jewelry of any kind. He didn't want anything to distract people from looking at his body."

"How was he strangled?"

"With his own karate belt."

"I bet Bateman's worried about the bad publicity."

He grunted in amusement. "Not exactly. You see, Carlson really outdid himself in this town. The fix was in. And I mean heavy. Probably too heavy for his own good."

I said, "You don't mean that . . ."

"Precisely. In normal circumstances, Carlson's death would be, at best, suspicious. But since Carlson took such good care of the local cops, they're still willing to go along with the original agreement: Let the carnival take care of its own messes, as long as it doesn't spill outside the lot."

"So what's the police report going to say?"

Every time he tried to talk, he broke into laughter. And every time he broke into laughter, he began to sweat more and get redder in the face, causing me concern over his physical condition. Finally he was able to utter the word that he found so irresistibly funny. "Suicide."

I saw a red light flashing up ahead in the carnival trailer court. I guess that Mary Trunzo was right after all. Carlson was the best. There wasn't anything the man couldn't fix. Even the investigation of his own murder.

CHAPTER THIRTY-ONE

Betty, the ticket seller for my magic show, looked at me with concern. "Are you okay?"

"What? Yeah. I'm fine."

I was sitting cross-legged in the cramped space behind the curtain of my performing platform. On my lap lay the stack of papers I had "borrowed" from Bateman's office. Taped to the back of the curtain was one of the twenty-year-old photos from Zig Mulvaney's archives. I slid the pencil from behind my ear and scratched a few words on my notepad.

The barker outside shouted, "Lay-dees and gen-tull-men . . ." as he began to round up a new crowd for my next show.

Betty decided to ignore her ticket selling for the moment. She said, "That was quite a shock tonight about Jacques Carlson, wasn't it?"

I nodded and continued my scribbling.

She said, "What are you doing? Working on a new trick?"

I laughed to myself and said, "Sure. That's exactly what I'm doing."

"Since you've been here, I've seen a lot of the same faces coming back show after show. The marks really like your magic."

I continued to write, and that irritated her. "Look, I'm trying to say that if you're really good, you shouldn't stick with this punk outfit. You should try for something better. You know, like TV."

"Television. Now, that would be a smart move. I just might take you up on that idea. Soon."

Betty looked at the photo taped to the curtain. "Who's he?"

The young man in the picture was in his late teens. He was saluting the camera with mock respect, holding his hand at an exaggerated angle across his forehead. His youthful skin was white and unmarked, and he wore his dark hair in bangs, with narrow sideburns that stopped level with the corners of his mouth. There was a folded piece of paper in the pocket of his button-down oxford shirt. The writing on the exposed portion of the paper was too faint to read, but the insignia in the upper corner was a smiling devil.

She asked again who he was.

"Nobody," I said. "Just someone's brother." From the yellow envelope beside me I slid out another photo and held it up.

"Hey, same guy," Betty said. "Wait, that's the exact same picture. Why do you have two copies?"

"That's what I'd like to know."

I went back to writing on my pad. My cryptic answers annoyed Betty, and she was afraid to ask if the pictures had something to do with Carlson's death. Even if she had, I couldn't have given her a straight answer. Not yet.

As I slipped the duplicate picture back into the envelope, she said—without really meaning it—"Have a great show," and left to sell her tickets. In a few minutes I'd have to set aside all my thoughts about murder so I could play the role of a fun-loving magic man . . . a guy whose biggest tragedy in life was to accidentally cut a hole in a borrowed handkerchief and then have to restore it with a wave of his hand.

As the crowd filed in, their laughter and chatter increased. And I continued writing, brainstorming for ideas. As the minutes dragged by, the audience's impatient coughing gave way to loud complaints. Some of them stomped and whistled. The barker stuck his head through the curtain and said, "Better move your ass. Just because Bateman has his hands full tonight doesn't mean you can goof off."

I shrugged.

"Your funeral," he said, leaving.

I stood up and faced the photo on the curtain. I returned the young man's comic salute. "We'll get to the bottom of it, Willy. Even if it takes another twenty years."

At the last minute, I realized that my cards and rope and scissors were in all the wrong pockets. After rapidly rearranging them, I stepped out onto the platform, which was now vibrating from all the stomping and clapping. I recited the necessary lines and mechanically executed all the proper moves. Somehow I got through the show.

And felt guilty when the crowd liked me.

With my last show of the evening finished, I spread out the papers over the entire platform. I hunched forward on my hands and knees, reading a series of carnival purchase orders for the month of July, twenty years ago. My moneybag lay on the corner of the stage, its contents uncounted. No fixer would be around to collect dues tonight.

I tapped my pencil impatiently on the first page of my notes. The tear-down crew would soon be laboring into the predawn hours, packing up the carnival for the journey to the next town. If I didn't come up with a plan by then, it would be too late. In the meantime, I had questions to ask and phone calls to make.

"Jeez, you look like hell. Need some help?"

Christine's voice startled me. She had changed from her fortune-telling costume into jeans. She had done her best to erase the evidence of her tears, but her eyes were still a dry red.

I said, "I'm sorry about—"

"No need to be. I don't intend to say nice things about the dead that I don't mean. All the other carnies will be doing that soon enough. Before long, Jacques Carlson will become just another name for the old-timers to reminisce about. Face it: Even though he did a good job for the carnival, Carlson was a louse. There isn't one carny here that he didn't trample over at least once."

She stepped up onto the stage, carefully avoiding the sheets of paper strewn in her path. She looked over my shoulder, reading my notes. "That name you just wrote down—Ray Kirkham. Who's he?"

"Just another name for the old-timers to reminisce about."

"He must have been before my time."

"Did Carlson ever tell you about his first job with the carnival?"

"Yeah. He was a Bozo—a dunking clown."

"Ray Kirkham was his predecessor. I want to find out more about him."

She looked at the photo of the young man that was now propped up on a folding chair in the front row. "And who's he?"

"I can't be one hundred percent sure, but I think his name is Willy Sanders."

"Was he with the carnival?"

"Yes, but only for a brief time. One evening, to be exact. But not as an employee."

"Oh, a mark," she said, looking away from the picture, no longer trying to recognize him.

"And a dead one, too. The Bateman Carnival was the last place he was seen alive. His was the only picture in Mulvaney's files from that month that had two copies. He never came back to pick up his photo."

"It's such an old picture. What difference could it make now?"

I explained what Lee Sanders had told me about the disappearance of his brother Willy. Then I said, "Because Willy was on his way to join the army, I figured that he might have stopped at the mug booth to get his picture taken to commemorate the occasion. That also accounts for the funny salute."

"And you think Sanders's death is tied in with Roth's?"

"Yes. And Carlson's, too."

"How do you figure?" she asked.

"Both Arlen Roth and Ray Kirkham quit the carnival very shortly after Sanders's disappearance. It's all here in these papers." I coughed from the smoke and knocked over my coffee cup with my elbow. I snatched up the papers that were in the path of the spreading puddle.

She tucked her fingers under my chin and lifted it until I was staring into her eyes. "I hope I don't look as bad as you," she said. "Could you use some help?"

"Yeah. That would be nice."

"What can I do? Ask more questions? Make some phone calls?"

"At the very least. We need something concrete to give to Bateman before this show rolls in the morning."

"What?"

"I need you to do some fortune-telling."

"But you don't believe in that stuff. Neither do I, for that matter."

"Not *that* kind of fortune-telling. I'm talking about making guesses based on limited facts . . . making two plus two equal six, as you call it. Remember?"

"What do I do first?"

"Why don't you show around a copy of Sanders's picture and see if you can find anything more about him? I'd also like you to contact Warner Huston, Roth's ghostwriter. I don't think you'll get through, but try anyway. Then I need to know if there's a pharmacy in the town of Tolley, Indiana. If there is, ask the owner if there was a suspicious theft there twenty years ago. Twenty years ago next week, to be exact."

"Anything in particular you think was stolen?"

"Yes. Poison."

CHAPTER THIRTY-TWO

After Christine left to make her phone calls, I decided to get some fresh air before driving back to my room. I had a long night ahead of me. The crowd on the midway had thinned to just a few die-hards—those who believed their gambling luck might still change, even at this late hour.

I observed a bearded man chewing on a toothpick as he watched five jumbo dice tumble down felt steps onto the counter of a game booth. After each loss, the man withdrew his tooth-pick, spat noisily, then plunked a few more dollars onto his favorite number. His wallet was attached to his belt loop by a metal chain of half-inch links. It would take a stronger chain than that to prevent the operator of Amelia Halfhill's dice game from draining what was left in his wallet.

The operator, a puffy-cheeked boy with carefully curled hair, was wearing a maroon runner's jacket with white stripes down the sleeves. It was zipped up only halfway, revealing a hairless chest. He pulled back his sleeve to check his watch. Time was now his biggest obstacle to cleaning out the mark. I decided to stick around to see how he played it.

Instead of rolling the dice again, he motioned the mark closer and whispered to him. The mark nodded, and the operator loudly announced that the game was now closed for the evening. He turned off the lights in his booth, and the small crowd drifted off, leaving just the mark with the big wallet.

The operator checked out the midway to make sure the coast was clear. Then he ducked behind the counter and came up with three matchboxes. I moved closer to hear his pitch.

He shook one matchbox, and it rattled loudly. He opened it to show that a penny inside had made the noise. He opened the other two and showed them empty. He shook these two, and, of course, they didn't make a sound. He then switched the matchboxes back and forth, moving two at a time, mixing them up. His hands moved slowly, making it easy to follow the box with the penny—the "rattler," as he called it. Three times in a row the mark guessed which box contained the penny, winning himself a quick thirty dollars.

But as the operator continued to shuffle the boxes his hands gradually became a blur. It was getting harder to follow the rattler. The mark began to miss now and then, slowing down his winning streak. As I walked away from the booth the mark was beginning to lose more often than win. It was a pattern that I had grown familiar with over the past few days. The box with the penny in it was becoming more and more elusive. Shortly, the mark's wallet would be reduced to nothing but credit cards and a driver's license.

I looked back at the operator as he again rattled the correct matchbox. Another loss for the mark. As I headed back to my tent I rattled some of the coins in my pocket, puzzling over the secret to the matchbox scam.

Bill Bateman was waiting for me in front of my tent. His face was pale and drawn. "Good to see you," he said. "I was afraid you had packed it in for the night."

"No, I was just letting this night air revive me. Is there something I can do for you?"

"No, I just want you to know I've heard good things about your show. In my opinion, you're a real carny."

Having just watched the game operator mercilessly hustling the mark, I might have not taken that as a compliment. But I did.

"We'd like you to stay on," Bateman said. "Although we'll be on the road tomorrow, we'll have a free day when we arrive at our next date. Since we won't have to rush our setup, it'll give us time to hammer out a longer-term agreement."

I wondered who the next fixer would be—the one who'd make sure that I upheld my end of our new agreement.

"I'm glad we're taking a day off," he said. "As you probably heard, we had some—shall we say—difficulty tonight."

"I heard. Everything okay?"

He smiled wryly and gave me the okay sign with his fingers. "It took a little, uh, fixing, but the Bateman Carnival will be rolling out of here tomorrow. Free and clear."

I looked up the midway toward the main ticket office and saw two men in suits standing beside a plain blue sedan with a whip antenna on the trunk. I said, "The police still tidying up their work on Jacques Carlson?"

Not detecting the sarcasm in my voice, he looked at the two cops. "Them? No, they're different cops. From out of town. The town of Maylene, I think. They're here to ask some stupid questions about some guy who worked here twenty years ago. Jeez, I've had my fill of police tonight."

Maylene . . . the town where Roth had been murdered . . . where I had left my old calling card. I clapped my hand to my mouth and began to cough. I doubled over and turned my back to the police. When I finally calmed down, I pulled a cigarette out and cupped my hands to light it, covering my face.

"Jeez," Bateman said, "with a cough like that you'd think that the last thing you'd want would be a cigarette."

I exhaled smoke and started hacking again.

"Let's go into the ticket office. I'll get you some water."

"No, no, I'll be all right." After recovering, I said, "It's just a mild allergy. I've got some medicine back in my van. I'll be okay."

"If you're sure . . . ."

I waved him off and went inside my tent. After a few minutes, I walked back out and saw Bateman talking with the detectives. They were smiling, shaking his hand, and patting him on the shoulder. Bateman had a small white card in his hand. Looking nervously in my direction, he crumpled it into a tiny ball and let it drop to the ground, where it joined the rest of the litter blowing along the midway.

I don't know what kind of deal he had struck with the detectives, but Bateman must have told me the truth. He must have *really* liked my magic shows.

Gibsonton, Florida—fondly called Gibtown—is famous for being a settlement for retired carnies and a winter home for those still active in the business. The directory assistance had a Gibsonton listing for Ray Kirkham, Carlson's predecessor as the carnival Bozo.

When Kirkham answered the phone, I heard a crowd cheering in the background. A ball game on the radio. I apologized for calling at such a late hour.

"Speak up," he said, although he made no effort to turn down his radio.

As I toyed with the matchboxes that I had bought at an all-night convenience store on the way back to the motel, I told Kirkham I was writing a magazine article about carnival dunking clowns.

"What a perfectly stupid idea," he said. But then he proceeded to tell me his life's history, starting with his first carny job at age ten. As he rambled on, my mind tuned in to the radio announcer, who was giving a breathless account of a late-inning pitching duel. Only periodically did I prod Kirkham to speed up his account.

When he finally reached the Bateman Carnival era of his life, I asked, "So why did you leave that job?"

"Beats me. I don't know what happened. I thought everything

was fine. But one day I suited up and headed for my tank and the son-of-bitchin' thing was gone. They tried to say it needed repairs, but that was a lie. I always made sure my tank worked properly, otherwise I might have gone belly-up with a lungful of water some night. But Walt Galloway and Arlen Roth, the guy who did magic tricks, tried to keep me quiet, telling me that my tank would be back in a day or two. I wanted to be reimbursed for all the money I was losing, but they balked at the idea. So I laid low and watched them. That night I discovered my dunking tank—what was left of it—all smashed to hell and left for the junk man. I put up a big fuss, and the next thing I knew, I was given my walking papers. I figured that one of those two must have had a little influence with Bill Bateman. I later heard that the carnival hired some muscle-bound goon for the new Bozo. Damnedest thing that ever happened to me. I was glad to get out of that loony bin."

"Was Galloway the carnival wirer even back then?"

"Wirer? Is that what he's doing now? Hell, he was just doing monkey work in those days. Imagine that. Galloway a wirer."

I remembered that Galloway had told me himself that ride monkeys were the lowest form of carnival life. "I guess you could say that Galloway is the carny version of the self-made man."

"Huh? If you say so. Anyway, it's good to see Galloway doing something he was cut out for. He never was comfortable working with the public. Not like me. But I can tell you this, all my years as a Bozo has really paid off. It's certainly made my retirement more comfortable."

"How do you mean?"

"I get treated with a lot more respect than most retired folks. Hell, nobody ever crosses me more than once. Just give me just a bad seat in a restaurant or throw my evening paper on the lawn, and by the time I'm done with all the insults, you'll never treat me wrong again."

"I bet. But doesn't it raise some eyebrows when you wear your clown suit into restaurants?

He spoke rapidly without pausing for a breath. "I bet you're so ugly that your face once stopped a sundial. You're so dumb, I bet you stand in front of a mirror just to see what you look like when you're asleep. I bet you're ugly enough to—"

I hung up the phone. Before I could dial again, the phone rang. It was Christine. "I've made some progress," she said. "I was able to get hold of—"

"Why don't you come over and tell me about it."

"Now? It's past midnight."

"I want to show you something."

Christine yawned as I dropped the three matchboxes on my bed. She said, "Hey, show's over. You can take your coat off. Aren't you warm?" As I lined up the boxes in a neat row, she reached into her purse, saying, "I did well tonight. First I got an irate pharmacist out of bed and—"

"Shhhh. Watch"

I showed her that one of the matchboxes contained a penny. I closed the box, rattled it, and put it back on the bed with the other two boxes. I then thoroughly mixed them, keeping my hands in motion for a full half minute.

She said, "I get it. You want me to guess which box has the penny. Like the shell-and-pea game. I bet it's a lot harder to slip a penny into a closed matchbox than a pea under a walnut shell."

"Oh yeah? You think that's how it's done?"

Using cellophane tape, I tightly bound up the box containing the penny. I tossed the tape to Christine, and she did the same with the remaining two boxes. I then played the game of pick-the-rattling-box with Christine. Unlike the game operator, I didn't try to hustle her. I didn't let her win even once. After only a few minutes of constantly picking the wrong box, she gave up in frustration.

She dragged a chair to the edge of the bed and rested her chin on her hands, determined to stare at the matchboxes until she deciphered the secret. I knew that feeling well.

"Whew," she said. "Mind if I open the door? It's hot in here. How can you stand it with that—" As she looked at the long sleeves of my tux coat, her face relaxed into a self-satisfied smile. She shifted her gaze to my eyes, hoping to distract me, but I was ready for her. She shot out both of her hands at once, trying to grab my wrists. I rolled away, across the bed. The matchboxes bounced onto the floor.

When she saw that I—like any good magician—was not going to let her look up my sleeves, she picked up the matchboxes. One by one, she shook them. Not one rattled. Having figured out the secret, she triumphantly threw the last box onto the bed.

I rolled up my left sleeve to show a fourth matchbox taped to my wrists. I shook it, and the penny inside rattled.

I again shuffled the three boxes on the bed. "Go ahead. Choose a box."

She did, and I picked it up—with my right hand—and shook it. No rattle. She chose another one. It didn't rattle either. I picked up the one remaining box—this time in my left hand. Lo and behold, it rattled. I tossed it to her, and she undid the tape. It was empty. The box strapped to my wrist supplied a rattle any time I desired . . . making it impossible for the mark to win.

She asked, "What happened to the penny you put in that one box in the beginning?"

"I palmed it out right after I slipped it in. Then I got rid of it when you weren't looking. See?" I reached down and plucked the coin out of my pant cuff.

"You aren't thinking of working for Amelia Halfhill, are you?"

"No way. Besides, one of her men is already using this scam. After watching him tonight, I figured out his method. Only I didn't catch on as fast as you."

She smiled at my compliment and then asked, "Don't you have enough to do without taking time out to play with carny swindles?"

"I couldn't get this matchbox game out of my mind. Then I realized why. You see, it reminded me of . . ."

As I explained my theory she didn't yawn once. When I finished, she said, "It's beginning to make sense now." She took a notepad from her purse. "I don't know if what I've found will be as helpful. I tried to contact Roth's ghostwriter, but a recording answered, saying that the phone had been disconnected. I called that bar you said he hangs out at, but they don't know where he is."

"I didn't think you'd find him. Now, what about the pharmacist?"

"At first he was angry that I was calling so late. But then he softened up because my question intrigued him. He said that there had indeed been a robbery at his drugstore twenty years ago. It had baffled him because the crook had passed up all the narcotics, taking only a bottle of Inderal, a heart medicine. A notice on the box clearly warned that an overdose would be lethal. In the days following the robbery, the pharmacist was afraid he'd read in the papers that somebody had OD'd on the stuff. But it never happened. Gradually, he forgot about the incident. Until I called him.''

''Anything else?''

''I think. Could I use your mirror?''

I laughed and pointed to the dresser mirror. ''I'm a magician. I do everything with mirrors.''

''No, not that kind. I was hoping for a mirror that makes images appear larger. I thought you'd have one for your magic.''

I nodded. From my suitcase I took out a three-way mirror that was the size of a thin phone book. I unfolded it and set it on the dresser. ''I use this one for practicing close-up tricks. It makes my hands appear bigger and helps get the angles right.''

She took her copy of the Sanders photo out of her purse and held it up to the mirror. ''Look.''

''What exactly what am I looking for?''

''The piece of paper sticking out of Sanders's pocket. The mirror makes it easier to read the writing.''

''Oh yeah.'' The enlarged image, now turned around backwards, said *100*. ''So what's it mean?''

''I was hoping you'd know.''

I turned the picture around and stared at Willy Sanders, his hand frozen in a salute that poked fun at the army he never got a chance to serve. ''Actually, I think I do now.''

I picked up the phone.

''Who are you calling?''

''Dr. Terry Swanson, a friend of mine who's an expert in magic history. You can bet he knows someone that collects carnival memorabilia. And after that I'm going to call Bill Bateman, Jr.''

Christine started for the door.

''Hey, where are you going?''

When she turned, her smile was one of resignation. ''It's strange. When I first met you, deep inside I hoped I'd end up here alone with you. But tonight's changed all that. But even if it hadn't, I have a feeling—if I call it mind reading, you'll just laugh—that there's someone else in your life.''

Had I mentioned my former assistant, Cate, to her? I couldn't remember. Maybe she *had* read my mind.

She said, "Whoever she is, she means more to you than you realize." She opened the door. "Madame Sirolli has just made her final reading for the evening."

"Stay. Please. I really need your help. Bateman won't believe that I know how and why Arlen Roth was murdered. I'll need you to persuade him that the carnival must play an unscheduled date tomorrow, one it can't afford to miss."

She closed the door and handed me a slip of paper from her purse. It was the number of the temporary phone hookup in Bateman's motor home. She pulled up a chair and sat down, waiting for me to call.

I wondered what she meant when she said that tonight had changed everything. I thought she was referring to the death of Jacques Carlson. Which shows how little I knew. I just wasn't as good a mind reader as Madame Sirolli.

CHAPTER THIRTY-THREE

In the few days since I'd met Bill Bateman, Jr., our roles had reversed. I now sat behind the big desk in his trailer office, my heels propped up on it. I took mighty puffs from one of his personal cigars, trying hard to enjoy it. Two crystal bowls, filled to the rim with an orange-colored punch, crowded the desktop. I offered Bateman a cup of punch, but he shook his head. My lips were dry, but even if I'd been dying of thirst, I wouldn't have drunk any of that punch. Bateman was sitting in the visitor's chair, clearly uncomfortable with its meager padding and low height. I looked under the desk to make sure that my bag full of empty bottles was still hidden from him.

I could sense the nervousness in the muffled talk of the carnies in the room behind me. Bateman had summoned them to his office to hear an announcement, and they were afraid that the carnival was going to close. Bateman and I had yet to iron out the exact wording of his announcement.

He fiddled with the package in his hand, a small padded envelope the size of a brick. He said, "Are you sure we have to play it this way?"

"It's your choice. After all, it was Jacques Carlson himself who struck that deal with the local cops. You can always let them deal squarely with Carlson's death. But they've got the power to shut your show down. How long can your carnival sit idle before going out of business? But somebody has to do something about Carlson's death . . . and it might as well be you. Think about it: The murderer is probably one of your own carnies. If you ignore Carlson's death and try to conduct business as usual, what's going to happen to the morale around here? Everyone will be worrying about who the next victim will be. And do you think the marks won't notice? They won't want to spend money in a fear-charged atmosphere."

"Do you really think we can get into that—that place?"

"Don't sweat it," I said. "Those joints are designed to keep you in, not out."

"But why . . . ?"

"Why there? Something happened nearby that place a long time ago that's directly connected to the murders of Roth and Carlson. Besides, it'll be the safest place to pull off my scheme."

"But the carnies aren't going to believe I'm throwing a party."

"You'll have to convince them. They've got to be distracted enough to not realize that the carnival's gone off route."

As Bateman reached for his cigar box I slid my feet out of the way. "But why the liquor? Everyone knows I forbid drinking on carnival property."

I ground out my cigar in the bottom of an empty punch glass. "We'll tell them that you're throwing a special celebration."

"Celebration of what?"

"We'll think of something. Just listen to them in there. They're murmuring like mourners at a funeral. When you give them the good news, they'll be so relieved, they won't question your motives."

"Everyone except the murderer."

"That's part of the idea."

I stood up and carefully lifted one of the punch bowls. Bateman stuck his cigar in his mouth and slid his package across the desk.

"Almost forgot," he said, his cigar wiggling in his mouth. "This overnight package came for you this morning. It's from a rent-by-mail video company."

"Great. I was hoping this would come in time."

"But you don't even own a TV, do you?"

"You've got a VCR, don't you?"

"Yes, in my motor home. But—"

"How about letting me ride in your motor home during the trip? Then I can use your VCR."

"Well, all right. But you'll miss the party."

"I'd have to miss it anyway. I've been up all night making arrangements. After I watch this film, I'm going to get some shut-eye."

It was obvious he didn't like the idea, but he shrugged and picked up the other punch bowl, moving slowly so that none of the punch spilled on his suit.

After we set the punch on the coffee table in the back room, Bateman tapped a ladle against the side of a bowl to get everyone's attention. Ernie and Christine were sitting on the sofa along the wall. Although Christine was right next to Ernie, due to his sheer bulk their two heads seemed far apart. She wore a short skirt with a flimsy strawberry top that stopped several inches above her midriff. She looked so overtly seductive that I at first thought it was part of her fortune-telling costume, except she wasn't wearing one of her trademark necklaces. With her hair pulled back, she looked fresh for so early in the morning. She showed no signs of having spent the entire night helping me prepare for the "party."

Standing at the far end of the room was Walt Galloway. Face pressed to the window, he was watching his crews complete the final stages of packing up the carnival. Next to him were Zig Mulvaney and Amelia Halfhill. Mulvaney handed a twenty-dollar bill to Halfhill, who then taunted him by waving it close to his face. While Mulvaney shook his head in disgust, Halfhill picked up a soda-pop bottle from the floor and shook out the penknife from inside. She slid the knife and the twenty into her jeans pocket. I spotted the nick in the ceiling where she had inserted the knife blade. Word traveled fast in this carnival.

As everyone quieted down to listen to Bateman, Mary Trunzo moved to his side. I noticed that Ernie and Christine kept smiling at each other and that her hand had disappeared in the clasp of his big hand. I looked at Galloway, but he was so absorbed with the work outside, he didn't seem to notice the affection between the two.

Bateman explained to everyone that he wasn't here to deliver bad tidings. As I had predicted, the mood in the room immediately brightened.

"So what's the occasion?" Ernie asked.

As Bateman stumbled for an explanation Mary asked, "Yes, what are we celebrating?"

Bateman said, "I, uh, I . . ." He looked to me for help.

And I obliged.

Maybe it was due to the early hour, but for the first time since I had met Mary, she was showing her years. The lines on her face seemed deeper, and her skin was gaunt. I saw only a glimmer of the good looks that had made her the top exotic dancer of the carnival twenty years before.

Or perhaps it was the way that Ernie and Christine were beaming at each other.

And I suppose it was because I also missed Cate, my former assistant . . . the one that Christine thought I was pining for.

For all these reasons, I said: "It's understandable that Bill Bateman is choked up at a moment like this. I'm sure he won't mind my speaking for him."

He nodded and smiled faintly.

I said, "Ladies and gentlemen, Mary Trunzo and Bill Bateman, Jr., after all these years, are finally going to be married."

There followed a lot of clapping and cheering. I continued to speak over the tumult. "As I understand, they have not yet set a date. Right, Mary?"

She shook her head. Weakly.

I continued. "Of course there'll be a huge celebration later on that will include all the members of the carnival. But for now, Bill wanted to have a small private party for you, the key members of the Bateman Carnival. It's his way of thanking you for making this whole show a success."

The room erupted into applause and congratulations and handshaking and backpatting. As I hoped, everyone in the room, except Christine, began to hit the punch bowl. "Drink up," I said. "When this trailer starts to roll, you don't want this stuff spilling everywhere."

As Ernie downed one cup after the other, Christine looked at me dubiously. I mouthed the words "It's okay." She nodded, understanding that with Ernie's huge size, it wouldn't affect him much.

Mary looked at me quizzically. I winked at her and extended my congratulations to her and Bateman. Bateman started to say something, but Mary gave him a long, passionate kiss. Bateman filled his cup and took a long drink. Then he slammed his cup down on the table so hard that ice cubes flew out.

He smiled.

Oh, how he smiled. Wide and full, with plenty of teeth. Such a big smile that his cheeks trembled and his eyelids flickered. But it failed to conceal the look in his eyes that said, *I want to strangle you, Harry.*

CHAPTER THIRTY-FOUR

When I saw who was driving Bateman's motor home, I wondered if I'd get any sleep at all. Sitting at the wheel was Gabe, the operator of the Ferris wheel on the day that the car had almost hit me. He was wearing a sleeveless undershirt that had probably been white at some time in history. Clamped to his ears were

foam-covered earphones connected to a miniature tape player.
Even from several feet away I could hear the squealing guitar
riffs. Every time I spoke to him, he had to peel away one of the
earphones. I had a vision of him sitting on his Ferris wheel
operator's stool, eyes closed and snapping his fingers to the beat,
while hundreds of terrified riders begged to be let off.

He leaned his free ear toward me and said, ''What did you
say?''

I pulled the cord out of his tape player. ''When will we get
there?''

''Beats the hell out of me. I'm like an elephant in a parade,
Harry. I just follow whatever's in front of me.'' The motor home
was now chugging up a hill in low gear, following a trailer with a
carnival poster plastered on the back window.

''Well, see you later,'' I said. ''I'll be in the back, watching
television. That won't wreck your concentration, will it?''

His answer was to let his headphone spring back over his ear.
He plugged it back into his tape player and began to sing along,
knowing only a few of the words. The motor home picked up
speed as it headed down the other side of the incline.

As I walked away I saw him raise a glass of orange liquid to
his lips. I spun around and lunged toward him, snatching the
glass away. We drifted a few feet off the road and back on again.
After sniffing the glass, I tossed it out the window like a live
grenade.

''Man, you're stricter than Bateman about booze,'' he said.

''Where'd you get that drink?''

''Galloway handed it out the window of Bateman's trailer. He
told me to write it on my calendar because Bateman never gives
away drinks. It looked like they were having a party in there.''

''How many did you have?''

''Just a few sips. I was saving it for the drive.''

I relaxed, knowing that I wouldn't have to take over the
driving. I looked out the windshield, making sure that the vehicle
ahead still had a Bateman Carnival poster on the back. From now
on, I wasn't taking anything for granted.

As we roared down the road I heard a clinking of glass coming
from the paper bag I had stashed in the garbage can—the empty
bottles of Jacques Carlson's Ener-Charge elixir. I inserted the

cassette into Bateman's VCR, switched on the wall-mounted TV, and settled down on the leather couch. My eyelids immediately felt heavy.

The film, entitled *Carnaval*, was a French documentary made over twenty years ago. The company I had rented it from over the phone specialized in rare films for hard-core movie buffs. I pushed PLAY on the remote control and the screen filled with French names. The credits dissolved into a scene of the Bateman Carnival midway twenty years ago. I was amazed at how many of the rides were still in use today.

Because the film had subtitles, I thought I'd be able to understand it. But I was wrong. The subtitles were in French, not English. The filmmaker had assumed that English-speaking people wouldn't need any subtitles, but because the sound quality was poor, I had to strain to hear the people being interviewed. The subtitles didn't help a bit. My knowledge of French was limited to two years in high school, almost entirely forgotten.

The film opened with an interview with the operator of the Ferris wheel, a tobacco-chewing man who constantly interrupted his demonstration of the ride's controls by spitting on the ground, sometimes too close to the cameraman.

The camera next ventured into the freak show, which was populated by several exhibits no longer in the current show. The camera lingered on a man with three eyes. He leered into the camera, blinking one eye after the other. Then he donned a pair of sunglasses with three lenses.

The scene switched to a shot of Ernie, then somewhat lighter, playing Ping-Pong with a midget named Binky, who stood atop the table to play. Ernie seemed embarrassed by the exhibition, but Binky was dead serious, fiercely slamming the ball into the far corners of Ernie's side of the table. But the little man's speed could not make up for the big man's force: Binky lost by two points. He leaped over the net and shook Ernie's forefinger in congratulations.

The next scene puzzled me. It showed a man on a stretcher being loaded into an ambulance. A hand kept trying to cover the camera lens while the cameraman shouted in protest. The filmmaker was attempting to interview the man in the stretcher, but unfortunately little of the conversation was audible. The victim's face was scratched and his arm was bandaged. Every time the man mumbled something through his swollen lips, French words flashed onto the bottom of the screen. The word that appeared most frequently was *singe*. I racked my memory but couldn't remember what it meant.

The camera then panned to the man trying to block the filming. It was Walt Galloway. The meaning of the word *singe* sudden came back to me. I was fairly sure it meant "monkey." In this case, it was obviously a loose translation of the carny term "ride monkey." Galloway, a lowly ride monkey in those days, was trying to cover up an injury caused by one of the show's badly maintained rides. Even back then, his loyalty to the carnival was complete.

Other sequences in the film included an interview with Bill Bateman, Jr., on the problems of managing a carnival; Ray Kirkham—the Bozo dunking clown—trading barbs with the marks throwing baseballs at him (Kirkham said that the cameraman was so short, he would have to milk a cow standing up); and a camera's-eye view of a hair-raising roller-coaster ride. The filmmaker also tried to crash the gate at the *Mysteries of the Orient* strip show, but the manager barred his entrance. Alas, Mary Trunzo's act of yesteryear would have to remain a mystery.

Next was a quick shot of a fresh-faced Arlen Roth performing a graceful waterfall shuffle with a deck of cards. I reran the tape several times until I saw that Roth's cards were stapled together. At this point in his career, he wasn't yet concentrating on sleight-of-hand feats. I suppose it was asking too much to think I'd see Roth performing the dagger trick in this film.

I struggled to stay awake. The final minute of the film was a montage of carnival shots intercut with scenes of famous American monuments—a cheap attempt to use the American carnival as a metaphor for the entire country. I again read the description of the film on the cassette box. It didn't surprise me that it didn't list any awards or positive quotes from reviewers.

Gabe lifted one of his earphones. "Did you say something?"

He shifted into a lower gear, and the motor home bounced off the highway and onto a narrow blacktop road with a wobbling, single white line. As we rounded a sharp bend I could see much of the carnival caravan snaking ahead.

"Do you speak French?" I asked.

"Huh?"

"Do you know what the French word *singe* means?"

"Huh?"

The truck in front of us still said *Bateman Carnival* on the back. But I was sure that even if it had said *Lemmings*—and was heading directly for a cliff—Gabe would still have cheerfully followed it.

I decided to get some sleep anyway.

CHAPTER THIRTY-FIVE

I straightened my bow tie and tried not to look down at my coat which I had borrowed from Eddie, the barker. With it's broad orange stripes, I felt as if I were wearing an awning.

I watched the workmen put the finishing touches on my platform. Three hammers pounded away while a man tested the microphone by tapping on it. These men were extremely loyal to Bateman. He had told them this morning to follow my orders, and no one had yet bugged me about why they were setting up the whole carnival twenty miles from the nearest highway, where the population of the nearest town wasn't much over a thousand.

One by one the rides started spinning. And spinning would be all they would do today. There would be no customers to load on the rides. No marks to rake over the coals at the gaming booths. The midway looked as it might an hour before opening time. Even Jacques Carlson's performing platform and his booth to sell Ener-Charge were set up.

Only when I looked beyond the immediate horizon of rides could I see anything unusual about this location. Instead of the normal fencing that surrounded the carnival grounds, there were walls—forty feet high. Strung across the top of the walls were triple strands of barbed wire. In the distance I could hear the sound of rushing water.

No marks would be strolling down this midway today. And no carnies would be leaving.

As ragtime music poured from the kiddy rides I stepped off my special platform and walked across the midway to Bateman's office trailer. When I opened the door, the sound of gunfire made my shoulders go rigid. More rifles cracked, followed by clanging bells and cheers. I relaxed. It was just some carnies passing time at the shooting gallery.

Inside the trailer, everyone except Ernie was asleep. Amelia Halfhill sat cross-legged, back against the wall, facing Walt Galloway, who was sprawled on the floor. A pile of money covered with loose playing cards lay between them. They were both snoring. Dozing in a chair by the window was Zig Mulvaney, his double-reflex camera slung around his neck.

Ernie was still sitting on the couch beside a sleeping Christine. Her head rested in the soft pillow of his shoulder.

"Did she . . ." I made a drinking motion with my hand.

Ernie shook his head. "A little water, that's all. I think she's just exhausted. As for the others"—he glanced around at the slumbering partiers and grinned—"let's just say that you missed one hell of a party."

I looked at the punch bowls. Bone dry. Ernie said, "It's a shame that stuff ran out. It tasted great. What was in it?"

"Nothing unusual. Some of the ingredients are actually quite healthful." I thought about the reported sedative effect of Jacques Carlson's Ener-Charge. It had worked quite well.

Ernie squirmed away from Christine, trying not to waken her. She mumbled and stirred. He tried to stand but couldn't send the correct message to his legs. He giggled and plumped back down. "I need more of that healthful punch."

"No, you've had enough."

Ernie looked out the window. "Jeez. The carnival's all set up. Where the hell are we anyway? That doesn't look like much of a fairgrounds out there."

"Actually, we're playing a special date today. A benefit."

Ernie looked at Mary Trunzo and Bill Bateman sitting on the

floor in the corner, asleep in each other's arms. "Hah! Benefit show? Him? That'll be the day."

"Not when the beneficiary is the Bateman Carnival itself."

Christine yawned and blinked her eyelids. Her eyes softened and a contented smile played across her lips when she saw that the big man was still beside her. When Ernie tried to get off the sofa again, Christine nestled closer, telling him to relax.

The way that she was caressing Ernie's arm made something roll over painfully inside of me. I didn't want to call it jealousy. Maybe I just didn't want to see Ernie get hurt.

I spoke more sharply than I intended, regretting it immediately. "Before we go on, I want to know what you were doing in Galloway's motor home last night . . . and why you were kissing him."

She showed no signs of surprise and instead looked at Ernie to see his reaction. Suddenly he had no trouble standing. I didn't like the way his forehead wrinkled. Nor did I like the way his eyes narrowed to the point of disappearing. He teetered toward me. To win any fight, all Ernie had to do was fall in the correct direction. I stepped back.

Christine tugged on Ernie's shirt, trying to sit him back down. She said, "Dammit, Harry. You're beginning to sound like Jacques Carlson. You aren't bucking for the fixer job, are you? What went on between Galloway and me the other night has nothing to do with the investigation. I was there was to—"

Ernie brushed away her fingers from his shirt. "Enough, Christine. You don't have to explain yourself. Harry, if she says it was harmless, it was harmless."

"But, Ernie darling, I think you should know—"

"It's okay!" He was shouting now, causing the others in the room to stir. "You don't have to say a thing." He searched through his pants pocket and found a handkerchief for his dripping forehead.

"If you say so." Christine shrugged and tried to change the subject. "Is everything set up, Harry?"

"We're as ready as we'll ever be. Why don't you wake everybody up, and I'll summon the rest of the carnies who didn't attend the party."

As I left, Christine was still trying to explain to Ernie her visit with Galloway. His hands were pressed tight to his ears.

*   *   *

When I saw the office trailer door open, I walked up to my microphone and tapped my cane on the platform. "Hurrrrrrrry, hurrrrrry, hurrrrrrrry. Step right up, ladies and gentlemen. Show time in a few minutes. The show is about to begin."

One by one the sleepy partiers emerged. As they stretched and looked around, shock registered on their faces. Even Bateman himself seemed agog at how claustrophobic his carnival was when devoid of customers.

As I continued my patter, smacking the platform with my cane, the carnies who hadn't attended the party joined the rest in front of my platform. I spoke with a clipped chatter that allowed little time for breathing. I was speaking their language—the language of the sideshow. "Ladies and gentlemen, it's a show of a lifetime . . . a show that makes you wonder what people won't do for money and revenge . . . a show that brings back the horrors of the past to haunt you again . . . yes, a show where you get exactly what you paid for."

When the crowd was fully assembled, I moved to the edge and smiled congenially. I tipped my straw hat to the audience and then tossed it in the air. It flipped over several times, landing square on my head. Someone started to applaud, but the cold stares of the others cut him short. That lone round of applause reminded me of my first performance with this carnival. It seemed years ago.

One voice in the audience said: "Where the hell are we?" It sounded like Zig Mulvaney.

I said, "We're actually standing in a part of historic Indiana. Up until twenty-five years ago, this was the exercise yard of the Spanier Prison, a maximum-security penitentiary. Over the years there have been attempts to convert the old prison to good use. There was even an aborted plan to turn it into a park." I looked into the distance where several trees were growing in the middle of the carny trailer court. "But alas, the abandoned prison has served no good purpose since the day it closed. Until today. You see, about twenty years ago something happened near the prison grounds that has a bearing on the confusing occurrences of the last few days. We hope to clear up that confusion today."

Walt Galloway spoke up, his voice still groggy. "To hell with you and whatever nonsense you have up your sleeve, Harry. We were having a nice little party during our trip over here. Anybody who wants to continue the celebration, just follow me into the next town." A few people seconded his motion.

"Sorry to disappoint you, Walt, but you've forgotten where you are. This is a *prison*. Before the workmen set up the carnival, they sealed off all the exits, even replacing some of the razor wire along the top of the walls. And if that's not enough to make you stay, just listen. Do you hear it? That rushing water in the distance is a quarter-mile-wide river that wraps around the northeast corner of the prison. A half mile downstream that river funnels into a long stretch of white water and treacherous rocks. There is only one road that leads out of the prison, and it's blocked by over half a dozen carnival tractor rigs. Why don't you stay awhile and enjoy yourself, Walt?"

Galloway looked to both sides and then behind him. The stone and brick walls dwarfed even the Ferris wheel. On all sides, sections of new barbed wire sparkled in the afternoon sun.

As the crowd stirred I tossed my cane into the air. In midflight it turned into a shower of shimmering spangles.

"I'm afraid that none of you are leaving until we determine who killed your fellow carnies Jacques Carlson and Arlen Roth."

Amelia Halfhill shook her head in disbelief. "My god, you're treating us like a bunch of . . . a bunch of . . ."

"A bunch of marks," I said.

CHAPTER THIRTY-SIX

While waiting for the grumbling and cursing to die down, I noted that those who had attended the party in the trailer were huddled near the front of the platform. They were dead silent, realizing it was no accident that they had been singled out for

Bateman's "celebration." As prime suspects, any protest from them would draw even more suspicion their way.

"As you can see, the carnival has been set up as closely as possible to how it was last night. Because of the tighter confines of the prison yard, it was necessary to move some rides and tents closer together. Plus, we've positioned the trailer court nearer to the midway, by that little grove of trees."

"So what's the point? Why go to all this trouble?"

Although low-pitched, the voice had a feminine lilt to it. When I looked to the back of the crowd, I saw that the speaker had a full beard. And wore a dress. The Wolf Girl.

"It's already been established that Jacques Carlson was killed sometime between nine and nine-thirty last night. In a few minutes, we want everyone to go to the exact places they were last night during that time period . . . and re-create what they were doing."

"Wonderful. You expect the murderer to waltz right into Carlson's trailer so that you can nab him? How dumb do you think we are?" It was Eddie, the barker. "And while I have your attention, Harry, I want my jacket dry-cleaned before you return it."

"Don't worry, I'll take care of all the blood stains and bullet holes. As for your question: Of course, the killer isn't going to just walk in and give up. But he—or she—has to go *somewhere* during the next half hour. It's vital that all of you keep your eyes peeled for anyone out of place—anyone who's trying to fake an alibi. I—"

I was interrupted by the hooting of calliope music from the merry-go-round. Bateman signaled for one of his men to shut it off. I pulled the microphone closer to talk over the music. "Please, leave it play. It's important to simulate as closely as possible the carnival as it was last night, including all the sounds. That way, you'll all be sensitive to anything out of the ordinary."

"No, no! Everyone listen to me. We can't let him do this. Are we not all brothers and sisters in this carnival? We can't let him turn us against ourselves." The man shouting and waving his hands was Gabe, the ride operator. He was holding his headphones in his hands.

I held up a placating hand. "Don't you see, Gabe? We're trying to *prevent* the carnies from turning against each other.

How long can this carnival create an atmosphere of fun when there's so much fear in the air? Let's get this over with while the memory of last night is still sharp. If we don't, I firmly believe that in six months the only thing left of the Bateman Carnival will be a for-sale ad in *Amusement Times* magazine.''

I saw several nods of assent. Then Gabe yelled, ''Your Honor, I will not have this sideshow turned into a courtroom!''

After several people groaned, Gabe looked sheepishly around him and said, ''Sorry. I've been waiting for a long time to use that line.''

I slipped out of the barker's jacket and enjoyed the rush of the afternoon breeze. I was surprised at how just those few minutes onstage had quickly overheated me. I looked at my watch. ''As of now, we all have ten minutes to assume our places. A half hour after that, we'll regroup here. If you see anything suspicious, feel free to come back earlier and report it to one of the maintenance crew standing guard.''

Eddie the barker spoke again, his voice sounding at home as it reverberated along the tents and booths of the midway. ''What do *you* plan to do in the meantime?''

''Like everybody else, I'll do precisely what I did last night between nine and nine-thirty.'' I neglected to add, however, that I wouldn't be doing it in exactly the same *place*. ''By the way,'' I said, ''you seemed worried about your jacket. I think I'll return it now. Here!''

I crouched down and held the jacket up to cover my face. With an upward flick of my wrists, the jacket sailed into the air and the planks beneath me gave way. I plunged downward. Everything went black. My stomach did a quick flip, as though I were on the carnival roller coaster. I was now looking up at the rafters in the underbelly of the platform. Thin slits of light surrounded the trap-door that had just sprung shut. The last image I remembered before vanishing was Amelia Halfhill hurriedly writing on slips of paper and waving them in the air to her fellow carnies.

I heard the crowd finally react to my magical disappearance. A few people laughed in surprise. Some were discussing how they thought I had done it. But no one applauded. I heard someone say, ''Guess we'd better go.'' There was a long silence, followed by the sounds of shuffling feet and angry muttering as the carnies slowly scattered.

Finding the piece of canvas I had left there earlier, I unfolded it on the ground and sat down. I snapped on my penlight, leaned my head against a wooden joist, and stared at the minute hand on my watch as it twitched its way around the dial.

My watch hand had made five revolutions when I heard the roar of more rides starting up. The game operators began to mechanically repeat their spiels for the benefit of invisible marks. The sounds of the carnival, against the background of the wind in the trees and the rushing of the neighboring river, all enhanced the ghost-town air of the Bateman Carnival.

My musing was interrupted by a crunching sound and a quick flash of light as someone stepped under the rear canvas apron of the platform. I played my penlight in that direction and saw Christine duck-walking her way toward me. "Don't hit your head," I said.

Joining me, she said, "Not bad. They all left for their posts right away. All except Gabe. He was listening to his tape player again, and Bateman had to tear off his headphones and shout in his ear what he was supposed to do."

"What about you? What will you be doing the next half hour?"

"I guess I'll stick with you. If I followed your directions, I'd have to wait outside Bateman's trailer with my heart in my throat while you're inside rifling the file cabinets. That's what we were doing last night between nine and nine-thirty, right? It also means that I'd have to relive those awful moments of seeing people running toward Jacques Carlson's trailer. And I'd have to ask what's going on, and they'd have to tell me that Jacques was dead. No, thanks, I'd rather not go through that again."

"I'm sorry, Christine, but it's vital that you go there. Only, this time, don't take off for Jacques Carlson's trailer. I need you to wait for Mary Trunzo and do your best to waylay her. When you explain why you're still there, she'll understand. But you must do everything possible to delay her going into Bateman's trailer. When she discovers that I'm not inside, she's going to think I'm the murderer."

"So where will you be?"

"Breaking and entering, just like last night. Only somewhere else."

"Oh, that's just great."

"Look, we still have a few minutes. Why don't you sit down and make yourself comfortable?"

She settled down on the piece of canvas, being careful to keep several inches between us. We listened silently to the grinding of the ride engines. After a few seconds, she said, "Ernie really surprised me today. I don't know why he was so protective when I tried to say why I was at Galloway's last night. After you left, I again tried to tell him, but he refused to listen, acting like I was making a sordid confession. Believe me, Harry, there was nothing sordid about it."

Feeling awkward, I wished her and Ernie the best. She thanked me and said, "It'll work out. After all, he and I are both carnies. Something you'll never truly be, Harry. It's just not in you. There are other things you should be doing with your life."

I turned my penlight off, not wanting her to see the regret in my face. After a long silence, she said, "You know about Galloway's hobby, don't you?"

"The miniature carnival in his workshop? Yeah, I've heard about it."

"He had told a lot of people about it, but I don't know anyone that's seen the whole thing, only sections of it. Last night he stopped in at my tent and offered to show it to me. On top of that, he asked me to pose for some sketches that he would use later on to make a carving of me. He was so nice, I couldn't turn him down. After all, no carny here loves the carnival as much as Galloway."

"And that's why you were there last night? Posing for sketches?" She nodded. "Did he show you any of the drawings?"

"No, he's waiting until he's all finished, so he can surprise me. But I did see his miniature carnival. Very quaint and lifelike."

"Did he let you look inside any of the tents or booths?"

"No."

For the first time I noticed a white piece of paper in her hand. "What's that?"

"Oh, this?" she said. "Amelia Halfhill was passing them out." She handed it to me. It was a list of names, mostly people who had attended the party in Bateman's trailer. "Amelia is covering all bets on who the murderer is."

It was gratifying to see my own name nestled near the bottom. I grinned. "Amelia doesn't miss a trick, does she?"

She took the slip and wrote her name at the bottom.

"You're not placing a bet, are you?" I asked.

"Sure, what do I have to lose?"

"Only your dignity. And your reputation as Madame Sirolli, who sees all and knows all."

She turned away so I couldn't see who she was betting on. I made a grab for it, but she jerked the paper away from my grasp. "Later," she said. "Then we'll see how good you really are."

We heard a dim voice outside that gradually got louder: "Mr. Cotter. Mr. Harry Cotter. Can anyone tell me where I can find him? A package for Mr. Cotter."

A second voice said, "Hey, you. If you're lookin' for Cotter, he disappeared."

"Can you tell me which direction he went?"

"Are you deaf? I just said that the dude disappeared. And I mean *disappeared*. We're talkin' thin air here."

I reached up and pulled the latch on the trapdoor. I eased the door down and fastened it with another latch to keep it from springing back. Bright light poured down. I stood up straight, sticking my head through the opening, bringing my shoulders level with the top of the platform. I rapped my knuckles on the floorboards to get the deliveryman's attention.

"I'm the guy you're looking for."

"Package, sir." He wore a blue jumpsuit. Emblazoned across his chest were the words *Fleet Delivery* and the insignia of a bare foot with wings growing out of it. With a graceful leap, he was on top of the platform, as though he had, well, wings on his feet. He bent down and thrust his clipboard in my face. After signing it, I tried to climb out of the hole in the platform.

"Sir!" the deliveryman said crisply. He put his clipboard under his arm and bent over, offering me a hand. After my feet were firmly on top of the stage, I said, "Wait. There's someone else coming too."

"No, thanks," Christine said from below. "I'll leave the way I came in."

The deliveryman handed me a big yellow envelope with the name Harry Cotter on it. After I thanked him, he stood by patiently, shifting his weight from foot to foot.

"Oh," I said. "Your tip's been taken care of. Check your left pocket."

"What?" Humoring me, he poked his hand into his pants pocket . . . and pulled out a new, unfolded ten-dollar bill.

After examining the bill and giving it a snap, he said, "Pardon me, sir, I can't help but notice how bad business is." He looked up and down the customerless midway. "Do you think the low turnout is due to your locale? After all, you've set your carnival up in a deserted prison in the middle of nowhere."

I shook my head. "I know what you mean, brother. But we don't have any choice about locale."

His eyes focused on the loops of barbed wire strung along the tops of the walls, and on the rows of barred windows in the buildings that used to house prisoners. His eyes widened. "My god, I thought they closed this place down long ago."

"They did, but it's open again. We're a new rehabilitation program. Instead of making brooms or license plates, we run this carnival. But it's not working out at all. The public doesn't trust us. I can't figure out why."

He looked at the empty rides going round and round, and at the seedy-looking booth operators leaning on their counters looking at their watches. "You mean that everyone here is a . . . ?"

I nodded. Rapid gunfire erupted from the shooting gallery, and he ducked, looking all around him. The man from Fleet Delivery then lived up to his company's name, pumping his arms hard in a hasty retreat from this prison yard cum carnival. I called after him, "If the guards at the gate hassle you on the way out, let me know."

I opened the envelope and pulled out a single, unfolded sheet of paper. I said, "Son of a bitch." I folded the paper and slipped it into my shirt pocket.

"You're popular today," Christine said, crawling out from under the back of the platform. She climbed the back steps onto the stage.

My face felt cold, and she must have noticed its lack of color. She asked what was wrong. Then she saw the envelope in my hand and the paper in my pocket. I had folded it exactly as Willy Sanders had twenty years ago while sitting for a picture in Zig Mulvaney's mug-shot booth.

The dark printing faintly showed through to the back side,

revealing the mirror image of the figure *100*. Too dim to show up in the picture, but visible to the naked eye, was a dollar sign next to the *1*.

"Who sent that?" she asked.

"It just came special delivery. Terry Swanson, the magician/doctor I told you about, persuaded a collector of carnival stuff to part with it."

She plucked the paper out of my pocket and unfolded it. It was a handbill, printed in thick black type.

She shook her head and said, "Son of a bitch."

"Precisely my sentiments."

CHAPTER THIRTY-SEVEN

Walt Galloway's motor home needed airing out. In the midday heat, the smell of his flowery, almost feminine, after-shave was everywhere. I tucked my paper bag under my arm and locked the door behind me. Taking short, quiet steps, I headed for his workshop.

The carnival worker who had driven Galloway's motor home from the last town had parked it too close to the copse of trees. The branches made annoying scraping noises on the roof.

When I turned the workshop light on, the overhead decorative netting cast a crisscross shadow on the floor. I slid open the sunroof, cooling off the room. Galloway's miniature carnival still sat on its table, covered with a white sheet. Wood shavings were scattered over the workbench and the floor. I carefully lifted the sheet off the display.

The little carnival looked the same, except for an ominous

piece of artillery on wheels sitting in the corner. I lifted the top of the tent marked *Mysteries of the Orient* and saw that Galloway had created a wooden caricature of me. The magician figurine was wearing a tux that was bursting at the seams. The pant legs were several inches too short, revealing a pair of shiny white socks. The bug-eyed magician, with spittle running down his face, was taking great delight in throttling the rabbit that he was pulling out of his top hat.

I lowered the top of the tent and lifted the top of Madame Sirolli's. The figurine of Christine sat at a round table, giving a reading to a customer. She was nude from the waist up, and her monstrous breasts lay across the tabletop. While the customer stared lasciviously at her, tongue lolling, Christine's superelongated arm was reaching under the table and into the mark's back pocket for his wallet. Her other hand innocently clutched her bare neck.

"Walt Galloway is certainly no Norman Rockwell," I said to myself, lowering the tent.

I looked in Galloway's closet and saw that the steamer trunk was now moved away from the wall. Its massive padlock was gone and the lid would no longer close tight because the latch had been bent. I opened it and trained my penlight across the interior. Its sole contents were a tan leather suitcase. Creeping closer to lift the case out of the trunk, I felt the motor home sway slightly. I figured the vehicle must be parked on uneven ground or across a rut. Good, I thought.

The combination lock on the suitcase had been badly smashed. One end of the case was dented, as though it had been rammed against something hard. As I carried the suitcase out of the closet, the lid flopped open.

And all the bones fell out.

I turned my head away and tried to figure out how to get them back into the suitcase. It was hard enough to look at the bones, let alone touch them. I found a pair of work gloves on top of Galloway's shop bench and began to scoop them back inside. Although I'm no anatomist, I didn't think they were from more than one body. In fact, several key bones seemed to be missing. I saved the skull for last. Shutting my eyes tight to ward off dizziness, I lowered the suitcase lid. It wouldn't close. I shook the grisly contents back and forth until finally the latches engaged. Blinking sweat from my eyes, I stowed the suitcase back in the closet, inside the steamer trunk.

I opened the middle drawer of the workbench, wondering if the small hypodermic needles were still there. I spotted a hand towel wedged between two cans of bolts in the back. I lifted it out. Something heavy was wrapped in it. Unfolding the towel, I found a small gray pistol with a hard plastic handle. There was a lever on the handle for pumping air into the gun. At first I thought it was a BB gun, but then I realized that the little hypodermics were animal tranquilizer darts . . . meant to be shot from the pistol.

Within the folds of the towel I also found a tattered set of instructions that explained how to load and shoot the gun. But they didn't explain how to disable it. I'd have to figure that out myself.

After a few minutes of fumbling, I rewrapped the gun and put it back. I then opened the bag I had brought with me and took out my last bottle of Jacques Carlson's Ener-Charge elixir. And went to work.

I was pouring myself a small drink of Ener-Charge when I heard the clicking of a key in the lock. I pulled a chair over to Galloway's miniature carnival. Seeing that there were still footprints on the seat, I brushed them off and sat down. I lit a cigarette and flicked the switch that set into motion the model amusement rides. The plinking music from the merry-go-round and the clatter of the little roller coaster filled the room.

Footsteps moved unhurriedly toward the workshop. The door swung open and Galloway stood in the doorway, blocking my escape. His face crinkled into a smile and his eyes flashed with delight, as if he were eyeing up the surprise dessert of a three-hour meal. I took a nasty drag on my cigarette and watched the swirl of smoke disappear up the skylight.

He said, "How rude not to rise when the owner of the home you've just broken into enters the room. Tell you what. I'll pardon your poor manners if you pardon mine. I'm afraid that under these circumstances I'm not going to offer you a drink."

"Fine with me. I've already had a little nip." I held up my glass. "I needed a little bracer before talking with you. But don't worry. I was careful not to overdo it, unlike everyone at Bateman's engagement party.''

He looked at the bottle on the table. ''Ah, the famous Ener-Charge. So that's what you spiked our punch with. A wise choice. The booze and the fruit juice completely covered up its sulfury taste. With the death of Ener-Charge's creator, I'd say the market for that stuff has declined.''

He moved closer to his carnival display. I was relieved when he didn't notice the small wet spot on the floor. ''Admiring my little avocation, were you?'' he asked.

''Your miniature carnival? Yes, I'm enjoying it immensely. Your high regard for the Bateman Carnival is heartwarming.''

''Glad you like it. It's a soothing way to take the edge off a hard day's work. I've only let a few people see the model, and then only the outside. The inside of my little carnival is for my own private enjoyment.''

''Unfortunately, that's not true, Galloway. It really didn't stay private, did it?''

He ignored my comment and looked at his rows of tools, checking for anything missing. I was afraid for a second that he would notice that the grinding wheel on his bench was still warm. ''Just what the hell are you doing here?'' he said. ''I thought everybody's supposed to be where they were during the time of Carlson's murder. Or did you exclude yourself from that weird order?''

''Only partially. I am doing what I did last night, just in a different place. Instead of breaking into Bateman's trailer, I broke into yours. With your macabre sense of humor, I figured you wouldn't try to hide somewhere, that you'd actually return to the scene of your crime. But what are you going to do now? How are you doing to fill the rest of the half hour? After all, you can only murder Jacques Carlson once.''

He gave up trying to maintain his smile, and his face frosted over with cold hatred. He shook his head. ''I don't follow you. Carlson was killed in his own trailer, not here.''

''No. Carlson's body was *found* in his trailer, but he was murdered here. I wasn't the only one to witness Christine's visit here last night. Carlson did too. He came back here to question you, and since you had no idea if Christine had told him about posing for you, you told him the truth. But that was a mistake, because then Carlson wanted to see your work. You refused. You didn't dare show him your cruel depiction of the woman he loved. Of course she had posed with her clothes on, but you wouldn't be able to convince him of that. So Carlson tried to find the figurine himself. He assumed that it wasn't inside your miniature carnival, because you wouldn't have had time to finish it yet. So he started rooting through all your personal possessions. You were heartsick when he started going through your closet . . . particularly when he smashed into your steamer trunk and found that suitcase. Since the suitcase was locked, he thought he was on the right track and he broke the lock on it. When he discovered all those bones, Carlson had sealed his fate. You had to kill him. There were many ways to explain Christine's visit here, but no way to explain all those bones. With Carlson's influence over Bateman, your carnival career was at an end.''

Galloway began to edge closer to me, but he seemed off balance, like a man who had been bedridden for a month. "Finding those bones means nothing. You've forgotten something, boy. This is a carnival. There's all kinds of strange people here. Why, we even got a guy who eats glass and metal for lunch. Oh, a few might think that my bones are strange traveling companions, but in the end they'll just think of me as an old carny with a few eccentric hobbies. As long I keep the carnival machinery running, they'll humor me.''

"I'm afraid that murder is not on most people's lists of quaint hobbies.''

"You have no idea where those bones came from.''

"I have a damn good idea.'' From my pocket I took out and unfolded the photograph of the young man with the brash smile and the jaunty salute. Galloway took the picture and held it at arm's length. He tried for a totally blank expression, but his eyes were too wide and unblinking. His face trembled from his jaw being clinched too tightly.

"Keep looking at it,'' I said. "It'll all come back. You probably forgot what his face looked like before it was bruised and scratched, before that look of overconfidence was replaced by rage.''

I tapped the paper in my shirt pocket and then pointed to the duplicate paper in the pocket of the man in the picture. I unfolded the real paper. "Haven't seen one of these for a while, have you?"

Printed in thick, blotchy type, the handbill offered one hundred dollars to any man who could win a wrestling match against Josie, a trained chimpanzee. I said, "You used to own Josie, didn't you?"

"What if I did? You know I've done a lot of different jobs with the carnival."

"Actually, that's the very thing that confused me. This morning I watched the documentary that Frenchman made about the Bateman Carnival. Did you ever get to see it?"

He numbly shook his head no.

"You didn't miss much," I said. "It was awful. I think your scene would have amused you, though. You kept trying to shield the camera from filming an injured man being wheeled into an ambulance. What threw me off was that the subtitles kept featuring the French word *singe*. I knew that it meant 'monkey,' so I assumed it was referring to the carny term for a ride operator: ride monkey. Considering that you now repair amusement rides, I figured that you were a ride monkey back then. But I was wrong. The injured man in the film didn't fall off any faulty Ferris wheel. He was a loser in a match with Josie the chimp."

A warm look of nostalgia swept across Galloway's face. "The marks were always suckers for that hundred-dollar offer. They assumed that all chimps were harmless little imps, just like on TV. They could never figure out how I could offer that much money just to dance around a caged ring with a cute monkey. But under the proper conditions, chimps can be vicious, efficient fighters. Even the guy that sold me Josie had to learn to sign his name with his left hand after Josie turned on him and bit off a few fingers. But that chimp never got mean with me. I knew how to treat him. Josie and I had an understanding."

"What do you mean by proper conditions for fighting?" I asked.

"The cage had to be small and the bars the right size for the chimp to grasp. People don't know how strong a chimp really is. Once Josie latched on to the bars, the challenger was doomed. There was no place in that cage to escape Josie's kicking.

Nobody ever lasted longer than fifteen seconds in the ring with
him. Now this guy in the picture—''

''Willy Sanders. My god, you don't even remember his name,
do you?''

''—he was the kind of guy I liked to see coming. Cocky.
Loudmouthed. He wouldn't even wear the protective helmet that
we offered the challengers. I can still hear him bragging to the
audience about how he was going overseas, that there'd be time
enough over there for wearing helmets. Then the swaggering son
of a bitch informed everyone that he wasn't just going to beat
Josie. No, he was going to kill the chimp.''

''Willy Sanders was just a scared kid, Galloway. He was on his
way to join the army and then go to war. He had a bad night. The
girl he picked up in a bar dumped him. And going to see the
carnival strip show by himself made him feel worse. Even getting
his picture taken at Zig Mulvaney's didn't pick up his spirits. By
the way, that's how I know this picture is Sanders. His photo was
the only one with two copies in Mulvaney's files for that month.
Sanders never came back to pick up his picture. That was
because of his match with Josie, wasn't it?''

Still gripping the photo, Galloway moved to his workbench.
He nearly stepped on the wet spot on the floor, and I held my
breath until he passed it. He made an elaborate display of smooth-
ing out the picture, as though removing the creases might somehow change the events of the past. ''This Sanders guy made all
kinds of threats to Josie. He said he was going to rip out the poor
chimp's heart with his bare hands.'' Galloway began to choke on
some of his words.

''Sanders's brother said that Willy was always a big talker,
and that he hated to lose.''

Galloway's face darkened with the memory. ''So I ordered
Josie to work him over good, showing no mercy. Before the bell
even rang, Josie lit into him tooth and nail. The match was over
in five seconds. The crowd loved it so much, I decided to let
Josie continue. Even when the crowd began to boo, I let it go on
for another half minute. Nobody talks to my Josie that way.''

He slowly crushed the picture of Willy Sanders between his
hands.

''I saw how you handled that runaway monkey the other night.

You were very good. Did you ever work with animals after Josie?"

"Never. Josie and I were close. We were buddies. Since I had already given up working with people, I became a wirer, where all I have to worry about is equipment. Believe me, the laws of mechanics are a hell of a lot easier to understand than the laws of human nature."

"So why bother staying with the carnival?"

"Because I love this place." His left hand dropped to his side and began to slowly open the middle drawer of the workbench. He pressed himself close to the bench, trying to mask his action.

"Oh yeah?" I said. "Your little model over there leads me to believe otherwise."

"No, I *do* love it here. Moving tons of equipment from town to town. Nursing broken rides back to health. Always a challenge. No, I like the carnival; it's the damn *carnies* that I hate. They're always spouting off about brotherhood, but then they stab you in the back every chance they get. They have the nerve to talk about the marks like they're some kind of foreign enemy. But just who is a mark anyway? Hell, to a carny, *everyone* is a mark. Even his fellow carnies."

I nodded with understanding, hoping that some of the rancor would leave his voice. "What happened to Josie, Walt?"

He pinched the upper part of his nose to stop the tears. "The morning after Josie's match with Sanders, I went to feed him. But he was dead. I checked his food. It didn't smell right, and I was sure that he'd been poisoned. I asked around, and a few carnies said that they saw a guy hanging around my tent after closing time. Their descriptions fit Sanders."

"You're right. Sanders did poison the food. He gave him an overdose of a heart medicine." I noticed that my cigarette was smoked down to the end. I wanted another, but I feared that reaching into my pocket would make him nervous. "Were you referring to Arlen Roth when you talked about carnies stabbing you in the back?"

He slammed the drawer shut, rattling the tools on the wall. "Yes, indeed. I used to think we were close. I helped that man build a lot of his magic equipment, and he coached me on talking to the crowds at my wrestling matches. We often got drunk together. We were supposed to be friends, but he turned out to be just like the others. Worse, in fact."

"Was he drunk the night he helped you kill Sanders?"

Galloway whipped his hand out from behind him. He pointed the pistol at my chest. As I stubbed out my cigarette on the track of his miniature roller coaster, two cars slammed into my finger and derailed. Galloway seemed disappointed that I didn't beg for mercy or bravely spring to my feet to defend myself.

He said, "As you may know, Roth loved practical jokes. To get him to help me, I painted the whole thing as one big prank. I never told him that Josie was dead, only that I wanted to teach some mark a lesson for threatening my chimp. After asking around town, we tracked Sanders to a bar where he was still nursing his wounds and drunkenly spouting off that his injuries were from a fight with a street gang. When he left that bar, he was so drunk we easily subdued him."

"You took Sanders to a clearing a few miles away from the abandoned prison here, didn't you?"

"How did you know?"

I didn't tell him about Pitlor's mother's odd reaction while riding past the Spanier Prison. Apparently Roth had told her his story before fleeing the carnival. I said, "You set up the Bozo tank in that clearing, didn't you?"

Galloway seemed irritated that I was robbing him of perhaps his only chance of telling his story. "Yeah. I tied Sanders to the stool above the tank. I can still remember Roth warning me that Sanders might drown if we weren't careful. But I *guaranteed* him that Sanders wouldn't drown. Then we had our little fun. Both Roth and I threw baseballs at the target on the dunking machine, getting closer and closer. Finally, at my urging, Roth walked right up and lobbed a ball into the target, point-blank. Sanders hit with a splash. He only came back to the surface once . . . to let out a long scream that disappeared into the forest. Then he went under again. The hissing sound that followed told Roth why Sanders had screamed."

"What kind of acid did you fill that tank with, Galloway? Was it the same stuff you use to dissolve grease from the ride machinery? Only undiluted?"

He nodded with approval at my correct guess. I asked, "What did Roth do after that?" The motor home rocked as the wind picked up outside. Not now, I thought. As if in answer, it died down.

I scooted my chair to the side, trying to move outside the aim of his gun. The barrel relentlessly followed me.

Galloway continued his story. "Roth ran like a scared animal. When he got back to the carnival, he took a few minutes to pack his bags and then kept running. And he's been running constantly for the past twenty years."

"Some friend he turned out to be," I said with sarcastic commiseration. "He left you with the job of disposing of the body. But you fooled him on that count, didn't you? You never disposed of it. You carried the bones of Willy Sanders with you all those years. Why?"

"So I could pay Roth back little by little for his lack of loyalty—the kind of loyalty that all these so-called carnies are supposed to have."

In my mind I saw myself opening the package in Roth's hotel room and finding the solitary bone of a human leg. I said, "You sent him a lot of packages during those twenty years, didn't you?"

He smiled, not trying to disguise his pleasure. "But why?" I said. In the distance I could hear the pings of the shooting gallery and oompah-pahs of the merry-go-round in the real carnival. Without waiting for his answer, I said, "You told me that you don't approve of the way that carnies secretly despise the marks. But isn't that what Roth became to you? Your own personal mark? Wasn't he someone you could harass all you wanted, knowing that he couldn't complain to the police any more than some poor sucker who loses a bundle on the chuck-a-luck wheel? After all, he was an integral part of the murder, even if it was unwitting.

"No matter where Roth went, you eventually figured out where he was staying. You kept your ears open for news of a man who performed a great card trick with a dagger. Sometimes other carnies passing through would give you clues to his whereabouts. And then you'd send him one of those bones to remind him of your power over him. You were able to locate Roth this last time because you read that interview with me in that outdoor entertainment magazine. You knew that the man I was looking for had to be Roth. When you called the editor of the magazine, he put you in contact with Warner Huston, the ghostwriter. That's when you found out that Roth's health was failing—that he no longer feared the law like he used to—and also that he was working on a book about his carny years. You knew you had to act quickly. Huston also told you that Roth was personally writing the final chapter of his book. You became convinced that he was going to give a detailed account of the Sanders murder. So, on a day the carnival was rained out, you raced across the state to the town of Maylene, arriving just ahead of me. And you permanently silenced him."

Galloway chuckled. "Oh, that's good. Very entertaining, indeed. I'd applaud, but it's hard to clap with this gun in my hand. But I have a good solution to that problem . . . ."

He pulled the trigger. The gun jerked in his hand, a reflex action due to the recoil that he had expected. He pulled the trigger again, but nothing happened. It was my turn to chuckle.

"Your workbench is very well equipped, Galloway. I especially like that epoxy glue of yours. That stuff really hardens quick. There's probably enough left to fill up five more gun barrels."

I visualized the path I would take: I would spring up, grab my chair, and swing it into his soft gut. While he was recovering I would zip out of the workshop and outside. Once I had the jump on him, he'd never catch me. I gripped the arms of the chair, ready to spring upward.

But I never got the chance. He reached up and pulled down the decorative overhead netting on top of me. And it was decorative no longer. The more I struggled to roll out from underneath, the more it ensnared me. The net was designed to hold animals ten times my strength. As I kicked and rolled and thrashed I felt the motor home rock back and forth. I stopped and lay calm.

Galloway stooped down until his face was inches from mine. "Don't be stupid. You can't fight it. Carlson tried. And that made it more painful for him."

The netting was wrapped around my neck, wrists, and legs. I felt as though a hundred little ropes were binding me. One salty-tasting strand of the net was strapped hard across my mouth, parting my lips.

I tried to talk but could only mumble.

"What's that? I can't understand you," he said.

I pushed the strand out of the way with my tongue. I began to talk like one of Amelia Halfhill's game operators. "A hundred dollars says I can escape from this net. What do you say, sport? Where's your guts? Where's your spirit of adventure, pal? Okay, I'll tell you what I'm gonna do. How's about double or nothing?"

Galloway smiled and said, "Well, what do you know. What they say is true. There *is* one born every minute."

CHAPTER THIRTY-EIGHT

Keeping well out of range of my kicking feet, Galloway bunched the ends of the net together and knotted them, making a neat parcel out of me. As he stepped back to admire his handiwork I started to frantically flop back and forth. I stopped when I spotted the tiny puddle on the floor. Galloway was now about three feet away from it. Looking up at him through several layers of net, I said, "Have you thought this through carefully, Walt? First of all, how are you going to dispose of—" I could not bring myself to say "my body."

"That won't be a problem."

"When Bateman discovers that I'm missing, he's not going to let anyone off the prison grounds without a thorough search of the premises. If you try to go over the wall, you'll have to eat a lot of razor wire."

"Oh yeah?" He laid his tranquilizer gun on the workbench and began to rummage through one of the drawers. After a few seconds he turned around. A length of electrical wire dangled from his fingers. "Using this is quite appropriate, don't you think? After all, I'm the wirer for the carnival." He wound it around his hands and pulled it taut. "You're going to be a lot less trouble than Jacques Carlson. After I subdued him with the tranquilizer gun, I stuffed his body inside my steamer trunk and hauled it to his trailer on one of the carnival's forklifts. Only then did I strangle him. It was his mistake to bust in on me last night, raising hell. By the way, how did you figure out that Carlson visited me last night?"

"Because you slipped up. That beaded finger ring found on his body wasn't a ring at all. It was the miniature necklace that you had made for the Madame Sirolli doll in your little carnival. Carlson must have secretly removed it when he found the half-finished figurine of Christine last night. I checked the fortune-teller doll in your model carnival, and she isn't wearing a choker necklace. The real Madame Sirolli always wears one with her costume. It's her trademark."

As he stepped closer to the puddle I struggled to gain slack. The strands of netting sliced into my wrists and pinned them to my sides.

"Galloway, if you do escape, what the hell are you going to do after that?"

"There are always a few down-and-out shows that'll hire a man without nosing into his past. And I can always change my name—and appearance—like you did."

He snapped the wire tight between his hands, testing its strength. I lowered my eyes to the floor and momentarily panicked. I had lost sight of the wet spot. Then I saw a tiny drop bounce off the top of Galloway's work boot: he was standing directly on top of the puddle.

I started to thrash about on the floor, desperately straining at the net. With feigned hysterics, I slithered around, banging my feet and elbows into the wall, trying to make it look like a last-ditch attempt for freedom. Soon the entire motor home was gently swaying from my efforts. Galloway grinned, savoring my struggle.

I rolled on my back and focused my attention not on Galloway's face but on the skylight above him. I had originally intended to let time take its course, but that was before Galloway had wrapped me up like the catch of the day. Now I had to speed things up. I was hoping the rocking of the motor home would stir up some of the branches that lay across the roof. The whole setup had been a last-minute idea, something intended for an emergency. Now it was my only hope.

Another drop of liquid plopped onto Galloway's shoe. As the scraping of the branches got louder I turned over and slammed my whole body into the wall, sending a sickening shock through my forehead, shoulders, and knees.

An instant later I heard Galloway let out a bellowing scream, followed by a string of curses. I rolled away from the wall and saw a knife buried in the soft part of his shoulder, an inch from the base of his neck. The dagger had finally dropped loose from the tree limb and fallen through the open skylight. The carved devil on the handle of the dagger smiled down at me.

He wrenched the knife from his shoulder and saw his own blood dripping from the blade. With eyes glassed over in anger, he flung the knife wildly at me. I flattened my face to the floor and heard the knife thunk into the wall behind me. With his face enveloped in pain, Galloway clapped his hand over the wound. Blood oozed through his fingers and ran down the front of his shirt. As he looked down at me his mouth moved but couldn't express his shock.

In my mind I saw him seize the knife from the wall and savagely plunge it into me again and again. My hands strained to reach the knife but came nowhere close. To reach the knife, I'd have to roll over twice. Galloway would easily beat me to it.

"Keeping throwing!" I yelled. "You didn't get him!"

Paranoia gave Galloway momentary leave from pain. He dropped his hand from his shoulder and looked up through the skylight. Then he realized his vulnerability and jumped to the side, as though fearing a rain of knives from unseen assailants. After spinning in a tight circle, checking each corner of the room for another attacker, he pulled a slip of paper out of his pocket. And fled outside.

I rolled over to the wall and raised my hand as far as it could go. Trembling against the net, it came to within an inch of the dagger in the wall. I rolled away, gained more slack, and tried again. This time I was able to wrap my first two fingers around the hilt of the knife, pulling it from the wall. It fell from my grasp and clattered to the floor. I then inched over to it, gripped it firmly, and began to saw through the net. Soon there was a hole big enough to poke my arm through. In a matter of seconds I shucked off the net and pulled myself to my feet.

I looked up through the skylight at the thick branch where I had stuck Roth's dagger. Then I looked down at the tiny puddle on the floor. Once again, I had found another use for Jacques Carlson's Ener-Charge elixir.

After shaking my arms to restore circulation, I headed for the door. As I reached it an explosion shook the walls of the motor home. Remembering that one of the new additions to Galloway's miniature carnival was a piece of artillery, I flung open the door, fully expecting to find the real carnival in ruins.

But all looked well outside. The rides of the Bateman Carnival still spun, the aroma of fried food still wafted from the cook-house, and the bells and bangs still emanated from the game joints.

I looked up in the air in time to see a white-tipped missile shoot over the north wall of the Spanier Prison. It reached its apex well above the snarls of barbed wire. For a moment, it seemed determined to challenge the thin threads of clouds in the sky. But then it lost altitude and disappeared on the other side of the wall . . . heading for the river that ran behind the prison. The sound of rushing water would cover up any splash it might make. But I knew it wasn't a real missile, unless they are making missiles nowadays that wear plaid shirts, work boots, and white crash helmets.

I walked slowly toward the midway. There was no hurry. My destination was the area behind the freak show and beside the main grab stand, where Bateman's men had set up Jacques Carlson's platform, where he used to wow his audiences with feats of superhuman strength. As I walked I rubbed my fingers and palms where the netting had made them raw. I started to yawn, tried to suppress it, and then let it out in a loud groan. It had been a long day. Only now did my glass of Carlson's Ener-Charge start to make me groggy.

Ernie sat on the platform with his back against Jacques Carlson's cannon. Beside him was a paper plate containing two uneaten ham sandwiches made from French stick loaves sliced in half. On his lap lay another plate and sandwich. Clutched in his hand was yet one more sandwich, which he was steadily devouring. With his mouth full, he talked loudly, sometimes shouting.

Sitting beside him, sipping from a paper cup and holding a

half-eaten hamburger, was Gabe, the ride operator. Ernie stopped shouting long enough to tear off a mighty bite of his sandwich. Gabe, still wearing his stereo headphones, looked at Ernie and said, "Absolutely, man. I couldn't agree more." Gabe seemed pleased to have found someone he could talk to without having to continually remove his headphones.

Ernie waved to me. I said, "What happened?"

He smiled and waved again. I said, "What happened?"

He said, "Huh?"

I lifted Gabe's headphones and said, "What's wrong with Ernie?"

"His ears. When the cannon went off it really did a job on them."

Ernie smiled blankly, as though Gabe and I were talking in a foreign language. I said, "Is he all right?"

"Yeah, I think the noise only deafened him temporarily. He's lucky. Hearing is a precious gift, you know."

"How true." I watched Ernie start to chomp on another of his French stick sandwiches. It was as big around as a baseball bat. "What the hell are you two doing here?" I asked.

"Ernie and I were just following your directions. Between nine and nine-thirty last night, we were both taking a break. We were eating sandwiches right here under the shadow of Carlson's cannon, where none of the marks would bother us. A really weird thing happened just a couple of minutes ago. Walt Galloway came barreling up to us, wearing a crash helmet and holding his shoulder like it was hurt. He rushed to the controls and cranked the cannon around. He kept looking at some coordinates written on a piece of paper, and he was mumbling stuff about air currents and trajectories and water currents."

After taking a nibble from his burger, Gabe said, "I looked at Ernie, and we both knew that Galloway had to be the murderer. Like you said: Look out for someone in the wrong place at the wrong time. I didn't know what the hell to do. Ernie just sat there, eating his sandwich and looking bored. Then Galloway crawled into the cannon. I could hear a ticking in the control panel, probably some kind of automatic timer. I ran away. I didn't want near that thing when it went off. I called for Ernie to follow, but he just sat there, polishing off his sandwich. When he finished, he wiped the crumbs off his lips and then walked over to the mouth of the cannon. He looked down inside. For a moment I thought he was going to get his head blown off. But then he began pushing on the cannon with both hands, putting his full weight behind it. I heard a creaking sound, but nothing happened. Ernie pushed even harder, wheezing and grunting and sweating like wild. Then I heard something snap. After that, the cannon moved easily to where it's pointing now.''

I saw that several metal bolts on the base of the cannon were bent. Three of them were snapped clean off.

Gabe said, ''Ernie was still pushing on the cannon when it blew. You'll probably have to write him notes for the next few hours if you want to tell him anything.''

I stood at the tail end of the cannon and followed the line of vision out over the wall. Ernie had diverted the cannon from Galloway's original coordinates. Galloway had probably intended to land in the river near the shore. Although the cannon was still pointed in the general direction of the river, it was now anyone's guess where Galloway had touched down. I remembered that Jacques Carlson had estimated that an untrained person would have only a one-in-ten chance of surviving a shot out of his cannon. If Galloway had landed in the middle of the river, he wouldn't have been able to swim ashore before being swept downstream to where the stretch of rapids water and sharp rocks awaited. In that case, the odds against survival were probably one hundred to one—odds that even Amelia Halfhill wouldn't bet on.

''I think that we've heard the last from Walt Galloway,'' I said.

Ernie, his mouth still full of sandwich, said, ''Huh?''

CHAPTER THIRTY-NINE

They all watched in silence as I washed the gray out of my hair in a basin in Bateman's motor home. My face still felt slick from the cold cream I had used to remove my makeup. As I wrapped the towel around my head Bateman said, "The men are still searching along the riverbanks. They found a crash helmet trapped among some drifting branches, but no sign of Galloway. Even if he is still alive, he won't dare show his face around any major carnivals in this country again." He looked up at Mary Trunzo, who was sitting on the arm of the chair beside him. From the way they were exchanging glances, he looked like he had forgiven me for springing that "engagement" party on him. He looked like he might even be grateful.

Zig Mulvaney sat on the edge of the sofa, smoking a cigarette that was as thin and white as his fingers. He said, "Harry, I understand everything that you've told us so far, but I still don't know how Galloway killed Roth and got out of that hotel room without you seeing him."

"Magic," I said.

"Come on, there's no such thing as magic."

Christine shook her head. "No, Zig, Harry is quite serious. Galloway knew a lot about magic. In fact, he actually helped design that bookcase illusion of Roth's."

I said, "When I first entered Roth's hotel room, Galloway was hiding inside the bookcase illusion. He slipped out of the room when I went into the bedroom and discovered Roth's body. It had never occurred to me that I wasn't the first to discover that the bookcase made a great hiding place. When I was inside the illusion, I kept smelling what I thought was the perfume of one of Roth's assistants. It was actually Galloway's flowery, almost feminine, after-shave."

Bateman squinted his eyes upward and wiggled his forefinger in the air, as though tallying a complicated math problem. "Wait a minute, Harry. That's impossible. Roth was still alive when you entered his room. There's no way that Galloway could have sneaked out of his hiding place and killed Roth without your knowing it."

"You're right. I didn't stumble onto the answer until the other night when I was watching a carnival game operator win a bundle from a mark. He was playing a game with three matchboxes and a penny." I explained how the scam worked, how an extra matchbox was hidden in the operator's sleeve.

Amelia Halfhill nodded with sudden realization. "I get it! Since you don't know that a fourth box exists, your mind tells you that the rattling sound is coming from one of the three visible boxes. In the hotel room, when you heard a muffled voice, your mind assumed that it was coming from the bedroom."

I covered my mouth to cough. And kept it covered. I wasn't as adept at the art as Galloway or Pitlor.

Bateman said, "What the hell does that have to do with—"

"*Hey, Bateman, you are one of the dullest guys I've ever met,*" a faint voice said.

Bateman looked around to see where the voice was coming from. The voice said, "Everything looks alike in here. Fifteen pairs of socks. And they're all navy blue. It's really boring in here. Why don't you at least buy a pair of argyles?"

Bateman said, "Huh?" and went to his dresser drawer and opened it. Of course, all he found were fifteen pairs of blue socks. And not one of them talked. He looked at me and said, "You did that, didn't you? You threw your voice."

"In a sense. It's actually impossible to 'throw' your voice, but many ventriloquists are skilled at creating the illusion of distance and muffledness in their voices. Chuck Pitlor told me he was making rapid improvement in learning to 'throw' his voice, because someone had been tutoring him. That *someone* was surely Walt Galloway. We already know that at one time Galloway had built and repaired ventriloquist dummies. In fact, he was refurbishing one for Pitlor when he left the carnival. Undoubtedly, Galloway picked up a lot of tips from the ventriloquists that he worked for.''

Ernie, whose hearing was beginning to return, strained to follow what we were saying. He leaned forward in his chair—the wood groaning from the strain—and cupped his ear, as if trying to coax more sound in. Christine sat on the arm of Ernie's chair, lovingly stroking his hair. When he spoke, his voice was still too loud. ''Let me see if I have this straight: Arlen Roth was already dead when you got to his hotel room. Right?''

''Yes. When I was talking to him on the phone from the café, Galloway had already sneaked into Roth's room. He probably overheard our conversation. Once Galloway learned that I was coming across the street to visit, he worked fast. He had only a few minutes to kill Roth and then to search his room for the last chapter to his autobiography, the chapter exposing Galloway's murder of Willy Sanders. By the time Galloway found the missing chapter, I was outside, knocking on the door. He didn't even have time to take with him the last bone that he had sent Roth. Galloway cleaned off the dagger and put it back, thinking that he could find a way to frame me for the murder. He then crawled inside the bookcase illusion and began talking in a rough impersonation of Roth. Since the only time I had ever talked with Roth was during our brief phone conversation, Galloway's imitation didn't have to be exact. He simply had to achieve the muted tone of a man talking from another room. My mind—as in the case of the penny in the matchbox—supplied the rest of the illusion.''

I removed the towel from my head and tugged a comb through my hair.

Mary Trunzo said, ''What about Warner Huston, the ghostwriter? Did Galloway kill him, too?''

''No, he's still living . . . quite well, in fact.''

Bateman snapped his fingers. ''My fifty thousand.''

''Exactly. Galloway stole the money to pay off the ghostwriter for his services. In return for the money, Huston promised to lie low and to go along with the story that someone broke into his home and stole Roth's manuscript. Galloway had also commissioned the writer to make alterations in Roth's book, inserting scathing attacks against all of you. That way, you'd all appear to have a motive for bumping off Roth. The only vicious chapter in the original manuscript was the last chapter that Roth had been writing himself.''

Mary Trunzo lifted the lid of a plastic yellow case and handed me the blow dryer from inside. I plugged it in and said, ''It looks like Warner Huston was ghosting the wrong book. Walt Galloway's life would have been the best-seller.''

While Christine held a hand mirror in front of me I turned on the dryer, working the comb and hot air through my hair for several minutes. When I was finished, Bateman said, ''Jeez. You don't look like yourself anymore.''

There was a knock at the door, and Bateman answered it. Two men wearing suits were standing in the doorway. I thought they might be police. Bateman quietly talked to them for a few minutes before closing the door and returning. He smiled widely, framing a big triangle of white teeth. It was a money smile.

I said, ''Who were they?''

''The town fathers from the village down the road. They came to investigate the commotion up here at the abandoned prison. I told them we were having a dress rehearsal for our carnival and that the show would be moving on soon. They said they were glad they caught us in time. They want us to stay and run the carnival for them tonight. It seems they haven't had live entertainment here for years . . . ever since the Bateman Carnival stopped coming here some twenty years ago.'' Bateman rubbed his hands together. ''I guess our little visit to the Spanier Prison won't be a total write-off after all.''

As I stood up to leave, Bateman said, ''Hey, where are you going? How about staying a little longer and doing just one more show? Come on. What harm would one more show do, Mr. Big L.A. Nightclub Performer?''

I shook my head. ''I'm sorry, but I'm so far behind in my rehearsal schedule already that—''

''Okay. Have it your way. I guess you're in such a hurry that you won't have any time to read this.'' He reached inside his coat pocket and handed me a wrinkled stack of paper. ''We found this stuffed in the waste can in Galloway's motor home.''

It was another chapter from Roth's book. Only this one wasn't devoted to any of his former carny friends. It was a detailed explanation—with sketches—of his dagger-through-the-card trick.

I plopped down hard in my chair. My hand shot into my

pocket and pulled out my deck of cards . . . the same way a
western sheriff reaches for his gun when there's trouble. The
people in the room continued their conversation about Galloway
and his crimes, but I no longer heard them. Their words were
overpowered by the words of Roth's manuscript. I couldn't wait
to follow his directions step by step. I asked Mary to get me a
knife from the kitchen.

She hesitated.

I said, "A *butter* knife, please."

CHAPTER FORTY

After explaining to Lee Sanders on the phone what had happened to his brother Willy, I mailed him the other copy of
Willy's photo, the one he'd never picked up from Zig Mulvaney's.
I hated telling Lee the news as much as he hated hearing it. He
said that he was relieved that he could finally retire as the
"fixer" for his family.

I was now shoving the last of my suitcases into my van. My
final show at the Bateman Carnival had gone well. With opening
night at the Magic Oasis now only a couple of days away, my
immediate plans were to drive to L.A., pick up my new doves,
shut myself away in a hotel room, and devote every free minute
to practice.

And after opening night, I intended to locate my former assistant, Cate Fleming. Nothing serious, mind you. I just wanted to
say hello. The image lingered in my mind of Christine Sirolli and
Ernie walking hand in hand down the midway. And of Bateman
kissing Mary at the engagement party.

Many of the people in the audience for my last carnival show stuck around afterwards, chatting with me as if I were a friend they had invited over to their house. I tried to imagine the jaded faces of the Magic Oasis audiences doing the same, but all I could picture was a smoky nightclub haze, penetrable only by resorting to quick—sometimes brutal—wit, and by performing faster and better than whatever tuxedoed conjurer had held the stage during the preceding five minutes.

Performing at the Bateman Carnival had been like a friendly game of penny-a-point pinochle, while working the Magic Oasis would be like having a nightly fencing duel to the death.

I started my engine. The carny who had driven my van for me today hadn't treated it with the loving care it needed. I'd have to spend a few minutes tinkering with the carburetor before starting my long drive.

I shut the engine off, picked up my moneybag, and took one last walk down the midway. The local village had certainly embraced the carnival during its surprise visit. The midway was jammed. I tried not to think of how much I would miss this place, of how much I'd miss this way of life.

With my makeup washed off, none of the ride operators, game-booth men, or grab-stand workers recognized me. The man in front of one of the gambling wheels looked straight through me while he chanted his pitch: "Spin and win." He was the same man who had run the dice game the night before. He was wearing long sleeves again tonight, prepared to play his match-box game at a moment's notice.

I looked behind me. A uniformed policeman from the local village was leaning on a grab-stand counter, nibbling at a tuft of cotton candy. "Evening, Officer," I said, walking over to him. I bought him a jumbo Coke.

I then took the moneybag containing my take from tonight's show and dropped it on top of the game counter. The operator stopped in midsentence and opened the bag. He looked at my face but didn't recognize me. He said, "What the hell's this for?"

"You said, 'Spin and win,' right? Well, go ahead. Spin the wheel."

"You're betting this whole pile of money on the even numbers? On just one spin?"

I nodded, aware that a crowd was already gathering on either side of me.

He pretended to be nervous. I could see that he was trying not to smile as he stepped back and spun the big wheel with his right hand. I was focusing my attention on his left hand, which was hidden from view by the countertop. His left wrist flicked quickly, probably tripping a lever under the counter. The numbers spun in a blur of color. As the nails that separated the numbers zipped past the metal ticker, I already knew what the outcome would be.

From my side of the counter it was impossible to detect that half the nails were shorter than the others. When the operator tripped his lever, it had drawn the whole wheel back a fraction of an inch. The ticker was now touching only the longer nails. The wheel was now rigged to stop on only odd numbers.

I motioned the operator closer. "What do you want?" he said. "Just a fair spin of the wheel. For once."

I reached over the counter and flipped the lever back so that the wheel now had a fifty-fifty chance of stopping at an even or an odd number. The operator tried to stop me but was jerked short. I had locked his wrist to the corner post of his booth with the handcuffs that I had stolen from the policeman. I leaned forward, blocking the cop's view of the operator's locked wrist.

As the wheel spun slow and slower, the crowd grew silent. When it finally stopped on the number eight, they cheered. The operator, knowing better than to buck the crowd, stretched toward his cash drawer and counted out my money with one hand.

"By the way," I said to the group clustered around the booth, "if this guy wants any of you to play a game using three of these"—I pulled back his sleeve to reveal the matchbox taped to it—"better make sure he's wearing short sleeves."

I looked back at the policeman at the grab stand. He had been intently watching my spin of the wheel, but when he saw me staring, he turned his head away . . . just like the carnival was paying him to. He was there to handle irate losers, not happy winners.

I walked farther up the midway, passing Madame Sirolli's fortune-telling tent, trying not to look inside. In spite of my big win at the gambling booth, a lonely feeling swept through me. I no longer felt like a carny.

I felt like a mark.

And probably would for a long, long time.

JONATHAN VALIN

NATURAL CAUSES   68247-8/$2.95
When ace detective Harry Stoner is hired to find out who killed a TV soap writer, he uncovers a slick world of high finance and low morals, the perfect setting for greed, jealousy, and murder.
"A superior writer...Smart and sophisticated."
The New York Times Book Review

DAY OF WRATH   63917-3/$3.50 US/$4.50 Can
Harry Stoner takes on the simple case of a teenage runaway—and finds himself on a bloody trail leading from the sleazy barrooms of Cincinnati to the luxurious penthouse of a well-known socialite.
"An out-and-out shocker." *Chicago Sun-Times*

DEAD LETTER   61366-2/$3.50 US/$4.50 Can
The Cincinnati private eye is pitted against the rivalries and plots of a hateful family, who soon have him involved in a gruesome murder case.
"A classic puzzle of motives." *Newsweek*

FINAL NOTICE   57893-X/$3.50 US/$4.50 Can
Private eye Harry Stoner must find a psychotic killer who mutilates art photos of beautiful women before moving on to living victims.
"One of the scariest, most pulse-pounding thrillers you'll ever read...A superior mystery." *Booklist*

LIME PIT   55442-9/$3.50 US/$4.50 Can
Harry Stoner tries to right the wrongs of a heartless city as he searches for a 16-year-old runaway who has disappeared into Cincinnati's seamy netherworld of prostitution and porn.
"THE LIME PIT is done right!" *New York Daily News*